Praise for Catherine Czerkawska's previous novels:

'Beguiling and enchanting ... Czerkawska is an excellent storyteller.'
The Scottish Review

'Czerkawska tells her tale in a restrained, elegant prose that only adds to its poignancy.' *Sunday Times*

'A powerful story about love and obligation.' *John Burnside*

'Moving, poetic and quietly provocative.' *The Independent*

'Heartwarming, realistic and page turning.' *Lorraine Kelly*

'Beautiful – lyrical and sensual by turns.' *Hilary Ely*

'A romance of Scotland's great Romantic. The Jewel finally gives voice to Jeany Armour, the girl who sang as sweetly as a nightingale.' *Sunday Mail*

'Take any aspect of the novelist's art and you'll find it exemplified here to perfection.' *Bill Kirton, Booksquawk*

Also by Catherine Czerkawska:

FICTION

The Curiosity Cabinet

The Jewel

The Physic Garden

The Posy Ring

Ice Dancing

Bird of Passage

The Amber Heart

Bitter Oranges

A Bad Year for Trees and other stories

Rewilding – a novella

NON-FICTION

The Way It Was

For Jean: *Poems, Songs and Letters by Robert Burns for his wife Jean Armour*

A Proper Person to be Detained

The Last Lancer

PLAYS

Wormwood

The Price of a Fish Supper

Quartz

Burns on the Solway

The Secret Commonwealth

POETRY

A Book of Men

Midnight Sun

HERA'S ORCHARD

Catherine Czerkawska

O love, what hours were thine and mine,
In lands of palm and southern pine;
In lands of palm, of orange-blossom,
Of olive, aloe, and maize and vine.

– Alfred, Lord Tennyson

Where there is love, there is pain.

– Spanish proverb

Published by Dyrock Publishing

Cover art by Alan Lees

Cover and book design by Lumphanan Press

ISBN 978-1-7384205-1-3

In Greek mythology, the Garden of the Hesperides was also called Hera's Orchard. It was said to be on an island in the west, where the mythical golden apples grew, guarded by a fierce dragon. Although there are various possible real life candidates, it has always seemed to me that the Canary Isles, with their beauty, their oranges, volcanoes and dragon trees, may have a better claim than most to the origin of this magical garden.

I therefore ask the reader to suspend her disbelief and accept this for what it is – a love story for the people we once were, in the place we once spent the happiest of times.

– Catherine Czerkawska

CHAPTER ONE

Bird you sang so well
upon the cypress bough.
Bird, I love to hear you.
Sing to me once again.

He was singing a Spanish folk song in a vibrant tenor voice with a passionate catch in it and accompanying himself on the guitar. Perhaps it was a Canarian song. She didn't understand enough of the language to translate it, but you would have had to be foolish or peculiarly insensitive not to realise that he was singing about love. Love and pain. There was a yearning quality about the notes that soared above the staccato rhythm of the instrument and tore at her heart. She looked around. No wonder the bar was busy, in spite of the virus and its lingering variants. Most of the singers in the restaurants and bars of Tenerife sang the kind of Latin hits that would appeal to tourists. But this was no ordinary season, and besides, he was different. If anything, he played better than he sang. She found the music both beautiful and moving.

She liked folk music, especially Scottish folk. Her ex-husband had kept her music strictly segregated from his, as though it would somehow contaminate his Mozart and Bach and Beethoven. He loved vinyl, frequented specialist shops in Glasgow's Byres Road, had a collection of discs that he would play on an old turntable, even though he sometimes had to put a coin on the arm to stop the stylus from jumping. It was one of the things she had loved about him when they first met: his insistence on playing what he called his records for her, sitting rapt, his whole body somehow involved with the music.

She smiled bitterly at the memory of how often he had come in and thoughtlessly switched off her music. 'Christ, Mags, how can you listen to this crap? I mean how *can* you?'

The insistently sensual tones of the singer recalled her to her surroundings. He seemed so different from the usual bar musicians, all of them amplified to the point of discomfort. He had a simple Spanish guitar – it looked like an old instrument from where she was sitting, more slender and shapely than most – the skill of his playing and a clear tenor voice. But it was his playing that enchanted her. Not that everybody appreciated him. People talked over him, laughed, went to and from the bar, greeting friends noisily along the way. She wanted them all to shut up so that she could listen. He didn't seem to mind. Once or twice, he glanced up with a rueful smile, raising dark eyebrows at nobody in particular.

Her colleague, Conor, stood up. 'Do you want another drink, Maggie?'

The musician had finished his set. Now he took a break, dipping his head in acknowledgement of the applause.

'Yes, yes please.' She held up her empty glass.

'Gin and tonic?'

'Yes please.'

The drinks were alarmingly large but the buzz of self confidence was worth the mild hangover. She had drunk two already and she could feel the alcohol beginning to throb in her head. When she went out with this crowd from work, drinking made her feel more at ease and less conscious of herself and her age. She was thirty five, a good ten years older than most of this group. They were almost all EU citizens from a variety of countries, working in property sales and rentals, everything from beautiful but shabby traditional villas to tiny studio apartments. The company was based in an open plan and mercifully air conditioned office. There were online videos of the properties, although as restrictions eased, Margaret would be sent out, suitably masked and sanitised at first, to show people around and try to persuade them to part with their hard-earned cash. There would always be a driver to drop her off and wait for her, for safety's sake, sometimes even coming in with her if there were any doubts about the client. The truth was that the majority of potential customers were middle aged or early retired couples, spending the kids' inheritance while they were still fit enough to enjoy it, either looking for a holiday apartment or even hoping to get the prized *residencia* if they were British.

She thought that she was employed mostly for her air of respectability. Her niceness. Her soft Scottish voice. It went with what she always thought of as her old fashioned name, although the alternatives, Maggie or Mags, were worse. Daisy would have been better. Clients of all nationalities seemed to find her reassuring. Not that there was anything wrong with the properties. In fact some of them were luxurious beyond belief. The rentals were, on the whole, well managed and maintained. But even here, with year-round sunshine, the new property market had come tumbling down. Buyers across Europe were cautious in the face of a rising costs. The pandemic had caused a predictable slump and the market was only just beginning to recover. Perhaps that was why she had been employed with so little fuss. Perhaps they were short of unattached people, willing to travel.

She had rented her flat from friends of her family in Scotland who had fallen foul of what she had come to think of as 'Bloody Brexit' and had to restrict their visits even now that Covid regulations were easing. She was one of the lucky ones, with an Irish passport, courtesy of her mother. Annie O'Brien had been born in West Cork, but moved to Scotland as a child when Margaret's grandfather found work in Glasgow. Every day, she blessed that simple accident of birth that had given her dual nationality, two passports, when so many people of her age had been summarily deprived of the freedoms they had been born with.

The apartment was part of a holiday complex, simply but comfortably furnished, with a tiny balcony overlooking a chilly pool. She had already turned it into a kind of home, with flowering plants, books and pictures. But there was no way of banishing the loneliness that threatened to overwhelm her each evening when she got back from the office. Unwilling to embrace the 'expat' community that had created a version of England in the sun, she was bereft of alternatives. She hadn't thought it would be so difficult to make friends of her own age. She hadn't thought about it at all, in her anxiety to get away, change something, anything, about her life.

She had been online in the library where she worked, newly reopened after lockdown, helping somebody to search for information about Spanish language courses, when the advertisement had caught her eye. She had always intended that her library job would be temporary, but that wasn't the way it had turned out. She could hardly remember now why she had first applied for it, quite soon after graduation, quite soon after her marriage.

'It'll suit you. You like books,' her mother had said. Perhaps Annie imagined that the work meant a lot more reading than it really did. But libraries involved so much more than books. And so much less. In the event Margaret had enjoyed it but only because she liked her colleagues, even liked working with the general public. After the divorce, the very familiarity of it had depressed her. It seemed to belong to a part of her life that was over and done with. Then the pandemic and lockdown had come along, with fear for her mother, unfounded as it turned out, but with a growing sense of isolation, only partly relieved when the library reopened.

When she had seen the advert, it had seemed like fate stepping in and showing her a way out. On impulse, she had applied, and after what she considered an all too brief Zoom interview, had been offered the job. English speakers with the bonus of an EU passport were in demand and she could get a certificate of registration on arrival. She had been here in Los Cristianos for six or seven weeks, since just after Christmas, and although she didn't think she was particularly good at selling anything, the customers liked her. People trusted her. Believed what she told them. But then she generally told them the truth.

The problem was, said Stella, her supervisor, repeatedly and acidly, that it was possible to be a bit too honest. Margaret was always telling people to 'go home and think about it.' The older and more enthusiastic they were, the more her conscience would prick her into discouraging them from parting with their money until they had taken legal advice back home.

All the same, she managed the odd sale. Some of the properties were very attractive. In spite of austerity, people from all over Europe would come here on an extended winter break and decide to splash out on an apartment. More Scandinavians than Brits now, but they all spoke immaculate English. Few of them spoke Spanish. It seemed as though the sunshine got into their heads and addled their brains. The effect seemed to linger even after they went home. Not all of them came to their senses. She hadn't come to her senses either, hadn't yet fled home to chilly Glasgow. Her family had expected it. Sometimes she thought that was the only thing keeping her here: cheating their expectations of her. All the same, she had the feeling that if ever the company decided to cut back on jobs, hers would be among the first to go.

Her colleagues, whether they were in sales, employed to write glowing descriptions for the website, or in cleaning and maintenance, were a friendly bunch, but whenever she went out with them, she felt as though she didn't quite fit in.

Conor came back with the drinks. He was from Glasgow as well, with conveniently Irish grandparents, twenty two, gangly and charming. Sick of working from home, tied to a phone and a laptop, as soon as restrictions eased, he had come out on a cheap flight with enough cash to support himself for a while.

'I had to be off the drink for months to save up the money,' he told Margaret. 'And even then, I had to borrow from my mum.'

Conor had worked in a bar for a few months before getting a bona fide job with the property company. The kindly bar owner had fed him and let him sleep on a camp bed in the store room for a few weeks.

'Like Mr Fezziwig,' said Margaret, who was a great reader and very fond of Dickens.

'Who's that?' asked Conor. 'Does he work for us?'

Not for the first time, it struck her that she might be too old for the company she was keeping.

Conor's first position with the property company had been as a handyman. He had been employed in fixing window catches, cleaning pools, killing cockroaches. Then Stella – another dual national – had spotted his potential in sales, taken him under her wing, trained him.

'You see, you have to get on good terms with the clients. Ask them about themselves. Tell them a bit about yourself. Establish a friendly relationship so that they'll feel guilty if they disappoint you. And then you have to make it impossible for them to admit that they don't have the money without losing face.'

Conor had told Margaret all about it, anxious to pass on his new-found knowledge, which she knew was simply old-style marketing. She had been torn two ways, careful not to dampen his enthusiasm for the job, but rather sad too. He had seemed like such a nice lad when he arrived.

The musician had begun again: a guitar solo this time, his dark head bent low and lovingly over the instrument, absorbed in it. He played well. Even better than he sang. He wore faded denim jeans with a brown leather belt and a dark blue T-shirt in soft cotton with open buttons down the neck. His arms were muscular, as though he worked out of doors, or perhaps just worked out. She found her gaze riveted to his wrist and hand as it moved on the guitar, her attention caught by the brown skin, downed with little golden hairs, the long, strong fingers moving surely and confidently in a complex rhythm. Around his left wrist she saw the dark band of his watch strap. He wore no jewellery, not even a ring.

Watching him, she had a sudden sense of her own loneliness. Perhaps it was the music. All its passion seemed distant and un-attainable. She felt as though she were locked into some solitary bubble while the notes soared like birdsong around her. She drank a great gulp of her gin and tonic, the ice and lemon bobbing up against her nose.

It didn't help. Wrong drink, wrong time and place. She felt the treacherous tears prickling behind her eyes.

What will I do if I lose my job and have to go home? What will I do if I *don't* lose my job and have to stay here?

Both options seemed equally impossible.

She saw Conor glancing across at her anxiously, although the rest of the crowd were talking and laughing in a multitude of languages, switching easily between English, German, Spanish, and hadn't noticed her misery. She controlled herself with difficulty. Her body was always letting her down these days. She would be thinking of something quite separate from Alastair and their years together and then, without warning, her throat would be seized and shaken by the emotional impact of some recollection. It was getting harder to suppress the tears. The tears weren't for her ex-husband. She could acknowledge that now. They were tears of anger, of regret for her own wasted time, tears of rage at the casual deception.

'Are you OK, Maggie?' asked Conor. They always called her Maggie at the office. She didn't like it, but she didn't have the courage to tell them. Alastair had always called her Mags and she hadn't liked that either.

'Margaret,' she wanted to say. 'I'm Margaret.'

'Me? Oh, yes, I'm fine.' She fished a tissue out of her bag and blew her nose. Don't be silly, she thought. Don't make a fool of yourself in public.

'*Are* you OK, Maggie ?' asked Conor again. He waved his hand in front of her eyes. 'Hey – is there anybody there?'

'I'm fine. I was just listening to the music.'

Conor glanced casually at the musician. 'Don't they usually have to plug it in, somehow?'

'You mean the guitar. I don't think so. It's a proper Spanish guitar. There's an ordinary mic.'

'I suppose so. It's not what I'm used to.'

'No. You're used to being deafened.'

He grinned at her. 'You should come out with us more often. What's the good of being here in the middle of all this sunshine and cheap booze if you can't enjoy yourself?'

'I feel a bit old for all this.'

'You're not old!'

'Well, older than you. I'm a fish out of water, that's all.'

'But we don't make you feel bad, do we?'

'Not at all.'

They had welcomed her into their circle. The problems were all on her side.

'I've led a quiet life till now.'

She had got into the habit of gently mocking herself, but it was true. Sometimes it had seemed to her that there was a similarity about the mild eccentricity of her husband's professional colleagues, as though they were all formed from the same peculiar mould. They had more in common with each other than with anyone outside the world of academia. It wasn't so much that it was sheltered as that it was all-absorbing.

The years had slipped by and she didn't know where they had

gone. All for nothing, she thought bitterly, forgetting that there had been moments of joy and tenderness with the husband she had once loved. Latterly, all the good memories had been swallowed up by indifference and uncertainty. She had changed too. Sometimes it seemed to her as though she would never be free of the bitterness of that wasted time. The pain of it ate into her like a persistent toothache that no dentist could cure.

CHAPTER TWO

Out of three or four-score books which touch upon the archipelago or devote
every page between their covers to the islands, one could count on the fingers of
one hand those that give accurate and original information.

Olivia M Stone, 1887

She looked up at the singer again. He was singing another heart-rending folk song:

Maria, flor de un dia
Se fue para no volver
Y en mi corazón dejó
El puñal del padecer.

Something about Maria, who was a flower of one day and a dagger in his heart. Very Spanish, she thought. Tremendously over the top, but impressive. She watched him, his face shuttered and absorbed, as though his mind were elsewhere, locked in the time and place of the song, perhaps, and she shivered at his intensity. It was disturbing to see such concentration, such focus in the middle of the busy bar.

'Do you like this depressing stuff?' asked Conor, pulling a face.

'Well, yes. I like it very much. It goes with this place, don't you think? Well, the real bits of it, anyway.'

'I suppose so.'

'I'm going to have to pull my socks up, aren't I?' she said, wrenching her attention back to Conor with an effort.

'What are you talking about?'

'At work. I'm not doing very well, am I?'

He looked embarrassed. So she was right. They did discuss her failures in her absence.

'We all like you a lot,' he said. 'You're very popular. We think you're a nice woman.'

How damning! she thought. 'But?' she asked aloud.

'Well, it's just that you don't push people hard enough. I mean – Christ, Maggie – you even tell people to go away and think about it when they're on the verge of signing on the dotted line.'

'But I'd hate to think of them committing themselves to something they can't afford. You know fine what it's like out here, Conor. Especially the older people. Sitting on a nest egg they may need in the future.'

'God's sake! That isn't your problem. And besides, who's to say that they might not be better off with a little apartment over here? Warm winters. Sunshine. What would they be saving for? So that the state can take the cash to pay for their care in some hellish nursing home? I'd say they'd be better off spending it, wouldn't you?'

'But some of the Brits seem to have no idea that they can't just live here now. I worry about them. And sooner or later, they won't be able to buy anything at all here.'

'All the more reason for them to do it while they still can. You shouldn't worry. Worrying won't keep you in your job. You have to toughen up a bit. Do things their way.'

'Like you, you mean? You used to be a nice lad.'

'I *am* a nice lad. Just not as nice as you.'

'You were lovely when you first arrived,' she repeated stubbornly.

'Well, just between you and me and the *Cuba Libre*, I sometimes feel like I'm conning my gran out of her life savings. But it isn't like timeshare. People hang onto the apartments for years. Fly out here every winter. Send their friends and families out here. What's wrong with that?'

'Nothing, I suppose.'

'And the developers have had a hard time too.'

'Not that hard.'

'Oh I don't know so much. A lot of them have gone bust. We're doing our bit for the economy.'

'I suppose you're right.'

'And there are plenty of other visitors from Europe. Not just Britain. Ireland for one. Scandinavia. Meanwhile, I've got sunshine and a roof over my head and enough cash to go out to the pub when I want to. I couldn't get a job at home except a call centre or kitchen-portering on a zero hours contract and the Job Centre telling me it was only part time, so why was I taking it? I was well pissed off, I'm telling you.'

She had to smile at his intensity. Besides, she could see that he might be right.

'I take your point.'

'Mind you, I'm not sure what *you're* doing out here. Don't you get maintenance or something from your ex-husband?'

'No, I don't. I wanted to make a clean break. We sold the flat and paid off the mortgage and I took a lump sum. But it's not huge. It's in the bank, earning peanuts. I went back home to live with my mum for a bit before I came here. I need to keep some capital in case I want to try to buy a flat, but I couldn't afford one out here at the moment.'

Her family had been very surprised by her sudden decision to move to The Canaries.

'You need to be at home. You need the support of your relatives at a time like this.'

Her mother was genuinely worried about her.

'You can always come home,' said her sister-in-law, comfortingly.

'I'm sure it's not for you. You'll be back in three months. Or three weeks, more like.'

They had been sitting in Fiona's kitchen. She was trying out a new recipe: a spicy macaroni cheese with tuna. As well as teaching Food Technology at a local college, she gave demonstrations at WRI meetings: Feed a Family On A Budget. Margaret had often envied her efficiency. Fiona's freezer was always well stocked with neatly labelled packages. She would never, thought Margaret, find ten year old packets of frozen green beans at the very bottom of the chest, as she herself sometimes did, among the escaped peas and crushed berries lurking there. When Fiona had rice left over from dinner she would always 'chill it quickly and pop it in the freezer', not leave it in the back of the fridge, to be discovered a week later, when it had become a health hazard. Fiona would never know the shock of opening the last cake tin in the pile, only to meet a ghastly monster of thriving green and blue mould that had once been a Madeira cake.

Margaret had always managed to get along with Fiona by agreeing with almost everything she said, and then doing the opposite. It was a coward's way out and she despised herself for it, but at least nobody got hurt. Ian, her brother, was capable of rousing the same intense vexation in her, even though she was very fond of him.

When Fiona had heard about the Tenerife job, she had said, 'How can you *think* of uprooting yourself at your time of life?'

'But I'm only thirty five!' Margaret protested. '*You're* older than me!' Fiona was heading for forty.

'Well you're not a teenager to go gallivanting off around the world, you know,' said Ian. Her brother's idea of a holiday was a fortnight in Crieff or Peebles with golf every day and his children installed in whatever kids' club was available for their entertainment, while Fiona took herself off to the spa. It was no wonder he called Tenerife 'round the world'. Fiona had been trying to get him to take a golfing holiday in Portugal for years but he said he didn't like the heat. He made an exception for occasional conferences, but you could attend those and hardly ever set foot outside the air conditioned venue.

Margaret had ignored his advice but she couldn't help remembering his words now. For once he might have been right. She was unhappy. Homesick, even. Not even the winter sunshine of Tenerife helped. It looked as though, like it or not, she might be forced to return home, even before Fiona's predicted three months were up. She thought of the future, of maybe going back to her job in the library.

She remembered her old bedroom in her mother's house, to which she had initially fled with relief after the separation, but which had begun to seem stifling, especially during lockdown, full of soft toys, childish ornaments and books. She thought of a future involving a job that no longer interested her, free time spent on what? Volunteering, charity fundraising, coffee mornings, quizzes ... pickleball? That had been Fiona's latest suggestion. Pickleball. She thought of brief encounters with Alastair and his new wife. She thought of going back to all this and black misery descended on her.

'But why Tenerife?' Fiona had asked, in obvious amazement that anyone should want to go and work there. Why indeed, Margaret wondered, sitting in the bar with the beginnings of a headache from the gin and the buzz of conversation threatening to drown the music. The musician was playing something very intricate, very Spanish. He was *good*, for God's sake! Really good. Why couldn't they just shut up and listen?

The truth was that anywhere would have done, just as long as she could escape Glasgow, just as long as she could be sure of never seeing Alastair again. He had left her after some twelve years of marriage. They had met during Freshers' Week, had dated through their four years as honours students and married immediately after graduation. She had got a slightly better degree, but he had always assumed that he was the clever one and she had gone along with him. It was Alastair who had gone on to do a postgraduate degree. Alastair who had secured a lectureship, tenure and the prospect of a decent academic career, albeit not a particularly starry or well-paid one.

She had once heard him saying to a friend, 'Oh, Mags reached her peak at university, you know. She'll never go any further now.'

It had made her angry, but not angry enough. His degree was in Linguistics. She had done a rewarding but not particularly useful degree in English Literature. During the first years of their marriage, her job in the library had barely helped to fund Alastair's PhD, although she had studied for her diploma at the same time. Whenever she ventured to mention children, he would always reply that it was too soon, there was plenty of time, wasn't there? He had been on a fellowship back then, teaching and researching, but money was tight. They had to save every penny. Things had improved later, although when she looked back on it, those early days had been fun, scouring charity shops and salerooms for furniture, making curtains and cushion covers on her mum's old sewing machine.

Alastair had turned out to be quite good at climbing the academic ladder, good at the occasional backstabbing. She had thought him nicer than he was. Or perhaps the working environment had changed him, had changed the man she first fell in love with. The work was hard, the world of academia as much of as rat race as any other. Over the years, a tendency to intellectual snobbery had grown and blossomed in this man she had married. She remembered the way he would snap at anyone who had the temerity to disagree with him, his scorn of anyone who held an opposing point of view, his habit of explaining things, patronisingly. Sometimes she would argue with him, but all too often she preferred to keep the peace.

Eventually, they had relinquished their rented apartment in favour of their own small flat in Hillhead, not too far from the university. They could afford it only because the bank of mum and dad had given him some money. It meant that he could get up late and still make it to lectures on time. The flat was half way up a traditional Glasgow tenement, with pretty green tiles on the stairways, fancy cornicing in the rooms and original woodwork. There was a kitchen, a sitting room, a bedroom and a boxroom that Alastair used as a study. The fireplace in the sitting room had tiles too, rows of stylised lilies. It was a desirable little flat but Margaret hankered after outside space, a garden. Her desire for a garden of her own grew with every year that passed. There was a communal green at the back with clothes poles for the occasional dry day, but that was all.

'I couldn't be bothered with a garden, could you?' remarked Alastair, without ever waiting for a reply.

Margaret had to content herself with house plants, but the apartment was dark and very few of them survived. She put an aspidistra in a big pot on the table in the window. Indestructible. She polished its leaves, feeling like a character in a Victorian novel. Eventually, her hours in the library were cut and she applied for other, full time jobs but didn't even manage to secure an interview.

'Don't worry about it,' Alastair said. 'We're fine as we are, aren't we? We're fine just as we are.'

Most of their friends seemed to be Alastair's co-workers. From time to time, they entertained her husband's colleagues with supper parties. Nobody called them dinner parties now. The guests would sit huddled around the scrubbed pine table in the kitchen, like participants in a TV reality show, having intellectual debates and drinking a lot of wine, while Margaret scurried around with bowls and dishes, refusing all offers of help, hating the fact that everyone could watch her cooking. It made her feel clumsy and incompetent, although she was a good cook when left to her own devices. Eventually, she realised that she could probably have served them bread and cheese, so long as she kept the wine flowing freely. They came for the booze and the conversation, not the food. Latterly, she had taken to buying everything from Marks and Spencer or Waitrose transferring the food to her own dishes beforehand and hiding the packaging in the bin. Then she started going to Aldi or Lidl, because the prepared foods were just as good for half the price and it seemed like a small rebellion.

Alastair never noticed. Nobody ever did.

For a while, after her library hours were cut, she had led this quiet existence, going out to work for a few hours each day, shopping and cleaning. She had volunteered in a charity shop where the paid manageress patronised her, telling her that she 'really needed to learn a bit more about retail, dear.'

She felt old before her time.

One of her old university friends, Suzie, clearly worried about her, had persuaded her

to sign up for an art appreciation class and she had enjoyed it very much indeed. Suzie was a successful artist in her own right, and felt that her friend was vegetating, blaming Alastair, although she never risked the friendship by saying it out loud. Occasionally Margaret had found herself dozing off in the warmth and darkness, while the lecturer showed slides, praised this or that artwork, damned another with faint praise. But it had been a good class. It had reminded her that she had a brain, that other worlds were possible. It had reminded her of Italy and Spain and the little frisson of excitement she felt whenever she came across images of sunshine and flowers, orange and lemon trees, even if they drifted only across her Facebook page.

Older people told her that she was lucky to have such a good husband, a good provider, and she believed them, but there were no children to disturb their ordered existence. No children. Even here in the warmth of a Tenerife bar, bitterness threatened to engulf her and she pushed the words out of her mind as she always did, knowing that recriminations were useless. There had been no problem of fertility, or not so far as she knew. She had been on the pill, at Alastair's insistence.

'Not the right time.'

He had said it so often. Perhaps he thought she agreed with him. If so, she had only herself to blame. She found it hard to credit just how compliant she had been. How had that crept up on her, that compliance? When she finally found out that he had been conducting an affair, had deceived her for a couple of years, he had said 'I didn't want to hurt you.'

'How do you think I feel now?' she shouted.

He was shocked. She never shouted.

Her thoughts always followed the same pattern. The same image always came back to her. Six months after the divorce, she had seen Alastair and his new wife, Jenny. She had been one of his postgraduate students. He had been scrupulous about that, if not quite so scrupulous about adultery, only dating her after she had graduated. Not long after lockdown ended, Margaret had seen them walking along Great Western Road together, his arm cradled protectively around the young woman, helping her along, her face plump and rosy, her belly huge in the final stages of pregnancy, swollen beneath the smart winter coat. That sight had been the final push she needed to get away, to change her life and now here she was, selling property in Tenerife.

A few years ago, she and Alastair had spent a winter holiday here. Alastair had passed the entire two weeks lying beside the blue hotel swimming pool that was too cold for bathing, drinking large glasses of *Cuba Libre* – rum and Coke. The more he drank, the more he snapped his fingers at the waiters and treated them with casual rudeness. Perhaps it was here that she had first begun to wonder what she saw in him; here she had felt her affection for him begin to turn to indifference. She had never really managed to hate him, even in the middle of the divorce, but in Tenerife, she had seen him in a new light, the glaring sunlight of these islands. Perhaps he had felt the same about her.

Alastair had sunbathed until he was bright pink. He had spent a day or two in a cool bar, plastered in cream, recovering and drinking too much. Then he had resumed his sunbathing, albeit more sensibly. She had slept beside him under the shade of a big umbrella. Later, bored with lazing, she had walked about Los Cristianos and looked in shops at straw donkeys and keyrings in the shape of bunches of bananas, and then dawdled back to their hotel. Above all, she had wanted to go up into the mountains to see the crater of the volcano, Teide. Alastair had always postponed the excursion, finding excuses not to stir from the poolside. Just before their last day, they had argued about it.

'Go up there yourself, why don't you?' he said. 'I can't be bothered. It'll be full of tourists, anyway.'

To spite him, she had not gone, and then later she had bitterly regretted her decision. To her shame, all she had seen of Tenerife on that occasion had been the inside of their hotel, the swimming pool, the streets round about and the distant, tantalizing view of cloud-shrouded peaks. Was that why she had taken this job? To prove to herself that she could be adventurous?

Now, although she had been here for several weeks, she still hadn't seen the mountain, had hardly even set foot outside Los Cristianos, apart from a few taxi trips to view properties outside the town. Her work companions had all been to Teide before and she hadn't yet summoned the courage to hire a car and drive there along precipitous roads and on the wrong side of the road at that. She had heard stories about Canarian *bandidos* in the wild country high above the tourist coast and although she didn't really believe them, the innate caution of the lone female always got the better of her. It seemed that even when you managed to get away, you always took yourself with you.

Conor interrupted her thoughts, his mind still on her financial situation. Margaret seldom talked about herself, and her colleagues were curious about her.

'You've got a nice little flat though,' he said.

'It *is* nice. And I don't pay over the odds either. I'm renting off some friends. Well, my mum's friends, really.'

Niamh, who was sitting at the other side of the table, moved closer to Conor.

'What's all this?' she said. 'Secrets?' She was a slender Dubliner with long auburn hair that she was always pushing away from her face.

'No secrets,' said Conor. 'We were just talking about the job.'

'God, how boring.'

'It isn't boring. I enjoy it.'

'But Maggie doesn't. You can see that.'

Niamh was extrovert and pretty and she was very good at her job. It was amazing how many properties she managed to sell and she must be doing quite well out of it, since she earned a commission on each sale.

Niamh slipped a long, slender arm around Conor. Margaret felt faintly excluded, though they were still sitting opposite her, still smiling at her. The singer had finished his performance. He dipped his head in acknowledgement of their applause and wished them *buenas noches*. Then he made his way up to the bar for a drink. Most of his drinks seemed to be either on the house or paid for by the customers, especially the single girls. Understandably. Margaret found her gaze drawn to him again, to his arms, brown and strong. He leaned on the bar and drank a beer while he spoke to the barman in rapid Spanish, laughing about something.

She wondered about him, wondered if he came from the mainland or if he belonged here. She had met, or at least spoken to, few genuine Canary Islanders so far. There were the women who worked in the supermarkets, the thick-set security guards who lurked outside her block of flats, and the wiry men, wearing dusty, threadbare jeans and sweat-soaked vests or T-shirts, who worked on and around the various building sites. There was the bank manager, who slowed down his

Spanish so that she could try to understand him. And of course there were the waiters.

It disappointed her. Somehow, perhaps unreasonably in this tourist town, she had expected more, expected that she might be working with local people, getting to know them, making friends. Instead, it felt quite deliberately English. Colonial. The waiters seemed to know it. They smiled enigmatically all the time. They saw nothing demeaning about their work and they were right. These men – and they were almost always men, she noticed – moved with grace and dignity and a kind of superiority. Most of them were tall, with long nosed, haughty good looks and they employed their undoubted charm on a string of female tourists.

Whenever she came out with the crowd from the property company they usually finished up in this place, a bar and restaurant called La Paloma. It had a green and white striped awning over a cool terrace, with basket chairs around the tables. She had watched the waiters and admired them when they were plagued by rude, difficult or simply idiotic tourists who shouted at them to make them understand, whistled or snapped fingers at them to attract their attention, or sent meals back untasted because they themselves had ordered the wrong thing. The unfailing patience of these young men astonished her. Even good natured Margaret would have felt like tipping the food down a sunburnt neck. But they made no scenes, quickly adjusting their manner to suit the mood of the moment. Once or twice, she had glimpsed their faces as they spoke to each other behind a difficult customer's back, and their longsuffering expressions had made her smile, but they seemed to enjoy their work, accepting compliments and slights alike with indifference. Sure of themselves.

Tonight, however, it was the musician she watched, her eyes continually drawn to him. She couldn't help herself. She had read that the natives of these islands, the Guanches, had been killed by the conquering Spaniards, but intermarriage must have taken place, as had happened with the Viking invaders of Scotland and the women whose menfolk they had killed. Life and desire, perhaps even love would eventually have their way. Those original Canarian inhabitants had been of Berber ancestry. By all accounts they had been civilized and handsome and the genes had persisted. You saw people all the time, people who looked strangely beautiful, men and women both.

The musician was no exception, a fine featured man with high cheekbones, brown eyes and hair so dark that it looked black in the dim light of the bar. His name was on the poster outside the restaurant. 'Tonight, Luis Herrera Garcia plays and sings the romance of Spain.' Conor had paused outside to make vomiting noises and pull a face at this wording but there was no doubt the man was talented.

'Oho,' said Niamh, following her gaze. 'Got our eye on the singer, have we?'

Margaret shook her head. 'I was just curious about him, that's all. And his guitar.'

'It's just a guitar.' Conor shrugged.

'It looks like a very good one. An old one. You'd think they'd get fed up, wouldn't you? Playing in restaurants. Singing for the tourists. There can't be much fun in it.'

'I suppose he makes a decent living,' said Conor, dismissively.

Soon after that, the party began to disperse. As Margaret stood up, she realised that the alcohol had gone to her head. She felt unsteady, her hands springing away from her sides, her cheeks flushed. As they passed the bar, squeezing between tables and stools, she stumbled and almost fell. The *guitarrista* put out a firm hand, took her elbow and steadied her. 'Careful, *señora*,' he said, smiling at her. It was a broad smile. White teeth. 'Are you alright?'

'Yes. Yes, thank you.' She blushed hotly and rushed out of the bar in some confusion, aware that Niamh was giggling behind her.

'Are you OK?' asked Conor again.

'Yes. I'm *fine* thanks. It's the gin. I'm not used to such large measures and I haven't eaten very much today. I'm supposed to be on a diet.'

She was always starting a diet, promising herself that she would eat only fruit and vegetables and drink mineral water for a month instead of disguising her bulges with her usual sloppy T-shirts and elasticated waists, but her willpower wasn't very strong. Most evenings she would sit alone in her flat, listening to the babble of Spanish coming from her television, her mind thankfully seizing on the odd familiar phrase. She would play patience or spider solitaire on her laptop or read on her Kindle. Sometimes she would doomscroll on her phone, but the state of the world was depressing. As she did all these things, the temptation to drink cheap wine and eat chocolate was irresistible. She wasn't fat, only a little plump, but she envied Niamh's lithe slenderness.

Conor and Niamh walked her home. Conor insisted and Niamh seemed torn between admiration of his good manners and an impatient desire to have him all to herself.

'Would you like a drink?' Margaret was anxious to postpone the loneliness of the empty flat for a while longer. 'Wine? Or coffee?'

'No, thanks,' said Niamh quickly, before Conor could accept. 'We'd best be getting back, hadn't we, Con?'

'I suppose so,' said Conor. 'Goodnight, Maggie.'

He kissed her on the cheek, then put his arm around Niamh and turned to go. Margaret knew that she was inclined to mother him and that Niamh resented it. It didn't help that Conor liked to sit in her flat drinking sweet black coffee or beer after beer, talking about his ambitions to own a property empire. But lately, his visits had become shorter and more infrequent and she knew that was down to Niamh. She was relieved. He was so young, so raw. But all the same, she missed his company.

She half filled her kettle with bottled water and set it on to boil, to make herself a nightcap, something to counteract the effects of the alcohol. When she went into her tiny en-suite bathroom she put on the light first and then peered cautiously round the door. To her relief she saw that the white tiles were clear. Just occasionally, there would be a cockroach, a huge brown creature, squatting obscenely in the middle of the floor. The first time she had seen one, she hadn't known what to do and had eventually summoned the security guard from downstairs to dispose of it, but she hadn't liked the way he had grinned at her as she stood there in her cotton pyjamas and bathrobe, and ever since, she had managed to squash them herself and flush them down the lavatory or wrap them in wads of tissue paper and put them in her kitchen bin. She hated them.

To be fair to the company that managed the flats, the roaches were few and far between. The drains were fumigated regularly and the poor creatures that finally struggled into Margaret's bathroom were half dead and only coming up too late for a little fresh air. She supposed this was a blessing because the poison denied them a cock-roach's normal speed of movement.

At least they stayed still while she hit them.

Sometimes she left her bathroom light on all night in an effort to deter them. Once there had been a sickening crunch as she closed the door in the middle of the night and in the morning she had seen the squashed body where it had been horribly trapped, half way up between the door jamb and the inner edge of the door. Once she had gone in in the early hours of the morning and, sitting sleepily on the lavatory, had become aware of the large brown corpse at her feet being carried off by a posse of efficient black ants. After that, her night-time visits to the loo were always fraught with worry.

She took her tea to bed, plumping up the pillows to make herself comfortable. The bedroom was very warm after the day's heat. Soon after her arrival she had swapped her pyjamas for a big T-shirt. She lay back with her Kindle and began to read. It had been an unexpected and faintly ironic gift from her friends in the library where she had worked for so long. 'You can stuff it with eBooks,' they had told her and that was exactly what she had done. There was a dearth of books in English in Los Cristianos. She didn't know what she would have done without it.

She put down her reader and drank the last mouthful of her Earl Grey, an indulgence because it was quite expensive in the local *super-mercado*. She lay back on the pillows and closed her eyes. It was still early and she could hear the strains of music from the bar down by the pool, just drifting in at the window. Somebody – an Englishman, she thought – was singing. Amid scattered applause, he began 'Spanish Eyes'. She supposed that all over these islands at any time of day or night, there would be someone singing a version of that song. All over Spain, perhaps. Unaccountably she thought of the musician, Luis Herrera, and the raw passion in his voice and in his music that had made her shiver: a sudden intimation of something magical.

Presently, she drifted off to sleep. Ever since she had arrived in Tenerife, she had been dreaming in vivid and sometimes disturbing colour. It surprised her because at home, her dreams had always been vague images that slipped out of her waking consciousness as quickly as she tried to recapture them. But here she had no trouble at all in remembering every last detail of every bright, light-filled dream. She wondered if it had something to do with the vibrant colours of the landscape itself. She dreamed tonight, incongruously, that she was a lady, dancing at a ball. She was in love with an officer of some kind, a tall man with Alastair's face. But he no longer loved her. In the dream she knew that she didn't care. Her heart was light and free of him. She heard birdsong falling sharply into her head. There seemed to be few birds in the hot and overcrowded towns of southern Tenerife. Sometimes she could hear the dusty sparrows squabbling over bread in the streets but that was all. What she distinctly heard in her dream was the cut-glass sound of a blackbird singing in a thicket and she ran towards it in inexplicable but joyful anticipation.

CHAPTER THREE

Girl, you are so pretty
that I never tire of looking at you.
But how can I speak to you?
I don't know if you love me.

In early March, Carnival time brought a fairground to Los Cristianos. Men swarmed over the site, noisy and good humoured, transforming it within a few days. By day, it had an untidy, seedy appearance, but by night, it looked as though a little piece of magic had been wrought so that when you were in the middle of all the lights, the crowds, the music, it was joyfully disorientating, as though a fragment of some other, more vivid dimension had been superimposed there. There were dizzying rides, an octopus with small cars flung up and out, a big wheel, dodgem cars and a speedway, as well as row upon row of stalls offering prizes for shooting or throwing. There were *churros* stalls, long, thin doughnuts, greasy, hot and fragrant, freshly made and eaten with powdered sugar or dipped in chocolate. There were liquor stalls and hot dog stalls smelling overpoweringly of fried onions.

Luis had always loved Carnival. When he was a boy, his mother and father had sometimes brought the whole family over from their island home of La Gomera to nearby Tenerife at carnival time. They had stayed with his uncle and aunt in Santa Cruz, and they had gone out to watch the processions. He could still remember the excitement of so much naked flesh, the bright colours, the feathers and spangles, and the oddly syncopated rhythms. He could remember sitting on his father's shoulders, the better to see what was going on, and holding firmly on to his ears.

'My ears! *Güicho*, you're going to pull my ears off,' his father said, laughing and tugging at his small feet. He always called his son by that name, an affectionate and slightly mocking version of Luis but one that nobody else ever used, not even his mother, who sometimes called him *Lucho*.

His older sisters, Isabel and Antonia, were standing in front. They were wearing all their traditional fiesta finery: blue skirts with red and white petticoats, white lace blouses and jaunty straw hats with bright yellow scarves beneath. They were very proud of them-selves, and kept twirling around, showing off. Cristina was still a baby, but she was already sitting up in her buggy and making noises that were almost words. Luis was dressed as a matador in a black suit, with a white shirt, a black cloak and a hat edged with scarlet. He remembered the suit vividly. It had been very uncomfortable to wear because the trousers were too short for him. He had always been tall for his age. The suit had belonged to one of the Tenerife cousins who had outgrown it very quickly, and he had inherited it. He remembered his mother and his aunt dressing him up in the suit and then making him parade up and down while they admired him. Now, when he pictured himself strutting about, swirling the cloak around, he cringed with retrospective embarrassment.

As the only boy among three sisters he had been a little prince, and often wondered just how much of a spoilt show-off he must have seemed. He was being hard on himself. His elder sisters had always petted and protected him, but then Cristina adored him because he fussed over her. They were a very close family. His mother, Maria, loved all her children equally but Eduardo undoubtedly loved his only son if not more, then differently, investing more of himself in the boy, teaching him all that he knew and loved of the history and traditions of their home. It was his Uncle Paco who first taught him to play the guitar, taught him the old melodies of the islands, although later he had more formal lessons, and it was an old man called Pedro who had first taught him to whistle.

Luis and his father, Eduardo, would often spend a day together, fishing for sardines in the brightly painted wooden boat they kept, or walking through the mountains to meet with his father's friend Pedro – '*Peiro*' they pronounced it on the island – who kept a small herd of goats near Alajero. Pedro was a mountain man and a *silbador*, who knew the whistled language of La Gomera. The old Gomeros, the people who had lived here long before the Spaniards came calling and killing and intermarrying, had used the language, the *silbido*, to call to each other across the steep-sided *barrancos* or gorges of the island. Pedro seemed to know many variations, formed by placing his fingers in different ways in his mouth, and he taught Luis all kinds of useful whistled phrases such as 'when are you coming over?' and 'your dinner is ready and the wine is on the table'.

Sometimes, so many years later, among the holiday crowds of Los Cristianos and Las Americas, jabbering away in the alien tongues of English or German, expecting him always to understand them but seldom attempting to understand him in return, Luis would be transported back to that springtime hillside on La Gomera. He saw himself sitting on low stones among the palms, the starry *tabaiba*, the spiky aloes; resting beneath a moss-bearded almond tree with pale petals drifting down on to his dark head; eating lumps of *gofio amasado*, toasted maize meal kneaded into a stiff paste in an old goatskin bag ('the older the better,' said Pedro), with the little man whistling like a bird and showing him how to put his grimy fingers this way and that in his mouth. Luis vividly remembered the taste of his own fingers, slightly gritty from the rocks and nutty from the *gofio*. And he remembered too the deep vein of silence that ran beneath his own first feeble attempts at the strange language, the bleating of goats, the flat clank-clank of their bells, and the more distant village sounds of dog and cockerel and crying baby.

Pedro was not young even then. He had been of the generation before Luis's father. His grandfather's generation, really. He still used the traditional *astia*, the long pointed pole, with the aid of which he could leap about the *barrancos* like one of his own goats. When Luis grew tired of the *silbido*, and when the men were engrossed in talk of their own, he would take the *astia* and practise with it, falling often, but always getting up and trying again. Pedro would clap his hands and say, 'Bravo! – bravo, my Luis! Bravo, my little man!' and he would glow with pride, knowing that he was right not to cry, feeling manly and full of his own importance.

Pedro had lived to a great age: he was over ninety years old when he died. He had certainly outlived Eduardo who had died very suddenly and much too young, some six years ago. Now, whenever Luis returned to the island, and on the few occasions when he found the time to walk in the mountains, he half expected to meet Pedro swinging over the rocks towards him, smiling his big, gap-toothed smile and offering *gofio* in a goatskin bag. He wouldn't have been at all surprised. Rather the surprise was that he was no longer there. His grandson herded goats in the same place, but he had never bothered to learn the *silbido Gomero*. Neither did he use the *astia*. Luis was angry about it, unreasonably he knew. Here and there were still people who could and did keep up the old traditions and the children learned the *silbido* in school now, although the island probably needed more young people, more families prepared to stay. But the men who had grown up with the traditions were growing old themselves. He wondered whether there would be any to take their place. He would practise the few phrases of the old language he remembered, promising himself that when he came back to live on the island, he would certainly learn more. And if he had a child, he would teach him or her as well, the way Pedro had taught him.

Pedro's *astia* had been given to Luis on the old man's death. It was propped up in his mother's kitchen. Occasionally, Luis would threaten to use it and Maria would say, 'Mother of God, you'll break your neck, Luis! You leave it where it is.' Once, he took it out, and his mother was right. He did nearly break his neck, landed on a sharp rock and tore a deep cut in his arm. He still had the scar. He picked himself up, deeply ashamed of himself, looked around furtively to make sure that nobody had seen his fall, and after that he had left the *astia* at home, regretfully nevertheless.

All this ran through Luis's mind as he walked down towards the seashore restaurant where he was to sing that night. His way lay along the fringe of the fairground stalls, and he carried his guitar carefully in its case. It was his most precious possession. All along the roads leading to the fairground, traders had set up their wares, either on the pavement or on folding tables that they had brought with them. Visitors from the nearby Moroccan coast offered pottery, painted tiles, polished wooden elephants and strings of beads. Closer to the fairground there were counters piled high with nut brittle and coconut ice, dried fruit and nuts, salted almonds. There were stalls selling carnival hats and masks, cheap and cheerful plastic toys for the children, souvenir keyrings. The noise of the fairground was deafening: the thrumming of dozens of generators, the music from each stall, the squeals and shrieks of laughter from children, the barking dogs and the swell of voices.

He had come to this same fairground when he was twenty one and still studying at La Laguna University. He had been at home on La Gomera for the weekend, but when he travelled back to Los Cristianos he had brought Cristina, who was just sixteen, and her friend Teresa who, he realised to his sudden gratification, was dewy eyed with love for him. He had managed to win them both one of the brightly coloured carnival dolls called *chochonas* on the old camel race. Back then, the stall must have been refurbished and repaired over the years but like most of the fairground rides and games the design was traditional. *Chochonas* were big rag dolls with smiling faces and masses of luridly coloured hair in pink or yellow or blue wool. They were always dressed in gaudy clown's costumes and the stalls back then were full of them. This stall consisted of a miniature race track with, in every lane, a wooden camel with a rider astride his beast. Down below were alleyways with holes cut in them, each corresponding to a camel. People threw tennis balls so that they landed in the holes and rolled back down to each player. Some holes scored more points than others and the camels moved up the track. The prize for the winner was a *chochona*.

Luis had always been good at this game, partly because he had a steady hand and a good eye, but mostly because he didn't care too much whether he won or lost. There was a casual streak in him. He never tried too hard and, paradoxically, he often won. On that occasion, all those years ago, he gave the first doll to Teresa out of politeness, and because he was almost certain he could win another. Besides, she was very pretty and so obviously fancied him that it would have seemed unkind not to indulge her. Sure enough, he had managed to pull it off a second time, and soon Cristina had a pink haired doll to match Teresa's blue one. Cristina had flown at him and kissed him on both cheeks.

'Oh, Luis! I knew you could do it!' she said, lavish in her affection as always.

Then she took one arm while Teresa shyly took the other, and they walked through the fairground together, the two girls proudly hugging their *chochonas*. He was very aware of Teresa, warm and sweet, scurrying to keep up with his and Cristina's long legged stride.

'Don't walk so fast!' she would say, and they would slow down, laughing at her, but they were both very fond of her. She was tiny and dark, with unexpectedly blue eyes. She always looked even smaller beside Cristina's boyish, slender height. The two girls had been friends since babyhood. Luis had hardly noticed Teresa changing until he realised with surprise that during his absence, the wiry child had become a graceful and very attractive girl.

Some weeks after the fair, he had come home to La Gomera again for the Easter celebrations and one late afternoon he walked down into the town of San Sebastian from his parents' house. Luis was supposed to be on his way to meet a friend who was coming in from Hermigua to see him, but instead he was waylaid by Teresa, lurking almost furtively by the roadside. She had a jealous and very protective brother but then Luis was seriously protective of Cristina. It was just the way things were. Teresa walked down the hill with him a little way but when they came to the ruined house where the Cabello family had once lived, they stopped and went inside. The Cabellos, mother, father and three children, had emigrated to mainland Spain years before, and the house was a sad shell, with a litter of superfluous personal belongings scattered about: bottles and boxes, a few broken pots and pans and, rather incongruously, a pile of old wedding photographs. It was, thought Luis, as though they had wanted to leave the old, hard life behind, and their memories of it too. Sometimes it seemed to Luis that people were always leaving La Gomera. People had headed west to South America after the Civil War, but latterly they were more likely to go east to the mainland in search of money, in search of security, in search of greener grass, whatever that was perceived to be. It made him sad to think about it.

They found a threadbare, musty blanket in the ruins. Luis spread it out and they sat down together. They had hardly spoken to each other on the way down the hill. They had known each other all their lives, but it seemed to Luis as if his body had suddenly betrayed those years of familiarity with a huge and unexpected onslaught of desire for Teresa. He took her in his arms and kissed her. He felt her trembling and then responding hungrily to his kiss. She wore a thin lemon-coloured dress, a child's dress really, too short for her. He felt her small breasts pressing up against him, her slender arms reaching around his neck as she kissed him again. He ran his hand over her legs, then higher, feeling the skin downy soft against the roughness of his palm, and she shivered at his touch, but opened her legs just a fraction to allow his hand to move up. His own heart was pounding now.

Then, suddenly, she said, 'Oh, Luis, I do love you so much!'

Her voice was so young, so defenceless that he pulled back and looked into those trusting eyes. Her face was all open to him, the brown of her cheeks flushed with deep rose. There was a smudge of dust on her forehead; her hair was tangled and, looking down, he saw that her feet in tattered sandals were grubby from the dust of the road. He was seized by a sense of her vulnerability.

It was his essential kindliness that halted him.

He was older and he cared about her. He thought about Cristina and how he would feel if another man took advantage of her innocent affection. It wasn't possible. It wasn't right or honourable. He gently detached Teresa's arms and stood up. He saw surprise, momentary disappointment, then relief flooding her face. It was definitely relief. He stretched out his hands, grasped hers and pulled her to her feet. Then he kissed her gently on the forehead, where the dust was smudged on the smooth skin.

'This isn't right, *Teresita*,' he said. 'Because I don't love you. And you're not ready. Not really. I'm very fond of you, but I don't love you. Not like this, anyway. It would be all wrong and we'd be sorry about it.'

Her face fell, the lower lip thrust out like a child about to cry. It made him laugh, but he slipped his arm around her shoulders.

'I don't love anyone yet. Not in that way. I'm going to Tenerife. To work, this summer. Maybe to the Peninsula. Maybe through Europe. I don't know yet. It wouldn't be right to take advantage of you.'

'I wouldn't mind. It wouldn't be taking advantage. Not if it was you, Luis.'

'You wouldn't mind now, and it would be very nice. But you might mind later on, when I'm gone. There's plenty of time. You don't have to rush anything. Neither of us does.'

She brushed her skirt down, took a comb out of her pocket and set her hair to rights. She had resumed possession of herself with a completeness that astonished him. He saw that whatever women gave or seemed to give, they would always keep more, much more, hidden. For themselves. But perhaps men did that too. Perhaps he did it as well.

'Shall I walk you home?' he said.

'No. No, I'll go by myself, thank-you.'

She thrust her head high into the air, shoulders back, brave as a little soldier. She made him want to laugh. She made him want to love her. In the doorway he kissed her again, very tenderly.

'You're the first man I've ever let kiss me like that,' she said. 'The first man I've ever wanted to kiss me.'

'Thank-you!' was all he could think of to say. He watched her walking up the track towards her home, her head still tilted high because she was aware of his eyes on her, the short yellow skirt swirling about her legs. He turned back briefly and looked at the interior of the cottage, moved the blanket, folding it neatly over a box. The wedding pictures saddened him, the young couple looking even younger than himself, the girl only a little older than Teresa. The cottage seemed full of misery and defeat, of unfulfilled dreams. Impulsively he turned the wedding picture face downwards so that those bright, hope-filled eyes were no longer turned towards the gloomy wreckage, trapped for ever in the ruin that had once been a home.

CHAPTER FOUR

A handsome, light hearted people are these islanders.

Olivia M Stone, 1887

He glanced at his watch. He was interrupted by the realisation that, still clutching his guitar close, he had strayed further into the fair than he had intended. The weight of the good-humoured crowd pressing in on him from behind had carried him along. He was about to turn and fight his way out again when his attention was caught by a woman queuing at one of the stalls for a drink.

She seemed vaguely familiar to him, and he remembered that he sometimes saw her in one of the restaurants where he sang: the seashore bar called La Paloma, where he was going tonight. She came in with the foreign property crowd, but though she was with them, he always thought that she didn't really seem to belong. For one thing, she was older than most of them; they were all in their late teens or early twenties. She was probably in her thirties, he thought. Like himself. He had noticed her because she actually listened to his playing. Most of these restaurant and bar audiences tended to eat, talk and laugh, noisily, throughout the entertainment. Once upon a time it had irritated him, but not now. You got used to it. It was part of the job. All the same, he noticed those who listened. And he had also noticed her because for whatever reason there seemed to be an aura of loneliness about her, and he felt sorry for her.

She got her coffee and turned away from the stall, fumbling with her purse. He wanted to warn her to be careful. There were thieves about, opportunists who might be waiting to snatch bags, purses, passports. But he thought she might misinterpret his concern, so instead, he waited and watched, just in case. She was plump and pretty, with freckles and untidy fair hair, curling down around her shoulders. The sunlight had streaked it blonde at the tips. He thought that she looked very attractive, very foreign. Preoccupied, she glanced over at him and blushed. For some reason, this touched him even more and he smiled at her.

She turned away quickly and blundered into the path of a bunch of young men. He realised that they were English and very drunk, one of the many groups of stag parties that came here all year round, creating a certain amount of mayhem. They were mostly harmless but occasionally threatening, hunting in packs, alcohol and sunshine and other more illicit substances breaking down their inhibitions. Luis couldn't tell what they were saying to the woman, but she was looking around for some means of escape. Smoothly, he went over to her, aware as ever of his precious guitar. With his free hand, he took her elbow.

'*Querida*, I wondered where you were!' he said and, ignoring the catcalls, began to walk away from the group, ushering her away from the lads. They took one look at him, the height of him, his general air of fitness, and wandered off, nudging each other, laughing.

'I'm sorry,' he said, once they were out of the fairground, letting go of her arm. 'I thought you might need rescuing.'

'Thank-you. I did. It was very kind of you.' She seemed embarrassed, unsure how to respond.

'They're idiots. Don't I sometimes see you in the bar where I play?'

'You do. I work for one of the property companies. I come in there with my colleagues. It's their favourite place.'

'But you listen to me when I play. They don't.' He looked at his watch. 'I'm so sorry, *se ora*. I must go.' He gestured towards the guitar. 'I'm singing and playing tonight. You know?'

'Yes. Your name is Luis –'

'Herrera Garcia. Why don't you walk down with me. I'll buy you a drink.'

'I think I owe *you* one, don't you?'

He smiled down at her. 'No problem. My treat.'

They walked on together. The street grew darker as they left the music behind, although the distant sounds pursued them as far as the seashore.

The restaurants here were almost empty; everyone seemed to have been sucked into the maelstrom of the fairground, and the evening diners, even the Brits who ate early, would all be later than usual. It was impossible to pass the fair without going in for just a few moments.

They stopped on the terrace of the restaurant. Luis held a chair for her and then sat down himself, propping his guitar in its case beside him on a seat. He leaned across and shook hands with her, quite formally. 'So – I'm Luis and you are?'

'Margaret.'

'Ah Margarita. Like the flower. Are you English?'

'Scottish. I'm from Scotland. And I love your music.' She nodded at the guitar case. 'You must have to take good care of your guitar.'

He was clearly very solicitous of the instrument.

'For sure. It is very old, very precious to me. The most precious thing I possess.' He patted the case. 'It was a gift. My uncle taught me to play when I was a boy. And then I had more lessons in classical guitar here on Tenerife. I prefer playing really. I sing because tourists like the traditional songs, but I like playing better.'

He was always as aware of the guitar as he was of his own body. It had been a gift from his Uncle Paco, for his tenth birthday, a very old guitar but a very good one, slender and surprisingly light. It had a sound, as Paco said, 'to make the angels weep for joy.' He was much given to these overblown poetic expressions but in this case, it was probably true. It had been left behind in the house where Paco and his wife lived. They had found it when they first moved there. The house was long and low, with red tiles, wooden shutters and a traditional platform called an *azotea* on the roof. The house had been built a long time ago by some Spanish gentleman for whom both house and garden had been a retreat, perhaps the man who had planted the antecedents of the orange grove, as well as almonds, date palms, mulberries and small, sweet bananas. There was even a dragon tree. Paco and Luis imagined him as a man who liked to play his guitar during the warm nights. Maybe one year he hadn't returned to the island from some voyage to the mainland, and everyone had forgotten about the instrument until Paco found it so many years later in the crumbling house, wrapped in quantities of silk, encased in a sturdy wooden box and stored away in a locked cupboard.

Luis's mother had said that he was much too young for such a valuable gift but Paco had waved her objections aside and given him the guitar anyway.

'What did it cost me?' he asked. 'Nothing!'

It was an old Spanish guitar with a wonderful tone, and much later on, when he learned more of such things, Luis even wondered if it might have been made by the great luthier Antonio de Torres Jurado himself. Torres had never signed his instruments, although if it proved to be a Torres guitar it would be worth a fortune. A large fortune at that. But perhaps it wasn't so old. Probably a later copy. There had been plenty of imitators. The truth was that Paco and Luis preferred not to know. They hoped that it was a copy and conspired in a kind of mutual ignorance. They could never have brought themselves to sell it.

'It would be like selling your soul,' said Paco. 'Especially if somebody put it in a museum and didn't play it!' Luis agreed with him. An instrument like this was meant to be played.

Whatever the truth of it, it was a very good guitar indeed, quieter than some, but with a beautiful depths of tone. Luis felt that it was a part of himself and when it was in his arms he always felt himself relaxing, breathing more deeply and calmly.

A waiter came to their table and wished Luis 'Good evening!' glancing curiously at his companion.

Luis ordered a coffee for himself.

'What would you like?' he asked her.

'Orange juice, please.' She wondered if she should tell him that she was *se orita*. But perhaps not. What did it matter?

'Something stronger, surely? Vodka? Gin?'

'Well, maybe a piña colada then?'

'Whatever you like.'

The waiter brought their order and left it with the usual flourish. Luis looked out into the bay, watching the lights of the boats there, dipping and swaying slightly with the evening breeze. As always he sent a mental salute winging across to his island, to La Gomera. But what should he say to her?

'So – you sell property here?' he asked her, almost abruptly. She jumped, focusing on his face. She had been watching his arm, stretched along the back of the empty seat that lay between them.

'Yes. Yes, I do. It's quite big. A reputable company.'

'Not like those timeshare places then. They used to be a menace. Come and see our beautiful apartments and we will give you a free bottle of whisky or maybe a hire car. Or maybe a free meal. Then we will take your money in exchange for a week in the sun.'

'Well, we don't sell time. We sell apartments and villas. Mostly to people from the EU. I do viewings. And then I try to finalise the sales but I'm not very good at that. I don't think it's quite the job for me.'

'Who would be right for such a job?' he asked, ingenuously. Then he thought, lots of people. People who were content to sell small parcels of paradise. Small parcels of his country.

'Oh you'd be surprised. Some people make a lot of money in commission.'

'Where are your friends tonight?'

'Oh they're just people I work with. Not close friends. We're sort of thrown together. You know how it is when you work with people?'

'I do indeed.'

'If we were at home, we might not be friends at all.'

He nodded, remembering. 'I once worked as a waiter in London. In a big hotel. And then as a sous-chef for a while. It was many years ago when I was very young. We were all one big family. Well, we had to be. I was sharing a room with three strangers. Within a week they were not strangers at all. We must get on together or kill each other. So we became very friendly, very quickly.'

He had worked in that hotel for ten terrible months. He couldn't even remember the names of the people he had shared with, because it had been so long ago; all except little Simon, who seemed too old for the job he was doing, one of nature's victims. He remembered Simon with a mixture of affection and frustration. Whenever there was dirty work to be done, the man had to do it. He always obeyed and with a good grace too, singing and making jokes. There had been occasions when the way Simon was treated had so incensed Luis that he had threatened to rebel on the small man's behalf. Always quick tempered, Luis had felt his fists itching to connect with the head chef's nose, but Simon had always restrained him.

'This is my battle, Luis,' he had said. 'So let me fight it in my own way.'

So far as Luis could see, it was no fight at all. It was complete capitulation.

'That must be why your English is so good.' The woman brought him back to the present, smiling at him. She still seemed nervous. Why would she be nervous of him?

'I learn quickly. I was in England for almost a year. That was some years ago. But I had been travelling for a while before that. And then November came and I found that I couldn't stand another winter there.'

'If you think London is cold, you should try Scotland!'

'Where do you live in Scotland?'

'I'm from Glasgow.'

'Is it colder than London?'

'It's colder and wetter and it goes on for much longer. Especially in the spring. I always think people in London have no idea what it's like.'

'One winter was enough for me. Besides, I didn't really like London very much, so I came home for the winter and then went to the Peninsula again. To mainland Spain,' he qualified. 'I went to work in Barcelona for a while. I like Barcelona very much. In fact I love it. Most beautiful of cities.'

'So you're a chef as well?'

'In a way. I can cook. But also, I play. What does that make me? A *guitarrista* who cooks or a chef who is a musician? I enjoy both. Why not?' He grinned. It surprised him that he was managing so well with his English. He used it almost every day, chatting to customers in the restaurants where he worked, but he seldom had occasion to talk about himself. Usually he spoke about his music or the islands: telling visitors about the beauties of Teide or the lace made at Oratava or the times of the ferries to La Gomera. Now the speed of his thought sometimes outstripped his facility with words so that one tumbled over disconcertingly into the next, but it was becoming easier all the time.

'How do you bear the cold?' he asked her. 'I never got used to that cold. You wash your clothes but you cannot get them dry. You spend all your time and money and energy just to keep warm. The old people –' He gestured broadly. 'You let them die because they are cold. I can't understand it.' He looked across at her almost fiercely and then subsided into his chair. 'No. I don't understand it at all.'

He had always been quick tempered. He could feel the current rise in him, sparks of anger flashing and crackling around him. Injustice, wherever he found it, angered him, but then his temper would just as abruptly subside. On this occasion it was the uncertainty in her face as she stared at him that calmed him. She was a nice woman. He could see that. Quiet but nice.

'So you have not made good friends here?' he asked, more gently.

'Not many, no.'

'What do you do with your free time?'

'Oh, lots of things. I swim a bit. Read, walk, explore.'

Lonely pursuits, he thought.

'Where do you explore?' he asked. 'What have you seen? Have you been to Teide?'

'Not yet. I keep meaning to take a coach trip.'

'Ah. The men and women with umbrellas and you follow like sheep. Come along boys and girls!'

'Well, yes. But it makes it easy, doesn't it?'

'Why not in a car? They are cheap enough to hire for a day.'

'I think I'm a bit nervous of driving here.'

'Nonsense. We are the best drivers in the world!' He heard how absurdly self congratulatory that sounded and began to laugh at himself. 'Well, perhaps not the very best,' he relented. 'But we are good drivers. We have to be on these roads. We will not push you off the road because you are in a small car, if that is what you are afraid of.'

She laughed too. It wasn't that he was saying anything particularly funny, but that his manner of saying it, beneath the ebb and flow of his temperament, was quite light-hearted, as though none of it really mattered much to him. He laughed a great deal, swinging between good humour and gravity. She found it very engaging.

'Listen,' he said. 'I must go now. I have to play and sing in a while. I must get ready.'

Did he imagine it, or did he really see the quickly concealed disappointment cross her pleasant features? He saw that she had tiny laughter lines around her eyes. He made up his mind, but then paused, assembling the foreign words carefully in his mind before trusting them to speech. He didn't want her to get the wrong impression, didn't want to be misunderstood.

'I have a car,' he said. 'It isn't a very good car, but it goes. When do you have some time off work?'

'I have two days a week. Why?'

'But when?'

'Saturday sometimes. That's the day when people are flying in or going home.'

'I know. One plane after another.'

'And I have one other day. It varies from week to week. Actually, Friday is my day off this week. Tomorrow.'

'*Viernes*. Good. I have no work tomorrow either. So I will take you to see Teide, if you like. To see the *almendros*.'

'Almond blossom?' she asked, eagerly. Then, 'Oh, but I can't.'

'Why not?'

'I can't impose on you like this.' She gazed across at him, doubtfully.

'What is this *imposing*?'

'Well, I don't know you.'

'What else do you need to know?' He frowned. 'Listen. *Soy un buen hombre*. I'm a good man. No funny business. I'll just take you to see the mountain. You'll like it very much, I promise you.'

'I'm sure you *are* a good man.'

She didn't sound very sure. He thought that she was trying not to laugh. He felt a little hurt by her amusement.

'It is not right to say this?'

'No. I mean yes. It's fine.'

'So what is the problem?'

She glanced across at his guitar. People knew who he was. He wasn't a complete stranger.

'There's no problem,' she said.

If she amazed herself by her acquiescence, his own sense of relief took him by surprise. It had suddenly seemed very important to him that she should come with him.

'Listen,' he said. 'I don't even know your second name. You know that I am Luis Herrera Garcia.'

'And I'm Margaret Sinclair.' She had reverted to her maiden name since the divorce.

'Margarita,' he said again.

It was a pretty name, he thought. A pretty name for a pretty woman. 'Very well. You meet me here tomorrow at ten and we'll go for a picnic.'

'What do you want me to bring?'

'Nothing. You leave it all to me. I cook. It is what I do. I play and I cook!'

He caught her looking suspiciously at his fingers. Well he could hardly blame her. He wondered about her own marital status.

'I'm not married,' he told her. 'But it doesn't matter because I'm taking you only for a picnic. I promise. No funny business.'

It seemed important to reassure her and he was rewarded by another endearing blush. She got out her purse to pay for her drink, but he snatched the bill from the little glass and pushed her Euros away. 'No, no,' he said. 'You will be my guest, *señora. Señorita?*'

'*Señorita.*'

'You will not stay and hear me play? And sing?' he asked.

'I'd love to, but I think I'd better go. I have things to do at home. If we're going out tomorrow. But thank you for coming to my rescue.'

'*De nada.* See you tomorrow. Ten o'clock. You will come?'

'Yes. Yes, I will.'

'I'll bring the car and the food. You just bring yourself.'

He watched her go. As she walked, she hunched her shoulders, bending forward slightly. Don't look at me, she seemed to be saying.

That night, as he played and sang, she walked through his mind. He couldn't banish her, nor did he want to. It was a long time since he had been even remotely preoccupied with any woman. There had been plenty of girlfriends when he was younger: at La Laguna University here on Tenerife, and then later, when he had travelled through Europe, and in London, and back to Spain, but nothing that lasted very long. He had come back to Tenerife a few years ago and had begun to make a decent living for himself, singing and playing in various venues by night, cooking in a restaurant by day. He liked to cook and surprised himself by being good at it. It had begun as a hobby with him, but one for which he had a definite flair. His experience in London had helped.

When he left school at first, he had gone to La Laguna here on Tenerife to do a degree in Agricultural Biology, but the subject began to bore him and he left without completing the course. He doubted if he would have passed anyway. His father was furiously disappointed in him. As a small farmer, he viewed his son's learning with a mixture of suspicion and awe. It was he who had encouraged Luis to choose this particular course but it was, ironically, his father's attitude to it that had contributed in large measure to Luis's disillusionment. The gap between what he was learning and what his father seemed to expect of him was much too wide for comfort. Eduardo's experience seemed more valuable than the theory he was being taught.

'I'm more interested in music right now,' he said, stubbornly.

'But we've worked to send you to university, to let you make something of yourself. To make life easier for you than it has been for me and your mother. I wish Paco had never given you that damn stupid guitar. I should have put my foot down years ago!'

'That wouldn't have done much good, would it?' observed Luis, drily. 'I'd still have found a way to play!'

Father and son were alike in their capacity for rage, suddenly kindled, as suddenly extinguished. Later, Eduardo and Maria had come over to Tenerife to hear Luis play and had been very proud of him, recognizing his talent. His cooking impressed Maria as well, but she didn't say much to her husband about it, aware that he wouldn't really have understood.

Not long after that visit, Eduardo had died of a heart attack. He fell suddenly and without warning, out in the fields at evening, his face towards the setting sun, and Luis could think of worse ways to go, but it had been much too soon and Eduardo was much too young. After the funeral, Luis tried to take stock of his life, and what he wanted to do with it, but he simply didn't know. He knew what he loved to do, but not where he wanted to do it, nor where it might lead.

And then he met a girl from Barcelona, working on Tenerife. Emelina had also sold property, he remembered wryly. His fondness for her city, coupled with her homesickness, had brought them together. He fell madly in love with her and lived with her for two years. When she moved back to Barcelona, he had followed her there, finding another restaurant job. Every few weeks, he asked her to marry him. She always refused him. She was very sexy, very shrewd. But when he remembered the affair now, he couldn't imagine why he had so wanted her to marry him. It was the kind of madness that lust, disguised as love, could sometimes inspire. He had wanted her desperately, in every possible way. Marriage had just seemed part of the package.

'No, Luis,' she had said. 'No way.'

Their lovemaking had been passionate and exciting. It had taught him a great deal, but he had never been sure of her, never been really comfortable with her. Later, when the madness subsided, he saw that he hadn't loved her. Only desired her. Eventually, while Luis was at home on La Gomera, visiting his family, she had written to him to say that she had met somebody else.

'Dearest Luis, I'm such a city girl,' she written. 'You know, I couldn't live on your island for ever or even for very long. And I couldn't ask you to live here because much as you love this place, I don't see you as a city guy.'

He reflected that if she had asked him, during those years when they had lived together, he might well have agreed, but wisely, she had not asked.

For a year after that, he mooched around Tenerife, going home to La Gomera infrequently, getting drunk often. He had several girl-friends but none of them for very long. Because he was good looking and could be charming when he chose, he found no shortage of partners among the shifting tourist population of the islands. But he soon became disgusted with himself. He liked women too much. He had sisters, loved them deeply, couldn't help but identify with their joys and sorrows. He was a man of imagination. At last, he realised that his own hurt pride lay at the root of his anger.

Since then, all his relationships had been casual and friendly but very few and far between. Most of the women of his own age were married by this time and he found the young holidaymakers who flirted with him whenever he played in some seaside bar amusing but not what he wanted.

Time raced on and recently it had seemed to him that he was always hurrying, hurrying to catch up on life as he had expected it to be. After Emelina, after he had recovered some of his old confidence, his Uncle Paco had summoned him over to La Gomera, to the restaurant that he and Aunt Carmen ran, not far from the pretty little town of Agulo. He had no inkling of why they wanted to see him. It must be something important, because Paco was usually so easy-going, but they had asked him to make a special trip.

They sat on the terrace one morning, with a pot of strong coffee and home-made biscuits: Paco, Carmen and Luis. The orange trees were in bloom and Luis remembered the scent of them, powerful, sweet and astringent at the same time. What came next was unexpected.

'We'd like you to take this place over in a few years, Luis,' said

Paco. 'We're going to have to sell it, you know. We can't keep going for ever. We want to buy a house in Vallehermoso. We want to retire while we're still fit enough to enjoy life. But we'd really like to sell this place to you, if you want it. We don't want to put it on the open market. We don't want a stranger living here. Somebody who might spoil the place. You're the only one in the family interested in cooking. The girls aren't, that's for sure. And we hear that you have a talent for it.'

'How do you know?'

'Your mother told us. Music and food, she said. Life's essentials.'

He was speechless for a few moments. The proposal had taken him by surprise.

'I suppose so. I have some savings. But not enough for a deposit. How long can you wait? I don't know if I can afford to buy you out yet! This is quite a big undertaking.'

Paco and Carmen had children, but apart from one married daughter, Pilar, living in Vallehermoso, the others had all departed for the mainland. The offer came as a surprise to Luis. He tended to live from day to day, but he had been frugal too.

'Think about it,' said Carmen, squeezing his hand. 'Take your time, go away and think about it. It's a big decision, we know. If you can get a deposit together, maybe you could get a mortgage, a loan of some sort? This place does well enough. We want you to have it.'

The more he thought about it, the more attractive the idea of the restaurant became. Now, it seemed to him as though he had a purpose. The building itself was very old and very beautiful, if a little tumble-down, with whitewashed walls and a red-tiled, moss-encrusted roof with a traditional *azotea* or platform at one end, looking out across the terraced gardens. It had once belonged to one of the old Spanish families of the island, a rural retreat perhaps. An infrequently painted sign outside reminded visitors that the name of the restaurant was *La Manzana Dorada*: The Golden Apple, though it was invariably known locally as 'Paco's place.'

Tourists often visited the island, only a short ferry trip from Tenerife. Paco and Carmen already catered for the occasional coach party, storing folding tables in an outhouse. Luis had always felt that the citrus plantations, the orange groves around the house, as well as the fertile terraces on all sides, could provide more produce for the restaurant. There were palm trees that could be tapped for *guarapo*, sap that could be made into syrup: *miel de palma*, palm honey as it was called. His uncle and aunt already specialised in traditional dishes. He imagined sourcing even more local produce. At last his course, or the horticultural side of it, seemed to have some practical application. He could grow things and he could cook simple local food, as long as he had some help in the kitchen. But perhaps most of all, he would be able to play and sing there too.

After that first meeting, he had gone back to la Gomera as soon as he could, to finalise things with Paco and Carmen.

'We'll wait as long as it takes, within reason,' Carmen said. 'We don't want to fleece you. We'll have it valued, but we'd settle for less. You can even pay us something to begin with and more later if there are difficulties. You are family after all. It matters. We need enough to help keep us in retirement. Paco will do odd jobs in the town. I'll do a bit of cooking here and there. Help you out if you want. Or maybe just do some baking for you.'

Carmen's baking was legendary.

'We love this place,' added Paco. 'We'd rather keep it in the family but none of our lot are remotely interested. Oh I know you'll want to make changes. You'll have your own ideas. But I don't think you'd want to cut down the orange trees or vandalise the palms.'

'No. I certainly wouldn't want to do that.'

Everything fell into place. All his latent ambition became focused on that one aim: his own small restaurant. But his strong sense of fair play dictated that he must pay Paco a decent deposit and so he took work wherever he could on Tenerife: singing and playing by night, cooking by day, doing food preparation and even kitchen portering if need be. Soon, the restaurant would be his. For the past few years, he had been much too busy to think about women, apart from the occasional date, the infrequent casual affair.

His mind veered towards Margarita again. Her diffidence inspired a sudden rush of tenderness in him. He must be careful. She was a foreigner. He knew nothing about her except that he found her attractive and he didn't know why. It had been like seeing a familiar face in a room full of strangers. He finished his last set of the evening, nodded and smiled to his audience. Then he went over to the bar and ordered a drink. Tomorrow, he thought, with a sense of anticipation he hadn't known for years. Let's wait and see what happens tomorrow.

CHAPTER FIVE

If I knew and understood
that I had your friendship
I would split my heart in two
and give you half.

You don't have to go. Margaret woke up with the words running through her head. You don't have to go. She had spent a woefully disturbed night. Truth to tell, she could have stayed to listen to him singing and playing. Part of her had wanted to. But part of her had felt overwhelmed by the intensity of his personality, his energy. Now, she couldn't imagine what on earth had prompted her to agree to spend a day in the wilderness with a stranger. You don't have to go, she told herself in the shower. And again as she dried her hair, dressed in cool cotton and forced herself to eat a piece of toast. Nevertheless, she was ready in good time, and made her way down to the restaurant where they had agreed to meet.

Why are you doing this, she kept saying to herself. Why don't you just say that you've changed your mind, go home to your flat and forget all about it?

But the sheer bad manners involved in doing any such thing made it seem impossible. The time for refusing had been last night. She had promised. So with a certain grim determination she walked down to meet Luis Herrera Garcia. Uncharacteristically for both of them, he was early and she was a little late. He was sitting in the same place as last night, tapping his fingers on the table. He looked as nervous as she felt but when he saw her, he leapt to his feet, all smiles. She realised that he had been wondering whether she would turn up, and anticipating hurt pride if she didn't.

The car was an elderly Fiat with a slipping clutch. Luis loaded a battered sports bag into the back of it, installed her in the passenger seat and drove off, competently and courteously, she was reassured to note. He was right. The other drivers were more polite than she would have expected. Even the men who drove the overladen banana lorries would stop on the winding roads to let them pass. She could have hired a car herself and made the expedition alone. She would have been quite safe.

The car laboured up the steep side of the mountain with occasional revving sounds as Luis changed gear.

'Will it be alright?' she asked anxiously.

'Si, si,' he said. 'It is only the clutch.'

'I can hear that.'

'It is ... sleeping? No. Slipping!'

'That's right. Slipping.'

'Ah.' He nodded, glancing sideways and grinning at her briefly. 'Yes. And I know what is sleeping too!'

The car was very small and she was aware of his thigh close to hers, of his brown hand as he wrestled with the obstinate gear stick, occasionally brushing her knee. He said an abrupt 'Sorry!' and she was certain that none of this contact was intentional.

'Look back now,' he said. 'This whole coast is one long town. My mother remembers when there was nothing. Just the small fishing villages and the desert. Even when I was a boy there was not so much building although it was well under way. They say they are making the desert bloom.'

'With concrete blocks?'

'Well, you should know!' he said, and then shook his head. 'Lo siento. That was very rude of me. And there are flowers too. People make money out of you sun worshippers. That isn't so bad, is it?'

'I'm not a sun worshipper,' she said, defensively.

'Then what are you?'

She thought he was being rude again, but she doubted if any of this was intentional. It was just the way he was, the way he spoke. She fell silent, not knowing how to reply. They drove past abandoned cultivation terraces and deserted banana plantations.

'How sad,' she said.

'Perhaps. But these are small plantations. People would have scraped a poor living from them at best. Believe me, I know. The big plantations are still worked. There are market gardens. Tourists like to eat bananas and tomatoes and … *aguacates*?'

'Avocados, yes.'

'They like oranges. They like to buy roses in winter. And *strelitzia*. You know these flowers?'

'Yes. Bird of paradise. That's what they're called at home.'

'Well, they like those too.'

'Yes, they do. But I think I prefer the roses.'

Each week she paid a few Euros for a huge bunch of tightly curled rosebuds in pink, red or yellow. After a few days they would open out into beautiful blousy flowers.

'You see, what happened was this,' he continued, negotiating numerous bends in the road with the ease of familiarity. 'All those years ago, some guy came from London and he found a fishing village. Unspoilt. So pretty. That was what he said to himself. But so poor. And then the following year, he would come back and there would be hotels and apartments and he would be very disappointed. Oh, it's all spoilt now, he says. We'll have to find somewhere else. But he does not see that now their children are well fed and they have good clothes, that they are comfortable or perhaps they can afford to drive a car where they could not before. Not when my grandmother was young. Or even my mother.' He slapped the steering wheel with his hand. 'He does not notice any of that. So you see it's very hard for me to be sad about the tourists, even though our economy is such a mess. Like yours. Like all of us, I suppose. But now, nobody local can afford a house. So what are we to do? No wonder there is graffiti. And protests.'

'Do you find the tourists a bit … I don't know … a bit rude?' she asked. He was beginning to flash and sparkle with anger again and he made her nervous. Light blue touch paper and stand well back, she thought, not knowing whether to laugh or take him seriously.

'Certainly I do,' he said. 'They shout at me to make me understand, as if I am an idiot. They expect me to speak English when not a word of my language do they know, except *cerveza* or *paella* or *sangria*.' He rounded on her suddenly. '*Habla Espa ol? Me comprende?*'

'*Un poco*,' she said, thrown by the question. 'But I'm trying to learn more. I go online and do the lessons every day. *Intento*. I try.'

His English was becoming better as he spoke to her, she noticed, as though he had once been very fluent, but lacked real practice. His voice, like his singing, was low and light. Sometimes she found it hard to catch exactly what he was saying; the intonation patterns were still not familiar to her. His Canarian dialect, she thought, must be a very musical one.

He laughed, suddenly. 'I remember I was on a bus once. Just a normal bus. It was full of tourists coming into Los Cristianos from the Costa del Silencio, the big development along there.' He gestured behind them. 'I had been to visit my friend who lives in Las Galletas, and there was this woman on the bus. An English visitor. She got very angry with the driver because she couldn't make him understand. "You'd think they'd make some effort to speak the language, wouldn't you?" she said. She spoke very loudly so that the whole bus could hear her. Me, the driver, everyone.'

'*The language?*' she said.

He began to laugh again.

'Yes. You'd think they'd make some effort to speak *the language*, these foreigners!'

It was, thought Margaret, like something she could just about imagine Fiona saying. But perhaps she was maligning her. Not even she could be so crass, surely?

'Oh Lord,' she said. 'How rude! What did you do?'

'I was sitting just behind them. I put my head between the two women. I said "Madam, don't you realise that it is *you* who are the foreigner here? Perhaps you should make some effort to speak *the language* yourself, eh? Or perhaps you should stay at home in England where they can understand you."'

'Did you really?' She could feel herself squirming with embarrassment for the woman. 'What did she say?'

'She made a very strange noise. But there were some other English people on the bus and they laughed and said "Quite right" so I felt better then. But I should *not* have been rude and I was sorry afterwards it's true. *Mi madre* would have been *horrorizada*! I have a temper. You know? I lose my temper. Is that what you say? Well, I did. And then I found it again and I was sorry. Because after all, you may be quite right.'

'Right about what?'

'I don't know if it's better to have a little land and scrape a living from the earth in the sun, like my father did, or to drive drunks to clubs in a taxi, day after day, or serve them more drinks. Or try to sing and play to them when they don't want to listen, but think I'm just background *muzak*. These apartment complexes are like towns, you know. The big hotels too. Tourists come and never leave them. Never shop in our shops or eat in our restaurants. Only they use our water and electricity and put very little back. Not even very much of their money. Not enough control. Not enough planning.'

Margaret thought of the graffiti she had seen. 'Foreigners go home. This is our land.' She was silent for a moment. 'But you know we have the same problem in Scotland,' she said eventually. 'Well, parts of it anyway. Airbnb has a lot to answer for. Cities like Edinburgh. And the Isle of Skye. All the houses and apartments are rented to tourists. There are big holiday homes that people stay in for a weeks and leave empty for the rest of the year. People can't afford to live where their parents and grandparents were born. So local businesses can't get staff, because there's nowhere for them to live.'

'Then you understand what I mean.'

Luis stopped the car suddenly and threw it into reverse. She looked behind her, alarmed. 'What's the matter?'

'Nothing. Look. This is what you have come to see.'

She had been so absorbed in his conversation that she hadn't noticed it: a clump of almond trees in bloom. She caught her breath. The blossom was delicate pink and white, even more unexpectedly fragile after the vividness of the hibiscus and bougainvillaea down in the town.

'Oh look,' she said. 'Oh just look at it!'

The trees were beautiful, like so many slender girls in the hazy sunshine of the high country. Luis shot her a puzzled, sidelong glance as though surprised by the intensity of her response.

'I never imagined it like this,' she said.

'But you have such blossom, surely?'

'There are flowering cherries. Apples trees. May blossom too, out in the countryside. We have a lot of that in Scotland and it's wonderful. But I don't think I've ever seen anything quite like this. Blossoms in the desert.'

He smiled, quietly satisfied. 'Good,' he said. 'I'm glad you like it. But come on. First we'll see Teide and then we'll eat.'

As they drove, they saw more almond blossom in colours ranging from darkest to palest pink. And then they were in amongst pine forests with a jumble of rocks below them and when she wound down the car window, she could feel the chill mountain air on her cheeks.

'This is Las Cañadas,' he said, as they entered the vast and ancient crater. 'An inhospitable place. As you can imagine, before there were roads up here, it was a dangerous place as well.'

They came to the entrance to the cable car that ran to the summit of Teide, but there was a hopelessly long queue, so they sat in the cafe and had coffee instead. She tried to avoid his eyes, vaguely embarrassed by his proximity. She felt like a teenager on a first date. It must be lack of practice because he was courteous but detached, giving no indication that he felt anything other than a friendly interest in her wellbeing.

'Tell me about Scotland,' he said. 'I always meant to go there when I was working in London, but I never did. Never had enough time.'

'It's very beautiful. But very wet.'

'Have you seen Nessie?'

'I didn't think you would know about Nessie.'

'Oh, everyone knows about Nessie. Have you seen her?'

'No. I've only been to Loch Ness once or twice. It's a long way from Glasgow.'

'Is it?'

'Yes. People don't realise how big Scotland is. Most of the people live in the central belt. Everywhere else – well, there's a lot of wilderness. It would take you half the day to get to Loch Ness if you were driving from Glasgow. And the loch itself is very big, you know. And deep. Who knows what might be lurking down there.'

'But you believe in the monster?' He grinned at her.

'Maybe. I'd like to think it was true, wouldn't you?'

'Perhaps. Sometimes it's good to believe in things that you can't see. Impossible things.'

She was thinking how nice he was. She hadn't had a conversation like this, so easy and friendly and flirtatious, for so long. Not for years.

Everything had gone smoothly until now. Perhaps the landscape itself was to blame for what happened next. They were on their way down, stopping to look at the scenery every now and then. The crater of the volcano stunned her. It was so different from anything she had ever seen before. She didn't know how to respond or what to say. It seemed as though any comment would sound superfluous beside the sheer magnitude of this place. The earth felt very thin beneath her feet, a slender crust over instability. Her eyes soared up to towering rocks only to be drawn down again to flat gravel fields composed of green, pink and yellow sand, but very regular, as though some giant had created a vast parking lot for himself, or perhaps a high Zen garden, with each rock strategically placed on the fine gravel, and intensely pleasing. She could have gazed at it for ever. The air was so clear up here above the clouds that all the colours of the landscape seemed sharper and more true. She was able to pick out and appreciate shades that she had never seen before. Above them lay the conical peak of Teide, snow-clad and remote.

'I feel as if I'm on a different planet,' she said. 'As if I'm in another world.'

'Yes. I always feel like that up here too. It *is* another world.'

But the altitude was beginning to affect her. It made her feel light-headed, dizzy. She had the beginnings of a headache. They parked the car and walked off the pathway, clambering up beside a tortured tower of rock to look down on a field of lava and ash beneath. Someone had climbed precariously down, all the way to the bottom, and written a pair of initials there, lovers perhaps, though the next mountain storm would obliterate the fragile letters as surely as the tide takes away letters in the sand.

Just for a moment, standing there looking down, vertigo and breathlessness overcame her. With them came a sudden sense of fear, a loss of control. That was how she thought about it afterwards, although at the time it just seemed weird. She put a hand out behind her, expecting to meet solid rock, but instead, Luis caught her by the shoulders and steadied her.

'What's wrong?' he asked.

'Nothing. I'm fine. I was just dizzy for a second.'

'It's the height. We're well over two thousand metres and your head has not had time to get used to it. If we had walked you might not feel it so badly. Your body would adjust. What is the word for this dizzy feeling?'

'Vertigo.'

'Ah – the same word,' he said.

She liked the way he always asked, never afraid to admit that he didn't know something. And then he would say the new word over and over to himself a few times, storing it up for future use. Vertigo, she thought, staring out over the lava. Or was it more than that? As though the whole axis of her life had moved, adjusting slightly to a new orientation. A very strange feeling.

They went back to the car and drove on through the crater, into the pine woods again, looking for a place to picnic. A little way down, he stopped beside a clearing in the trees. She realised that somewhere along the way, they had diverged from the main road and the place was deserted. The silence was immediate and oppressive. He got out and went round to the boot to take out the bag of picnic things and a rug for them to sit on.

That was when, suddenly and unexpectedly, panic swamped her.

Afterwards, when she tried to rationalise it, she saw that maybe her depression about the divorce had never quite left her. Perhaps she hadn't really grieved for her lost marriage, for what she now thought of as all her wasted time. But there was more to it than that. She was afraid, suspicious of his motives. Why had he invited her on this excursion? What reason could he possibly have? She had slept so badly the night before that she felt on edge, her concentration slipping as badly as the car's clutch. And now there was this grimly beautiful landscape, the crater, the effects of altitude.

She got out of the car.

Whatever the reasons, it was as though a great black dog of anxiety leapt on her, gripped her by the throat and shook her. She was overwhelmed by terror, her perception of reality skewed. Who was she? What was she doing here? She thought that she might be going to keel over there and then, and fall down dead at his feet. Her heart was pounding, her breathing quickened. She could hear herself beginning to pant and the more she panted the more light-headed and panic-stricken she became. She couldn't blame him. His behaviour so far had been beyond reproach. Even though he was, for the moment, the focus for the horror that overwhelmed her.

She stood with her hands on the warm bonnet of the car, looking around, trying to calm her breathing, trying to remember who and where she was. The air seemed to vibrate around her head, full of small pinpoints of light.

Below this clearing, the land descended steeply. She could see light cloud beginning to seep up from the Orotava Valley. She could smell the sweet, resiny scent of the Canary pines. Somewhere high up in the trees, an unknown bird was calling, a single repetitive note. There was the faint swish of another car passing on the main road, high up above them, out of sight. Then all was silent again.

As a child, she had been afraid of dense woodland. Some book had scared her but she couldn't remember which one. The Hobbit perhaps? Gradually, as she grew older, she had managed to conquer the fear, but back then she had imagined nameless creatures lurking among the trees, blending with the branches and shambling along, always just beyond the edges of her vision.

That same primordial fear came sweeping over her now, intensifying her original panic. Luis was coming towards her, smiling. She didn't know the first thing about him, other than that he played his guitar in a restaurant and had driven her up here in a shabby old car. Why? What reason could he possibly have? How precarious was this? Being alone with him, on a deserted mountainside in the middle of a forest. No cars had passed them since they stopped. Not one. This wasn't a tourist road. You would have to be local to know about it.

And she didn't know him at all.

Off the road, the terrain underfoot was treacherously littered with jagged lumps of lava. She felt all her fears gathered together into one vast terror. He could murder her if he wanted to, extinguish her completely. There would be little she could do to save herself. It had happened to other women on other occasions. You read about these things every day. Saw them on the news. And although you were sorry and angry, you still caught yourself thinking that no animal would do this, but women did it all the time, conditioned to be kind. Endangered by their own politeness, their desire not to offend. Getting into elevators with strangers. Meeting them in far-from-public places. Getting into cars with them and driving along unfrequented roads. Never their fault, of course, but that was beside the point. Even a cat would be more cautious. Had they felt the same paralysing terror? All the fear of men she had ever known seemed to assault her on the mountainside.

He saw the look on her face and stopped, frowning.

'Margarita?' he said. 'What's the matter?'

Then he came towards her, looming over her. It was too much. Her mind released its grip on her body and a rush of adrenalin gave her the impetus to move. She turned and fled though the trees, slithering down the easier parts and stumbling over the sharp chunks of solid lava beneath the pines. She moved as quickly as she could, scattering huge pine cones before her. She could hear him some distance behind her, coming more carefully but dislodging stones in his path, small boulders that came rattling down beneath her feet, threatening to overbalance her. Sometimes she managed to stop just short of a tree trunk in her headlong rush to get away from him, but then she gathered herself together and ran on. She knew that the main road curved somewhere far below her, below the detour they had taken. In her confused mind was an idea that she must reach it and then run, where running would be easier. Run for her life.

CHAPTER SIX

Often we had to dismount while the horses climbed and scrambled up these mounds, jumping and picking their way over the rocks. By rocks I do not mean those firm, hard basaltic rocks to which one is accustomed, but masses of smelted earth, somewhat of the consistency and appearance of coke, but the size of rocks and containing not a square inch of smooth surface on either side.
Olivia M Stone, 1887

'Margarita!' He was calling her name, or his version of it, in puzzled exasperation, but she ignored him.

Then she heard his voice a little further off, as though he had paused and was looking down at her. She didn't hesitate. She struggled on until her left foot caught between two big lumps of lava and she fell headlong, saving herself with her hands but wrenching her ankle with her continued forward impetus. The rocks brought her to a jarring halt, and she gasped with pain. Then she heard him coming up behind her, picking his way carefully among the stones. Like a trapped animal, she struggled to get away.

'Margarita!' he said again. His voice was deliberately low and gentle, but it had no effect. With a desperate wrench she was free, though hardly less restrained by her wounded ankle. It was already swelling, a purplish bruise around her shoe. She turned to face him and put out her hands as if to ward him off.

'No!' she said. 'Go away. Leave me alone. Please. Leave me alone!'

He stopped again, uncertainly. '*No tengas miedo de mi*,' he said, half to himself, and then, 'Why are you afraid of me? What have I done? Are you hurt?'

He put up his hands in turn, a reciprocal gesture. 'You must let me help you. I can see that you are hurt. Let me help!'

She began to cry then and it was as if she would never be able to stop. Sobs tore at her throat, uncontrollable sobs that threatened to choke her if she didn't let them out. There were tears streaming from eyes and nose, tears that seemed to dissolve her whole face. She had not cried like this since the divorce. She had been dry eyed, proud of her self-control. Now she was crying as if the storm of emotion that beset her was beyond her means to halt or restrain in any way. Still puzzled and upset, he came and sat down beside her on the uncomfortable rocks. An intensely physical person, he had to stifle his first impulse to take her in his arms as he would have comforted a wailing child. There were a great many children in his family and he was used to handling their small woes, but she was rigid and untouchable in her adult grief. He let her cry for a long time, though she felt him giving her shoulder an occasional gentle pat, hardly a touch at all.

'*Mi niña, mi niña,* I mean you no harm,' he said, eventually, when the sobbing had subsided enough for her to be able to hear him. 'I'll take you home if you like. I thought you were enjoying today.'

'I was.'

She wanted to say that she was sorry, but she began to cry all over again. What on earth must he think of her?

'This isn't your fault. This isn't your fault, Luis.'

The renewed sobs so racked her that her words were quite incomprehensible to him. He felt in the pocket of his jeans and handed her a tissue.

'Wipe your eyes,' he said quietly.

She did as she was told, blowing her nose for good measure.

'I know what this is. *Un ataque de panico.* Do as I say and you will feel better. Take a breath in. Not too deep. Hold your breath. And now breathe out. All of it. Out, out, out.'

She obeyed him with difficulty, choking and gasping.

'That's right. And another. Breathe out now. Out. All of it. And hold your breath out. Just for a moment. Now breathe in. Hold. And out. Do it with me.'

She felt herself beginning to calm down, though her body was still rent by the occasional involuntary sob. Luis seemed to have decided that since he apparently had a madwoman in his care he must take charge.

'Now,' he continued. 'First we'll go back to the car and then we'll have a drink. I have some wine. Not too strong, but perhaps it will help. And then we'll see.'

He knelt, slipped off her shoe and examined her ankle, wiggling it about gently this way and that with capable fingers. She winced.

'Not broken,' he said. 'Or I don't think so. But I am no doctor. *Esguince*. Sprained, for sure. I must help you. I'm sorry.'

Rather formally, he offered her his arm, and she leaned on it. Half carrying her, he helped her to hop back up towards the clearing where the car was parked. The picnic bag lay where he had abandoned it. He left her for a moment to spread out a blanket, though he kept looking anxiously back at her as though he half expected her to make another crazy bid for freedom. Then he helped her to sit down, fished a bottle of red wine out of the bag, along with two glasses in a cardboard box, and poured them each a measure: a large one for her, a much smaller one for himself.

'I'm driving. But you must drink,' he insisted. 'You'll feel better.'

She drank a few mouthfuls of wine. She felt the comforting, rough and ready taste of it on her tongue. It was very good. She had that empty feeling that comes after crying for a long time. She mopped at her face with the wad of tissues and looked up at him.

'What must you think of me?' she asked.

'I tell you, *señorita*,' he said, shortly, 'I have no *idea* what to think of you. But perhaps you should try to tell me? Have I attacked you? Did I even *touch* you? No! So what makes you run away from me and half kill yourself? *Por que? Por que me tengas miedo?*' He was losing his English. She saw him becoming angry and, in her delicate state, found the tears beginning to prickle behind her eyes all over again. He saw them too and, reaching for the bottle, topped up her glass. He looked away while she drank and recovered herself.

'What's wrong with you, *querida*?' he asked more gently.

She was ashamed of how she must look. There is something ugly and heartrending about the fierce tears of an adult. She knew that her face must be swollen and blotchy, her eyes bloodshot, her nose shiny. She glanced up at Luis but he turned away. Tears are infectious. He couldn't bear to see them. Couldn't bear to see her so distressed when he could do nothing to comfort her.

'You ought to cry, you know,' her mother had told her when the divorce was going through, as though it were some sort of bereavement. Perhaps it had been. The death of a marriage. Perhaps her mother had been right. But she owed it to Luis to try to explain what was the matter with her.

'It's nothing to do with you,' she said, blowing her nose again. 'You've been so nice. And I'm very sorry. I got divorced a little while ago. That's my problem. I was married for quite a long time.'

'But you're not old enough for that.' His natural courtesy was reasserting itself even in this situation. She smiled wanly.

'Oh, I am you know. But you're the first man I've been out with alone since the divorce. I'm really out of practice. And I know this wasn't even going out. It was just a trip, wasn't it? You were just being kind. But still ...'

She had hardly been anywhere at all since the divorce. All the social invitations had dried up. She remembered how couples who had been in the habit of inviting Alastair and herself for meals had managed to forget about her. There had been a few invitations from her old university friends to summer barbecues or birthday parties. And then Covid had come along when nobody went anywhere. She wondered if the others still invited Alastair, but then he had quickly become one of a convenient couple again. So perhaps they did. It was easier that way. Besides, people seemed to feel that they had to choose between the husband and the wife in these situations. It was then that she had realised just how many of their so-called friends were actually Alastair's colleagues, the wives not always people she would have chosen to socialise with herself.

'I'm thirty five,' she said.

'Same as me.'

'I was married at twenty one. I'm not used to going out with anyone. I was nervous. And a bit afraid.'

'Of me?'

'Yes. Of you. But maybe I'd have felt the same with anyone. Any man.'

'Has somebody hurt you?'

'Not physically. No. I don't even have that excuse.'

'Then why ...?' He hesitated.

'I know. I think the mountain made me even more scared.'

'It can be a disturbing place. I know that. It's primitive.'

'And besides, I'm here in a strange place, well a strange place for me, doing a job I don't much like. And I'm so *lonely*!'

Speaking the words aloud made them seem real. But she hated the neediness in her own voice. She almost started crying again, but controlled herself with an effort.

'Yes. I could see that you were lonely. And perhaps a little unhappy. That was why I asked you. That was all. To let you see the mountain and the almonds. I would like to show you the orange blossoms on my island too, in season. I wanted to' – he shot a rueful glance at her and then started to laugh – 'to cheer you up.'

'Well it did. For a while. And it was very kind of you.' She was struggling now because she found it hard to explain this, even to herself. Besides, the lurking tears threatened again. 'You know, I think it was *because* you were so kind to me that everything suddenly overwhelmed me. I haven't cried before. Not properly. Not about the divorce. My husband left me for a much younger woman. She's expecting his baby. In fact she's probably had it by now. But I haven't cried until today.'

He frowned. 'So why are you alone here? What about your own children? Are they with your husband?'

She shook her head miserably. 'No. You don't understand. There were no children. We had no children.' She bit her lip and stared down the hillside. The mist from the valley was creeping closer. She felt chilled.

For a few years she hadn't wanted children and neither had Alastair. Then she had suffered with some small hormonal problem. Her GP had sent her to the hospital for tests. It was nothing serious, but it had given her a jolt, had brought her face to face with the possibility of childlessness, and she didn't like that possibility at all. She amazed herself by her sudden change of mind, by the strength of the maternal instinct that possessed her, body and soul.

'I've been thinking that we ought to have a baby,' she had said to Alastair, tentatively. 'I think we should try for a baby.'

Why had she expected him to change his mind, just because she felt differently?

'No children,' he had said. 'Too big a tie. Too big an upset at our age.'

She knew he meant it. At the time, she didn't know the reason why. He had blamed her for upsetting their contented life together. But the reality was that he had other plans, even then. She had believed him, even through the divorce, had been inclined to blame herself, until she had seen Jenny, pregnant with Alastair's child, their lockdown baby. She could hear him telling his friends about it. She had felt doubly betrayed. At least she might have had a child; at least he might have left her that. When well-meaning people, most particularly Fiona, said to her, 'Lucky there were no children,' she wanted to scream at them that it wasn't lucky at all, that she would have given anything for a child, something tangible from the marriage, some proof that the time had not been wasted. They would have reached some kind of peace between them, she thought. They could have done that, in spite of the divorce. And she would have loved the child.

Luis was looking at her in great surprise. 'No children?' he said wonderingly and then, recollecting his manners, didn't pursue the question further.

'It wasn't my decision. It was my husband. Anyway, it all just seemed to swamp me suddenly. I'm so sorry you had to be here. To see me lose it like this. I feel so pathetic.'

'You are not pathetic. But why did you run?' he asked, not quite satisfied with her explanation. 'I saw your face and it was full of fear. Why were you afraid of me? I won't harm you.'

She couldn't tell him because she didn't know. Later that night, lying awake, she realised that he had seemed to her confused senses to represent some great threat. She had thought him, in those few panic-stricken seconds, as primitive and pitiless as the mountain itself. She had been afraid of him and she had run in blind panic with the same feeling, the same prickling sensation at the back of her neck that she had felt as a child, when she had run upstairs at night. There was no rhyme or reason to it and the fear seemed to be older than time.

She looked at him, seeing only gentle concern in his eyes. 'I was afraid. I don't know why. You must think me very silly. I'm sorry, Luis.'

'No.' He made a dismissive gesture with his hand. '*De nada*. How is your foot?'

'I'm sure it'll be fine when it's bandaged. I'll need to bandage it up. I wonder where I could get an elastic bandage?'

It seemed embarrassing. She wished it didn't hurt so much. Wanted to pretend that everything was fine.

'I'll take you to a doctor when we get back to town.'

'Oh, you don't need to do that.'

'It's no problem. You must let me help you with this at least. But listen. Are you hungry?'

She was surprised to find that she was, and nodded.

'They why don't we have the picnic anyway?'

'Are you sure you still want to? With me?'

'Of course. Why not?'

He was, as he had said, *un buen hombre*. He had brought cold tortilla, cooked with new potatoes and fresh herbs. There were crispy buttered bread rolls with soft melting centres, small sweet bananas, and tart oranges with thin skins, oranges so sweet and scented that they seemed unlike anything she had tasted before.

She ate hungrily.

'Who made this?' she asked. 'The tortilla? It's wonderful. Who cooked it?'

'I did, of course. This morning. I told you. I like to cook. But this is very easy. The simplest thing.'

'You're a man of many talents.'

She was still embarrassed by the memory of her headlong flight down the mountainside. But he wouldn't let her dwell on it. Instead, he started to talk about himself. He told her about his time studying at La Laguna University and how he hadn't graduated but had gone travelling instead.

'I realised that there were only two things I wanted to do: play the guitar as well as I possibly could, and cook. My uncle taught me at first. I used to have guitar lessons on La Gomera, and when I was living in La Laguna I found a teacher there. But I was spending more time on the guitar than I was on my studies.'

'I don't think I've ever found anything that interested me like that. I wish I could.'

'What was your work?'

'I worked in a library.'

'And did you enjoy it?'

'Not much. It was a job, that's all. I always thought there must be something better for me. But I still don't know what it might be.'

'You'll find it one day. You have to keep searching.'

'Maybe. Where do you live now, Luis? Have you an apartment of your own?'

'No.' He shook his head ruefully. 'No. It's complicated. I rent a room in my friend's apartment. I help with his restaurant. I learned cooking when I was travelling. So I play and sing a bit. Well. I play a lot and sing a bit. And I cook. And I save. I'm saving up for something.'

'You're very good. At the guitar, I mean.'

'Yes. I suppose I am. Well, here I'm good. On the mainland there are many with more talent. I've heard them. Admired them. But I play in my own way. And the old songs of these islands – not many people sing those. So it suits me. I play and sing for my own pleasure as much as anything else.'

He leaned on his elbow, facing her, deliberately distracting her from her distress.

'I used to have a partner. But she didn't love me. Or perhaps only a little. We don't speak or even message each other now. So you see, I told you the truth. I'm not a married man.' He pulled a face. 'Although my mother is always telling me that I must find a nice girl, settle down and have children.'

'It's what mothers do, isn't it?'

'Well nice girls are very hard to find. Here, anyway.'

'I see plenty of nice girls. Very pretty girls.'

He pulled a face. 'Oh, we have a shifting population here. They come for a week, two weeks at most, and they go. I suppose some of them are very nice girls, but their expectations are … They are not what I want. Not now. You understand?'

'I think so.' She smiled a watery smile.

'I'm not really looking for a girl at all now.'

'Aren't you?'

She wondered what he was looking for. She drank more wine, feeling the warmth of it coursing through her. It was smooth and sunny, with an undertone of something spicy, peppery.

'It's local,' he said. 'Volcanic wine from Guia de Isora, not so far from here. It's like Lacrima Christi in Italy. Do you know that they found a big wine container buried in a vineyard near Vesuvius and they could tell what it had been? And they find that this is exactly the same kind of wine. The tears of Christ. I *love* that name, don't you?'

'So this is volcanic wine too?'

'Of course. The vines do very well here. And on my island too. On La Gomera. Although white wine is a speciality on La Gomera. There is a grape called *La Forestera* – not the same as the one in Italy, a different grape. Very rare. We use it to make some excellent wine.'

Margaret thought about her ex-husband who fancied himself as a wine buff. Keeping what he called his 'cellar'. She didn't think he would approve of this Tenerife red. It went straight to your head with a great *vivo yo* cheer. No pretensions. Rather like Luis himself.

'Do you like it?' He nodded at the bottle.

'Very much. But then I'm very ignorant about wines, you know. My husband knew a lot more.'

'Ah, you English!'

'I'm Scottish.'

'Scottish then. You make such an exclusive club of everything. Who the hell cares? There's no mystery. What you like, you drink. What you don't like, you don't drink. Whatever makes you happy.'

She saw that on all occasions he would treat things with the casual grace, even arrogance, of the Spanish male. There would be none of the agonizing over a menu that Alastair had faced when he took academic colleagues out, hoping to impress them with his sophistication, his worldly wisdom. Luis would eat and drink whatever he liked. He would always be at ease with himself, although perhaps that wouldn't make him an easy companion.

But it might make life exciting.

He was packing away the picnic things. 'Come on!' he said. 'I should take you back to see a doctor. Your ankle is very swollen. And then I'll see that you get home safely.'

They drove through the crater again, heading back to Los Cristianos. It was early evening now and the tourist buses were long gone. The crater was empty, apart from the occasional hire car passing through. The air was very clear and still. The setting sun was bathing the lava fields in an intense green aura. Far away, on a sea of cloud, floated the other islands: La Gomera, La Palma and Hierro.

'The Fortunate Isles,' she said.

He grinned. '*Si*. The Garden of the Hesperides. Guarded by a dragon. Hera's Orchard. Well, maybe.'

'A garden for sure. The garden of the gods.'

'Everything will grow here. Even the golden apples of the sun.'

'So what do you think they were? The golden apples?'

'I don't know.' He thought about his restaurant but said nothing about it. Not yet. 'Perhaps something very simple and good,' he suggested. 'An orange maybe. I've read the tourist books too, you see!'

They drove on for a while, but then he pulled into a lay-by, leaving the engine running. 'Look. Watch the setting sun for a moment. You may see something special. Maybe, maybe not.'

'What am I looking for?'

'Wait and see. The light is perfect today. We may be lucky. Wait for the sun to sink below the horizon. Watch carefully.'

Intrigued, she did as she was told, until the slender rim of the golden disc had almost disappeared below the horizon and then, as the thin arc slid from view, she saw it: a sudden and intense green flash. Like an explosion on the edge of the world. It was there and gone so quickly that if she hadn't been watching intently she might have missed it.

'Oh!' she said, very much surprised.

'What did you see?'

'A flash of green. Just after the sun went down. Is that what you meant?'

'Yes. Sometimes you can see it. More often not. We've been lucky today.'

'What causes it?'

'I don't know. Look it up. Or perhaps best not to enquire. Perhaps it's best just to enjoy. It just *is*.'

He started the car, drove on, keeping his eyes firmly on the road ahead.

In Los Cristianos, he took her to a pleasant, English-speaking doctor who waggled her foot very gently and told her that her ankle was probably not broken, just sprained. He bandaged it tightly and advised her to rest it for a few days but to go to hospital for an x-ray if it didn't improve.

'You were lucky, *señorita*,' he said. 'It is easy to break bones in the lava fields. You must go more carefully in future.'

Luis had been waiting for her. He took her home and pulled up outside her apartment complex. She had been wondering what to do, how to take her leave of him, for she supposed that he would be very relieved to see her go. She had made such a fool of herself. For the rest of the day, he must have felt obliged to do his best for her out of natural courtesy, but she expected that he would be very glad when she had vacated his car and his life.

'Are you OK now?' he asked.

'Yes, thank you. I'm fine. And I'm sorry if I spoiled your day.'

'No, it was a good day after all.'

A line of Shakespeare came unexpectedly into her head. She said,

'Why didst thou promise such a beauteous day, and make me travel forth without my cloak?'

'What?' he asked, puzzled.

'Shakespeare. I don't know why I thought about it. I've had too much wine!'

'Shakespeare. Well, why not?'

'Listen, I'd better be going. Thank-you. Thank-you for the picnic and everything. It was very kind of you.'

She would have opened the car door but he detained her, his hand lightly on her arm. 'One moment. I'll help you. I need to make sure you're safe.'

'Oh, I'll be fine. There's an elevator. I'll manage.'

'Listen to me. I have a lot of work for the rest of this week. My friend's restaurant in the day and playing at night.'

She smiled bravely at him. 'I do understand, you know.' Sometime she smiled so much that she felt as though her face might split in two with the effort involved.

'*Callate!*' he said, exasperated with her. 'For heaven's sake, woman, will you shut up and listen to me. I'm working for the rest of this week, but next week, I have some time off. Perhaps you will come out with me next Wednesday night? We can eat. If your foot is better we can dance. If it's not better we can sit and listen to somebody else's music. OK?'

'Yes,' she said, bemused into immediate agreement. This was so contrary to what she had expected that there seemed little else to do but say yes.

He made arrangements to meet her, got out of the car, opened the door for her and courteously helped her to the main entrance. There he saluted the security guard who seemed to be an acquaintance, patted her arm and left. She sat down on one of the couches in the entrance hall to wait for the elevator.

She was in such a reverie that the elevator had arrived and was standing there, its doors open, for some minutes before the security guard came and tapped her gently on the shoulder.

'*Señorita*, do you need any help?' he asked.

She jumped. 'Oh, no. Thank you. I can manage.' She got up and hobbled into the elevator, smiling at him. She was exhausted after the tempests of the day, so tired and confused that she felt, even as she smiled, the tears begin to course down her cheeks again. As the doors slid shut, she saw the man looking at her in astonishment, fascinated as always by the apparently endless eccentricity of the English.

CHAPTER SEVEN

All the girls called Margarita
are as sweet as caramel.
But I am bitter.
For a Margarita I am dying.

The following day, Margaret's colleagues joked endlessly about her bandaged ankle.

'What were you doing up there?' asked Conor.

'Just walking. I twisted my ankle. That's all. I don't know why everyone keeps going on about it.'

'Are you sure that's all you were doing? I mean he wasn't chasing you through the lava fields, was he?'

This was so close to the awful truth that she felt herself colouring at the memory, but it was only Conor after all, so she said, 'Don't be silly. I'm a mature married woman.'

'A divorced woman. It's a bit different.'

'You're on shaky ground, Con.'

'Nothing to the shaky ground you must have been standing on.'

She tried to put next Wednesday completely out of her head. Much to her own and everyone else's surprise, she sold an apartment in a holiday complex to a retired couple from Cork, with a big family of children and grandchildren who could all use it for holidays. It was a nice apartment at a good price and she felt pleased with herself, pleased for them.

Her supervisor seemed happy too. 'You see, Margaret, I knew you could do it if you put your mind to it,' said Stella. 'You just needed a positive approach. Every time you can get them to agree with you, it's one step nearer a sale.'

'I know, but it wasn't too difficult. The apartment was beautiful. I wouldn't have minded living in it myself.'

'The price was too low.'

'You know how difficult it is here – and back home.'

Stella sighed. 'I know. I know.'

'And the last viewing I did there were a couple of dead cockroaches in the bath. It didn't help, you know. The place was supposed to have been cleaned.'

'You should have got there early. Moved them yourself.'

Margaret shuddered at the thought. All the same, she knew that Stella was right. Her sales pitch must have carried more conviction this week. She had been genuinely enthusiastic about the beauties of the island. At any rate, she had earned herself a bit of commission. She decided to buy herself something pretty to wear. Even while she was trying on an Italian skirt and top in creamy linen, she was wondering if she should be trying so hard to look good. She thought Luis was probably being polite, proving that he wasn't the dangerous person she had so clearly thought him. It was such a long time since she had been on a date and she supposed this must qualify as a date. Or must it? She suspected he was just trying to make up to her for frightening her into a panic attack, even though none of it had been his fault.

Before her marriage, she had been interested in clothes, loved to scour charity shops or eBay for retro items. Her years with Alastair seemed to have dulled her enthusiasm. He dressed both shabbily and conservatively, as did his friends, as though too great an interest in clothes was somehow beneath them. His academic colleagues mostly favoured shades of grey, black and beige, people who had long ago ceased to care what they looked like. She didn't know where she fitted in. She had always liked vintage coats and dresses, but Alastair didn't approve of her bright colours, her old costume jewellery, her battered but beautiful leather handbags. He didn't approve of her charity shop finds at all. Why couldn't she, he asked, go to normal shops like everyone else?

He was a master of the low key put-down.

'Are you wearing *that*?' he would ask. She knew that she would have to go and change, otherwise he would sulk all evening. He had been a great one for the prolonged sulk. He could go on for days, weeks even. If she challenged him, he would tell her that she was imagining things. 'Why are you so needy?' he would ask her.

That was another thing she resented. On the few occasions when she had seen Jenny, her replacement, the younger woman had been dressed in bright colours, embroidered cottons, like a younger, fresher version of herself as she would have wanted to be. Alastair didn't seem to mind. In fact he seemed proud of his new wife.

Towards the end of their marriage, Margaret had found herself not caring what she looked like at all. Now, her renewed interest in clothes made her uneasy only because it centred around a man she hardly knew. Alastair's Calvinist streak must, she thought, have affected her more than she realized.

She gave herself a shake. Why can't you just do what you want, she thought? Like Luis. But what *did* she want?

After a couple of days, her ankle was more comfortable and by the end of the weekend she was able to take off the bandage. She had got off lightly. It might easily have been broken. It looked as though dancing on Wednesday might be feasible after all. But as her ankle healed, she felt more apprehensive. It wasn't that she didn't want to see Luis again, because she did, but she was apprehensive of the physical contact that sooner or later he would want, equally scared that she might be mistaken.

He might not want her at all.

Through thick and thin, Margaret had managed to maintain her essential optimism. But she had trusted Alastair, whom she had known for most of her adult life, and he had betrayed her. How much less faith could she place in this stranger, an attractive man who sought her out in a place full of younger women? That alone should set alarm bells ringing and it did.

Why me? She asked herself this question all the time, but she had no answer. She might even have suspected him of wanting a meal ticket, a way out of poverty. But Luis had already left and come back to the islands. He was well educated and cosmopolitan. So what *did* he want? She had no idea, but she had seen far too many dramas and documentaries about romance scams. The thought that he might simply be attracted to her hardly even entered her head.

Just once, in an idle moment between customers, Margaret allowed a daydream of Luis, or more precisely his hand holding her own, to enter her thoughts. She remembered watching his long fingers manipulating the strings of the guitar on that first evening. When she had sat on the blanket among the trees, weeping, and he had patted her shoulder, she had felt his palm cool and dry, through her thin top. Not quite a caress. Not like the way he handled the guitar. Not even like that. She remembered his hands moving capably on the steering wheel. Now, she imagined herself walking hand in hand with him.

At that moment, sitting at her sunny desk and staring out across the town, she had surrendered something of herself to him. Whatever she might later describe as blind chance was no such thing. How could it be when she was already beginning to imagine him as her lover, touching the pictures in her mind's eye, skirting around them and moving away again?

They went to a small restaurant, one she didn't know, nicer than most, tucked away down a side street. It was all dark wood and intimate tables; each had a single red rose in a stem vase. There was a tiny dance floor and a singer whose music was more romantic but less stylish than Luis's. He ordered food and wine, briefly consulting her about her tastes – they both liked seafood – but he insisted on choosing the wine.

'This is tourist food anyway,' he remarked as they ate. 'Not real Canarian food. Our food, our cuisine here is plain but very good. There are places where you can eat excellent local food. I'll take you if you think you might like to try it some time. Potatoes, fresh fish, lots of different salads. There's a way of cooking the potatoes with a lot of salt. A big bag of it.'

'Really?'

'Yes. They must be just the right size. Not too big, not too small. You cook them until the water goes away. And then you are left with potatoes, their skins all ...' He made the gesture with his hands.

'Wrinkly? They would go wrinkly with all that salt, wouldn't they?'

'That's right. But inside the skin, the potatoes are superb. *Papas arrugadas* we call them. In the old days, they would have been cooked in seawater. And a very spicy sauce to go with them. *Mojo picon*. And then, of course, there are freshly grilled sardines. Although when you've eaten a meal like that, you need a lot of beer to follow!'

'You like to cook, don't you? I mean you really like food.'

'I like simple traditional food. No fine dining for me. When I've saved enough money, and that will be quite soon, I plan to have a restaurant of my own.'

'What about your music?'

'I want to do both. Music and food. They're my life.'

'I like the sound of that!'

'And I'll serve real food.' He poked crossly at his meal. 'Not fussy things piled in the middle of the plate. You can come and eat in my restaurant when I have it, and you can taste real Canarian food!'

'I'll look forward to it. But this food is lovely.'

'It isn't authentic.'

'So where are you going to open this restaurant?'

'Oh it's open already. My uncle and aunt own it. I'm just going to take it over and make some changes. Not that there's anything wrong with it as it is. But I have ideas, plans, dreams of my own. Why wouldn't I?'

'Where is it?'

It's on La Gomera. My home.'

'La Gomera? You mean the island?'

'I'm sorry.' He shook his head. 'I think you know all about me, but you don't. That's my home, over there.' He nodded in the general direction of the sea. 'La Gomera. You saw it last week. When we were driving down the mountain.'

La Gomera was the nearest island to Tenerife and on clear days it could be seen from Los Cristianos, a distant and mysterious hump. Each day, ferries travelled to and from the main port of the island.

'I keep meaning to go over there on one of my days off. I haven't done it yet though.'

'But you will, in time. It's difficult when you move to a new country, I know. It's different if you're on holiday.'

'You're right. It's different then. You forget that when you're on holiday, real life doesn't intervene quite so much.'

Coming here, taking a job, changing her whole life – these things had been a huge hurdle for her. It was as though she had needed to pause, draw breath before challenging herself further.

'You haven't been here so long, have you?' he said.

'Not really, no.'

'It takes a while to settle down. You don't need to do everything in a hurry, do you? You can take your time.'

'I suppose that's true.'

He looked at her speculatively. 'What do you do tomorrow? Can you be off work then?'

'Actually, it's my day off. It was Friday last week. Thursday this week. It varies. And it depends on how busy we are. We often work weekends as well.'

'I was planning to spend a day on La Gomera tomorrow.'

'Were you really?'

'Yes. Really. To see my family. I go home when I can. Which is not often enough at the moment. Will you come?'

She surprised herself by saying, 'I'd love to! I know nothing about La Gomera.'

'It's bigger than you might think when you see it from here. And very beautiful. We wouldn't be able to see much in a day. But perhaps it would be nice for you.'

'Do you want me to come?' she asked, hesitantly.

'Why wouldn't I?'

'Well, you know, after last week.'

'Oh, that was nothing. It's over and done. Besides, it was a good day. Mostly good. And I think you know me a bit better now. I'm a good man.'

'I know, I know. And a good man is hard to find.' She laughed with him, suddenly elated.

'We could get an early ferry.'

'How long does it take to get there?'

'About forty minutes.'

'Is it different from here, from Tenerife?'

'Oh –' He was rendered speechless by the ignorance implicit in her question. 'Different?' he repeated. 'Yes. Yes, it's different. And so beautiful.'

'But it's beautiful here.'

'I know. I know. But –' He spread his hands. How could he tell her?

'Is wine different from water?' he asked finally. 'Oh yes, Margarita, it is different. There are parts which are so green for one thing.'

'So is Tenerife. Well, a lot of it, anyway.'

'Not like La Gomera. Oh God, there are such flowers and trees. There is *laurisilva* and *myrica faya* – a tree like a flame. And *cedre*. What is this tree? Very big, very old.'

'You mean cedar?'

'Yes. That's right. Cedars. I don't have the words to tell you in English what my island is like. Nor how beautiful it is. In Spanish, yes. I think I could tell you something in Spanish, but then you wouldn't understand. So I'll just have to show you.'

'You could speak to me in Spanish. I should try to learn some more.'

'I know. But this is helping my English.' He paused. 'On La Gomera we have a whistled language. The *silbido*. There are many steep-sided valleys so if you wish to speak to your neighbours and you have no phone, no internet, in the old days, you must whistle instead.'

'You're joking!'

'No. It's true.'

'Can *you* do it?'

'Just a little. I knew someone who was better at it but he's dead now. Our children learn it at school. People do it for the tourists.'

'Can you show me?'

He grinned at her. 'Not here. I think they would throw us out! I'll show you what I know some time. Perhaps on the island. It's like your Scottish bagpipes. Better out in the open, I think.'

After the meal, he said 'How is your foot for dancing?'

'I think it's fine.'

'Then we'll go very slowly and gently. You must be able to walk tomorrow when we're on La Gomera. It's a good place for walking.'

It wasn't hard to go gently. It was that kind of place. The music had changed, slowed. The dance floor was very crowded and there was no space to move very far or very fast. It was more a case of standing in one place and swaying in time to the music while leaning on your partner. This was the first time she had been so close to Luis. It seemed to her that they fitted together well. She was glad that she had bought the new outfit; glad that she had worn scent and make-up.

She hadn't danced like this since university. They had always kept the slow music for the last half hour or so. If you had the right partner it was wonderful. She dimly remembered when it had been wonderful to dance with Alastair. How was it possible for two people to change so much over the years? Alastair had been warm and funny and interesting. They had waited a while before going to bed together. She had wanted to be sure of him and sure of her own feelings. But because they had met when she was still very young, he had been her first, her one and only lover. When she talked about this to female friends, they couldn't believe it, but it was the truth.

'Weren't you curious to know what it would be like with somebody else?' they asked.

'Well of course. But what could I do? I only wanted Alastair at that time.'

After the divorce, she hadn't wanted anyone else, hadn't wanted to get embroiled with any other man. Until now.

What would Luis expect and how soon would he expect it? He must meet many women who were all too willing to jump into bed with him, girls who would have been just as inclined to love and leave him. Nice while it lasted. Not to be taken seriously. *Soy un buen hombre*, she thought, and the gravity of his repeated assertion made her smile. He might well be a good man, but he was a very foreign man. How would he treat her when he knew her better?

He held her firmly but not too close, her head at his shoulder, his hands resting lightly on her waist. He smelled very nice, of some faint, spicy, citrus cologne. Neroli, she thought. They moved with small steps in time to the music. There was no point in talking. Besides, it was something of a relief not to have to talk, but simply to move like this and relax into the rhythm of the music.

The restaurant closed in the early hours of the morning and the owner distributed roses to all the ladies. Then they wandered out into a tiled square down by the seashore. The sounds of the stag and hen parties and other revellers had faded. There was a seat, where a group of travellers had arranged themselves for the night, their heads resting on their bundles, their children cuddled up close. One of them was still awake, sitting cross-legged, playing an ocarina shaped like a bird, a small terracotta instrument with a clear, pure sound. As they walked towards the beach, the notes of the ocarina came floating back to them, very high and sweet. A full moon hung over the bay. They walked along the empty promenade and Luis reached across and took her hand.

They walked aimlessly and happily, swinging their arms together. Yachts were tied up alongside pontoons, some vessels finer than others. There was a splendid fifty foot catamaran with a lion's head painted on the side and a 'pirate ship' that took tourists on whale watching tours.

'I'd like a boat,' said Luis. 'My father used to have a rowing boat. He used to take me fishing. But after he died, and when I was still away from home, nobody took care of it, nobody maintained it and it fell to pieces after a while.'

He pulled her closer and tucked her arm through his as they walked.

After a while, they sat on a low wall and looked out at the bay.

'Was it a good evening?' he asked.

Something in his tone surprised her and she realised that he was still unsure of her. He really needed to know that she had enjoyed herself.

'Yes. It was wonderful,' she said truthfully. 'I haven't enjoyed anything so much for years. I feel as if I'm about nineteen again.'

He sighed. 'Age. Age. Why do you always talk about how old you are? Who cares? You're a young woman. You only feel old because you were married for so long. Now you're not married. You should get used to feeling young again.'

He put his arm around her shoulders and pulled her closer. Then, with his free hand, he turned her towards him and kissed her. His lips were firm and dry. He smelled of citrus and there was just a faint taste of alcohol about him, the wine they had drunk. The kiss was oddly without passion, very gentle, very cool. But at the same time and contrary to his apparent self control, she could feel his heart beating strongly and swiftly against her breast. He ran his hand gently up and down her back, then kissed her on both cheeks and stood up, pulling her to her feet.

'*Vamos*,' he said. 'I must leave you at your apartment. We'll be up early. For the ferry.'

He walked her home and as soon as he was sure that she had her key, he left her at the door. He didn't kiss her again that night, which left her feeling faintly disappointed, but he grasped her arms briefly and firmly, as though setting her right.

'Goodnight, Margarita. *Hasta mañana*,' he said.

CHAPTER EIGHT

They say that you do not love me any more
because I live in a hayloft,
but tiled roofs are also
swept away by the storm.

They saw dolphins on the way to La Gomera. They swam quite close, easily keeping up with the ferry and unafraid of the din of the powerful engines. Further off were porpoises.

'But they're shy,' said Luis. 'They never come near. Even if you are in a little boat. You can see the ...'

'The fins?' she suggested.

'Yes. You can see the fins and you know that they are out there looking at you, but they never come up to the boat. Not like the dolphins.'

He remembered one magical summer when he had come out here with his father in their boat and a pair of dolphins had come right up to them, craning out of the water to look at them, and then diving to bob up suddenly on the other side of the craft. He remembered one terrible occasion when they had gone out aboard one of the bigger fishing boats. They had caught a dolphin in the nets and it had drowned before the skipper could free it. He would never forget the screams of the animal. He had been very young, in his early teens, but the sound had haunted his dreams for months afterwards, although the skipper had taken it in his stride.

'It happens,' he had said. 'Don't let it worry you.'

But some of the older men, including his father, had blessed themselves and said that it was unlucky to kill a dolphin and strangely enough the skipper of that boat had died the following summer, tripping over a rope and falling into the harbour one night, unable to swim and too drunk to shout for help.

Each time the sleek creatures surfaced, Margaret fumbled with her phone, trying to get a picture of them.

'They're so beautiful that I find myself watching them instead. And then by the time I take the photograph they've disappeared.'

'Just watch them,' he said. 'Don't try to catch the moment. Just enjoy it.'

San Sebastian was the chief port of La Gomera, its buildings scattered about a valley that sloped down to a sheltered harbour. This was an ancient port. Columbus had left from here on his voyage to the Indies. Mellow old houses rubbed shoulders with starkly ugly new buildings. There were palm trees and laurels in the square and the whole effect was of a much more exotic place than Tenerife.

'Where does your family live?' she asked him.

'Oh, I'll take you there later on. We have plenty of time. Let me show you the town first.'

He was simply happy to be here. When he was away, the memory of his island and its people often seized him, filling him with its green and gold light, its breath-taking vistas, the breezes that blew there, the scents and sounds of it. Every time he stepped off the ferry he felt joy seize him all over again, and wondered why he couldn't find a way to move back immediately. But today he also thought of his home and her possible reaction to his family. It brought him down to earth with a jolt.

In the town, people greeted him volubly and cheerfully, delighted to see him.

'This place feels very foreign,' she said.

'In a good way?'

'Oh yes. In a good way. But just to me, it feels exotic.'

He looked around, seeing it briefly through her eyes. Here, in the old part of town, there were ancient stone houses with glimpses of cool green courtyards behind half closed doors, wooden balconies and casement windows set within carved shutters. A very old lady, with sunken lips in a pale, wizened face, leaned out of one window and, seeing Luis, waved a tiny hand at him and grinned, showing her gums. Luis waved back in genuine pleasure at the sight of her.

'I'm surprised she's still alive,' he said. 'Sometimes it seems to me as though whenever I come back here somebody else has died. People who were part of my childhood. But she just seems to go on forever.'

'Who is she?'

'Her name is Señora Gomez. Jacinta Gomez. She's very old. Well into her nineties, I think. She seemed like an old woman to me when I was *un niño*, although she would only be in her sixties then. She used to bake the best cakes and biscuits. In fact my aunt uses some of her recipes. She was kind to me. I think she knew my great grandmother. I never knew her, but she did! Sometimes she remembers things, sometimes not.'

'She seems to remember you well enough.'

'Yes, she does. She once said to me, "Luis, the memories come and go and I can't stop them!" Even her sons are dead and gone. There are one or two grandchildren but they don't visit much. She still arranges the flowers in the church though. I think the priest looks out for her. The priest and the ladies of the church. There are always ladies of the church.'

'Yes. In Scotland too.'

'Everywhere, I think!'

'Will you take me to see the church?'

'Of course. We could go there first. It isn't far from here.'

Inside the ancient building dedicated to Our Lady of the Assumption, she felt conspicuous in her sundress and sturdy sandals. But he hastened to reassure her. Nobody would mind. Still, she fished a light cotton jacket out of her bag and slipped it on. The church was dark and full of the scent of years of incense, layers and layers of it absorbed into the wood. The altars were all painted wood, but with the once-vibrant colours still glowing faintly in the darkness.

'We came here every Sunday to mass. My mother and my sisters still do.'

'Do you still go to church, Luis?'

'Like my father used to. Weddings, christenings, funerals. That's all.'

'Me too. I was brought up as a Catholic but I wasn't married in the church. I don't think my mother approved of that. She was born in Ireland.'

'Ah. That's why you have permission to live and work here?'

'Yes. I have the priceless Irish passport. Half our politicians suddenly dug up an Irish mammy or granny you know, even the ones that voted for Brexit.'

He raised his hands as though unwilling to enter into a political debate.

'You're lucky,' was all he said.

'I am. Anyway, my husband's family were Church of Scotland but we got married in a registry office. I don't think he has any religious belief at all now.'

'An atheist? And what about you?'

'I'm not sure what I am. Not an atheist anyway. It irritates me when people tell me how comforting it must be to believe in something. But it must be far more comforting to be certain, mustn't it?'

'*Talvez.* Perhaps. But I like this church,' he added. 'I like it a lot. I do find this place very comforting.'

'It's a bit like coming home, isn't it? Going into a church. Especially one as old as this. And I suppose most people are Catholics here.'

'Not all. Not now.' He touched the place where his heart lay. ' I am *catolico non fanatico*. It is just a small part of me that I cannot get away from. When I am on my deathbed you may send for the priest.'

'Don't.'

'Why not? It's true.' He had a sudden crazy vision of the two of them, he and this woman, grown old together here, a distant but clear image, like looking through the wrong end of a telescope. How foolish, he thought. She's such a stranger to me. I hardly know her and she knows nothing about me. Nothing important, anyway.

On one of the walls were the faded remains of a fresco showing sailing ships and the towers of a town.

'Is that Columbus and his ships?' she asked, peering at it through the gloom.

'No. Much later. It's to commemorate our great victory over the British.'

'Really?'

'Really. You didn't have it all your own way. You may have dealt with our Armada in the old days, although I think it was the weather that defeated us much more than you English.'

'I keep telling you. I'm not English.'

'*Lo siento*. I'll remember.'

Who did you defeat, then? What's this painting of?'

'One of your admirals. He was sent to take the town in seventeen something but we fought him off. The picture was painted afterwards.'

'Why did he want to take the town?'

'I don't know. Its position was important, I suppose. I forget. We used to learn this at school. And we learned about Columbus. He would have knelt in here to pray before his voyage.'

'Would he?'

'It's a very old church.'

'In fourteen hundred and ninety-two, Columbus sailed the ocean blue,' she recited, under her breath.

'*Que?*'

'My grandmother used to say it. Maybe even my mum as well. They used to skip to it at school. You know. Little girls, jumping over a rope.'

'Ah yes.'

'We didn't skip much when I was at school. They said it was too dangerous. So Columbus left from here?'

'Yes. He was in love with the widow of the governor of La Gomera.'

'Was he really?'

'Well, in something, anyway. She was not a nice lady. Bobadilla was her name. She had many people killed. Her husband had treated the islanders very badly so at last they murdered him. And then she took her revenge.'

There were, he thought, places on the island that were full of mystery and places that you visited with caution or not at all. He firmly believed that a sense of the past might cling to the land, might cling to the rocks themselves. There were tales of blood and cruelty, some more recent than others. But he couldn't begin to explain this to her and certainly not in English.

'What about you, Luis? What are your forebears? I suppose they must be Spanish.'

'We are all a mixture, here, I think. Guanche, Spanish. I am not sure that any of us are completely Spanish. Lots of North African blood as well. It's why we are so good looking!'

'And so *very* modest with it.'

He began to laugh.

'Hush. We're in *church*,' she said.

'I know. But they won't throw us out. You must know that you never get thrown out of a Catholic church. They always do their best to keep you inside. They never let you go.'

'Tell me more about your ancestry. I'm interested.'

He shook his head. 'All in good time.'

The church was very quiet and peaceful with just a few elderly ladies dressed in sombre black, kneeling in prayer before the various altars. He lit a candle, putting a few coins into a metal box. The candles were electric lights, coin operated. That was a change, he thought. But with so much tinder dry wood about, anything else would constitute a fire hazard.

'There,' he said. 'One for you and one for me.'

The sunlight outside dazzled them after the gloom of the church. The bright white houses cast the light back at them. Margaret turned her eyes longingly up to the cool hill that reared above the town. He followed her gaze.

'We can walk up there,' he said, quickly seizing on another excuse not to take her to his home. He was filled with sudden reluctance, as though once she met his family she would know too much about him. What would she think?

'Why do you have such small windows? In this climate?' she asked. 'Why are the houses so shuttered?'

'It's cool in summer, but warm in winter.'

'Winter? What winter?'

'This is our winter. Oh, I know our winter is much warmer than your summer, but we get used to it. We feel the change. Besides ...' he gave her a sidelong glance. 'Besides, some people used to live in caves, once upon a time, on these islands. Did you know that?'

'Yes. I'd heard that.'

'They were not Spanish, those first people. Wherever they came from, most likely North Africa, they were cave dwellers. So perhaps we have this from our forebears.'

She looked at him, clearly wondering if he was laughing at her, but he was perfectly serious. 'Come on,' he said. 'We must eat first and then we'll climb the hill. It's a wonderful view from up there. You can see Teide.'

'What about seeing your family?'

'Oh there will be time. *Hay mucho tiempo.*'

He took her to a cafe, where they ate *tapas* and drank cold beer. When they had finished, and were walking towards the hill, a gaggle of schoolchildren came rushing and jostling along the road towards them. A little girl in a pink tracksuit detached herself from the crowd and came running over. She was about eight or nine, with dark silky hair, neat features and big brown eyes. She rushed at Luis and butted him, shrieking with joy.

'Carmilla!' he said, distracted by his pleasure at seeing her. He picked her up and swung her round and round. When he set her down she stood back and berated him in rapid and emphatic Spanish.

'Luis, you haven't been home for ages and ages. I've missed you lots. Where have you been? Have you forgotten all about us? And who's this? Is this your *girlfriend*? Your *novia*. And you never told us!'

She shook a small finger at him, one hand on her hip, a caricature of an older woman. He laughed and tickled her and then tried to introduce her to Margaret but the child, in a sudden fit of shyness, hid behind him, dragging her school bag on the ground. At his bidding she went to rejoin her friends.

'My niece, Marie Carmen,' he said. 'She tells me I don't come home often enough. She's right. But I can't help it. I have so much work to do.'

It was a long haul up the hill, though he was clearly used to it. She walked behind him, panting, laughing, enjoying the climb. Occasionally he took her hand and hauled her up the difficult bits. They climbed quickly, leaving the scent of flowers and the bleating of goats behind them.

At the very top of the hill, looking down towards San Sebastian, in an attitude of stony compassion, was a massive concrete statue of Christ. He was meant to be blessing the harbour but two of his fingers had been broken off. He wore a rakish halo of lightbulbs and there were flowers and candles grouped around his feet.

'So that's who it is!' Margaret said as she came up breathlessly behind the statue. 'I thought it might be Christopher Columbus.'

'No, no! Cristobal Colon is in Barcelona. And Lisbon, I believe also. Although I suppose it could have been him, looking out towards America.'

'Where's your home?' she asked again, seeing the sun beginning to dip downwards. Far off, Teide floated astride a dense mass of cloud, a magic mountain, holding up the sky.

'We'll go there soon,' he said, but still he made no move. Instead he walked to the edge of the precipice and sat down on a rock. Up here, on the open mountainside, the wind was salty and chilly, coming straight from the Atlantic to temper the warmth of the sun. The hillside was full of prickly pears, spiky aloes and small *tabaiba* bushes that had seeded themselves on this moonscape, like miniature palm trees with stellate leaves.

'I thought you told me the island was green.'

'So it is, but not here. I'll show you one day, I promise you. Perhaps we could spend a few days here. If you think you would like that. If you are still here, on the islands I mean.'

'I don't plan to go home just yet. I don't think I could bear to go back to Scotland. The weather's awful there right now.'

'Good. I'm happy about that. About you staying, I mean.'

'Are you?'

'*Si!*'

He was happy. Helplessly happy. How could that be, he wondered, when he hardly knew her? But there was some quality of innocence about her, the ability to be delighted by new things. She had seemed very cautious and careful to Luis at first, so typical of her nation. But then, when she had sobbed and wept, he had wanted to take her in his arms and hold her close, rock her and comfort her, thaw her ice with his own sure warmth. He hadn't been able to do that. But she needn't have worried about his motives. He had asked her to go out with him again because she seemed different from all the others. Which, when he thought about it, was how love began. Wasn't it? With the perception that here was somebody special. Her face had stayed in his head. Whenever he sang a love song, she came walking quietly into his mind.

'Shouldn't we be going to see your family?'

It was growing chilly in spite of the sunshine, in spite of the beauty of the blue sea dissolving into a blue sky with the long line of cloud at the horizon. She sounded unhappy. Luis wondered if she had caught his melancholy mood.

'We'll go soon, but first come and sit by me.' He wanted to feel her close to him, to feel the warmth of her. He needed reassurance.

She put out her hand to sit beside him and inadvertently rested her palm on a small prickly pear, growing in a crevice in the rock. She had forgotten for a moment that it was not like home; that at home you were alert for nettles and brambles. She cried out and lifted up her hand. Fine prickles, like razor sharp hairs, were sticking out of it, dinning pain, disproportionate to their size, into her palm.

He turned around at her cry.

'What's wrong?' He caught her hand and pulled her down beside him, frowning. 'What have you done? Ah – I see. *Picos. Higos picos.* What do you call these plants?'

'Prickly pears, I think.'

'We say prickly figs.'

He raised her palm to his lips and she felt his teeth nipping at the spines, pulling them out and spitting them away, a certain sensuousness amid the pain. He felt it too, felt desire for her overriding all his other uncertainties.

'Better?' he asked.

'Yes, thank you. Much better.'

He held onto her hand for a moment, kissed her palm and then impulsively, he took her in his arms. He held onto her fiercely, not wanting to let go.

'Oh Margarita!'

He kissed her with open mouth, hard and long and passionately. He pressed his face against the softness of her breasts. He was aware of the delicate perfume of her hair and her body. But then he released her and stood up, pulling her to her feet. She stood shakily beside him.

'Listen, we must go to my home,' he said. 'If we don't go now, we'll never go. It will be too late. So now we must go to see my home.'

He set off down the mountainside, almost at a run, and she had to scramble down the path after him to keep up with him. He knew it and yet he couldn't slow down. When they joined the main road that curved up and out of San Sebastian, they hitched a lift on a tourist bus. Luis knew the driver very well. It was a relief to him to have someone else to talk to. He didn't want to speak to her, to answer her questions, not now, not yet. He wanted to speak in his own tongue, to speak about things that didn't matter. He stood up in the front of the bus, where nobody was supposed to stand, and chatted to his old friend, while Margaret perched among a group of elderly German ladies on a tour of the island. They smiled at her and offered her peppermints. Soon, the bus stopped just outside the town, beside a cluster of houses. Luis got off, held out his hand and helped her down and then waved to his friend as the bus drove away, down to the harbour. Almost immediately, he set off again, up a whole series of steps and stairways that climbed up the side of the rock. Margaret came after him. At last, she stopped, with a stitch in her side, calling after him.

'Luis! Luis – wait for me. I can't go any faster.'

He looked back, repentant.

'I'm so sorry,' he said. *'Lo siento.'*

He slowed down and took her hand, but still had to restrain himself, his inclination being to drag her faster and faster after him. Presently, they came to a neat white villa perched half way up the hillside. A woman was outside, watering her trailing scarlet and orange geraniums with a green watering can. She raised a hand in greeting and smiled, her face creasing into habitual lines of good humour.

'Virginia!' he called.

'*Hola*! Luis, it's been too long.'

The woman looked curiously at Margaret, but Luis was still disinclined to stop. He embraced her and kissed her on both cheeks. He had known her since, as a boy, he had come past her house on the way to and from school and she, childless herself, had given him sweets and home-made lemonade. She was great friends with his mother.

'We must go,' he said. 'Just a flying visit. We have a ferry to catch.'

'You won't have long then.'

'No. There's never long enough.'

They hurried on.

I thought that was your house,' said Margaret, breathlessly.

'No, no. That's a friend. That isn't my home.'

Soon they joined a back road from San Sebastian. They passed a tiny corner shop with a bar and a few shabby tables outside. A couple of workmen in dusty shirts and threadbare trousers leaned on the counter in the dim darkness of the interior, drinking small glasses of spirits. '*Hola*!' they too called as they caught sight of Luis, but though he returned the greeting, he didn't wait to chat to them. Now they were in open country, on a rough track, hardly a road, that ran past an old windmill with arms upraised in a salute to the sky. Children were playing in the dust but they stopped to follow the couple's helter-skelter progress. They passed a pig in a sty of stones and another enclosure housing two goats. The animals lifted their hooves on to the edge of the drystone wall and craned over, apparently recognising Luis.

'They know you,' she said, surprised.

'Of course they know me!' He was very impatient now, even angry.

Why would they not know him? He had fed them often enough. They were approaching a curious building with a stone front and a red tiled roof, built on to a dwelling, some of which seemed to be part of the rock itself.

'Oh look!' she said, before she could stop herself, for almost immediately the words were out of her mouth she saw the two women, one in her fifties or sixties, the other about the same age as Luis, or maybe a little older, coming out to meet them with broad smiles of recognition and greeting on their faces.

'This is my home,' he said. 'And this is my mother, Maria, and my sister, Isabel. Say "*Buenas tardes*," Margarita!'

Bringing her home to meet his family had become an insurmountable obstacle for him. He tried to blame her for her obvious surprise, for her shyness, but he knew that the real fear lay deep within himself. It was nothing quite so simple or so culpable as shame at their relative poverty. He loved them too dearly, was too proud of them to feel ashamed of them. If anything, he was ashamed for her to be meeting them hurriedly like this. Ashamed that he hadn't told her all about them earlier.

'My family are not rich. Not, perhaps, what you have been used to.'

But that was a difficult thing to say, difficult to explain, and besides, what *had* she been used to? He found it very difficult to visualise her home in Scotland. He had never been to Glasgow, knew very little about it.

He hid his discomfort as best he could behind a terrible mask of formality. The truth was that although he was a Gomero born and bred, with all the fierce family feeling, courtesy and good humour of the islanders, this had been tempered by his years abroad. Once he had been open, almost naive in his affections. Now this was overlain with a thin veneer of cynicism. He could see his loved ones through her unfamiliar and possibly censorious eyes. He still didn't know her well enough to trust her reactions. He worried that once she saw the poverty of his background she would suspect his motives in bringing her here. Would she see that he was offering her a gift of himself, plain and unadorned, or would she think that he perhaps saw in her a means of escaping from that background once and for all? Embarrassment made him cruel but he couldn't help himself.

CHAPTER NINE

The girls are simply pictures that one never tires of looking upon.
Perfect oval faces, generally dark eyes and a wealth of dark hair,
complexions fresh and delicate, the figures tall and well moulded
form nearly the perfection of womanly beauty.
Olivia M Stone, 1887

'This is my home. Say hello, Margarita.'

The harshness of his introduction bothered her more than his family. She had had no very clear idea of what to expect, certainly not a palace. But her natural diffidence made her seem more detached than she felt. The contrast between Luis's inexplicable coolness and his family's enthusiastic welcome confused her. She didn't know what to say. Even her small amount of Spanish deserted her.

His mother must have been very pretty; she still was, really, as was his sister. She recognised in both women the features she had seen on little Marie Carmen earlier that day, coarsened only by exposure to sun and wind; recognized the same intelligent sensitivity that enlivened Luis's own face. They were a handsome family.

'Come in, come in!' they said, ushering her in, rushing about, pulling out chairs.

'Where's Cristina?' asked Luis.

The older woman hugged him, embraced Margaret and kissed her on both cheeks. Social distancing had always been a non-starter here, thought Margaret. Fortunately.

'She should be home from work very soon. It's your fault if you don't see her. But she'll be disappointed. You never let us know when you're coming.'

That was as much as Margaret understood. The rest became a confused babble of syllables.

'Call me Maria,' his mother kept saying, though she spoke only a little English. 'It is a pity that Cristina is not here. Her English is very good.'

Isabel's two children danced excitedly around Luis: Marie Carmen and a younger boy called Miguel, dark and fine featured, like a miniature Luis, about six years old. There were two small brown dogs, typical squash-faced Canary dogs, going delirious with delight, chasing their plumy tails, chasing each other around the furniture, leaping up at Luis and trying to lick his hands. Maria shooed the dogs out of the room and made the children sit down. They had been eating bread with chocolate spread, and fresh fruit, bananas and oranges. Margaret did her best to understand what they were saying but the pace was too swift, although she gathered that there was an older boy, Domingo, who was out working in the fields with Isabel's husband as he did every day after school. She judged that Isabel was two or three years older than Luis. He had told her that he had another older sister, Antonia, a teacher, married and living in Vallehermoso. Cristina must be his younger sister.

Marie Carmen was asking for a gift. She always got something when Luis came home.

'Quiet!' said her mother. 'Don't pester your uncle!'

'Leave her alone,' said Luis. He pretended he had brought nothing until at last he relented and said well, yes, he might have something after all, what was this in his jacket pocket? He took out bars of *turron*, the hard Easter confection made with nuts and honey.

His mother wanted to send Miguel out to the fields to fetch Juan and Domingo but Luis said that there was no time. They had to catch the ferry. He paced up and down impatiently, jiggling his keys in his pocket and peering out of the door, wondering if Cristina would come.

Maria smiled at Margaret and said, 'How are you?' in English and then, 'Coffee? Cake?'

When Luis tried to say no, yet again, that they had to get back down to the harbour in time for the ferry, her face crumpled with disappointment.

Margaret couldn't bear it. 'But we *do* have time,' she said, glancing at her phone. 'We do. I'm sure we could manage some coffee.'

He relented and agreed that they did have time, half an hour, maybe even an hour.

Margaret watched him with a kind of shocked disbelief. Maria kept touching his arm as though to reassure herself that he really was there, and at last he persuaded her to sit down while Isabel made the coffee. He perched on the edge of her chair and imprisoned her hand in his own for a moment.

'But you never come home, Luis,' she said, struggling to be polite, to speak in English for Margaret's sake.

Isabel handed round mugs and brought out a plate of sponge cakes with yellow icing.

'If I had known you were coming and bringing a visitor, I would have baked something. These are just shop cakes,' Maria said reprovingly. 'I would have made something nicer.'

The coffee was very good, strong and rich, and Margaret ate one of the cakes, though she had trouble getting it down because it was very sweet. While they were drinking their coffee, Marie Carmen said in Spanish, 'Are you going to go away, Luis, and live in England with this rich lady?' and Miguel said 'And then he'll never ever come home again.'

At that, Marie Carmen burst into tears and flung herself at her uncle. Luis shook her, but kindly and said, 'Oh, don't be silly, Marie Carmen! I'm not going anywhere – do you hear? *No voy a ninguna parte.*

I'm not going anywhere except back to Tenerife.' He looked briefly at Margaret to see if she had understood any of this. She gazed back blankly, her cheeks flushed. 'Not anywhere!' he repeated. 'Do you hear me? *Ella es solo una amiga.* She is just a friend.'

Margaret smiled so much that her face ached with the effort. She looked around the room that smelled faintly of bleach. The house was only partly built into the hillside, with a big open-plan living room and kitchen. There were white walls and a stone-flagged floor relieved by brightly coloured mats. The room was quite sparsely furnished with a dining table, a couple of mock leather easy chairs, a bookshelf crammed with books and a carved wooden chest against one wall, the most beautiful item of furniture in the room. There was a statue of the Virgin Mary on a small table, one that Margaret recognised as Our Lady of Lourdes. Outside the window, three canaries twittered sweetly in a big cage.

'How many are there in your family?' Margaret asked Luis.

'I told you already. Three sisters. Two are older than me. Antonia is in Vallehermoso. The other is Isabel –' he nodded at his sister – 'who lives here with her husband, Juan. These are their children. And there is also Domingo who is out with his father. They make a living of sorts from the land. Sometimes Juan goes fishing as well. It's what he used to do before he and Isabel were married, before my father died. This is what island living is like.'

'Yes. I can see that. In Scotland too. It's just like that in Scotland.'

'I don't think it can be like this.'

'Yes it is,' she said, defensively. 'There are plenty of Scottish islands where it's very much like this.'

'Anyway, he's out in the fields just now. Fields!' He laughed. 'You would not call them fields. They are terraces. You won't see Juan today.'

She was relieved. So many voluble strangers at once was disturbing. But he saw her relief and misinterpreted it.

'And then there's Cristina.' His tone softened. 'The youngest of us.

I was hoping she would be here. I'd like to see Tina. She should be on her way up from work.'

'Where do they all sleep,' she asked and immediately regretted the question.

He pointed to a doorway covered in a heavy curtain. 'Through there. It's bigger than it looks. There are other rooms. One for my mother and Marie Carmen, one for Cristina, one for Juan and Isabel and a room upstairs for the boys. There are loft rooms up there. I told you – we all lived in caves once on these islands.'

'Oh but I didn't mean –' She looked at his face and broke off, not liking what she saw there. 'Why won't you translate?' she asked him. 'What are they saying? Tell me what they are saying?' but he only shrugged and wouldn't answer. He didn't want to translate. 'Just small talk,' he said. 'You wouldn't be interested.'

She was becoming irritated, but she couldn't show it in front of his mother and his sister. So she patted the dogs, which instantly turned over for tummy tickles, and smiled at the two children who had begun to overcome their shyness.

Just before they were due to leave for the ferry, another young woman burst into the house, embracing Luis and obviously scolding him at the same time. Cristina was tall and slender, dressed in a smart suit and long leather boots. Her black hair was caught up in a complex arrangement of combs, with shiny strands breaking loose here and there to frame her face.

What a handsome family they are, thought Margaret, enviously.

Then Cristina was embracing her, kissing her, saying, 'How do you do?' and 'You must come again. Make him bring you again. I would so like to speak in English. Oh, *why* didn't you tell us you were coming, Luis? I could have been home an hour ago. I only went for coffee with my friend. I hate you!' She rushed over to her brother and, her actions belying this statement, kissed him lavishly as a sort of hail and farewell.

When Luis was a boy, Cristina had exasperated him and delighted him about equally. For a while, when he was ten and feeling grown-up, she had embarrassed him by following him about and popping up at inopportune moments. She had been a tomboy, game for anything, and the other boys had expressed a grudging admiration for her.

'Luis, look at your sister!' they would say, and he would turn around to find Cristina perched high in a tree, making faces at him, or swinging upside down with her skirts over her face and her white knickers showing. She never cried and she never told tales. As he grew older, he had confided in her. When he went away, it was always Tina he messaged more than anyone else. He worried about her a good deal. She worked in a bank down in San Sebastian. It wasn't a bad job but she was a clever girl and he occasionally wondered if she wasn't wasted, living in this house, still tied to the island at the age of thirty and as yet unmarried. Not even seeing anyone, or not as far as he knew. He thought she would probably have told him if she had a boyfriend.

Their departure was imperative now, if they were to catch the ferry. 'Look, we really do have to go,' he said.

'Thank-you,' Margaret said, shaking hands with them, receiving kisses. 'It was very nice to meet you.'

She was relieved to go, puzzled and distressed by Luis's behaviour. They walked down to the ferry in near silence. Once aboard the craft, he sat morosely staring out of the window and said nothing. If she spoke to him, his answers were monosyllabic or in cryptic and rapid Spanish. She had not taken him for a sulky man. He seemed to be deliberately trying to shut her out. Once, she tentatively touched his arm but he muttered '*Largate!*' and shrugged her off. She didn't know what the word meant, but from the tone of it, nothing good. She moved away from him, staring at a stand of tourist leaflets, and didn't try again. She went on deck for a while but there were no dolphins and the air at sea was very cold. She was relieved when they arrived back at Los Cristianos.

They disembarked and stood undecided on the quayside. He had put on his jacket and now he thrust his hands into his pockets like a sulky child, but still he would say nothing, offer no explanation for his behaviour, for his unreasonable anger. How could he? Pride lay at the root of it and that same pride wouldn't allow superficial excuses. He set off down the road towards the town without even glancing in her direction. She was at a loss for a moment and then she went after him, scurrying to keep up with his long-legged stride.

'Luis,' she said at last. 'Please stop. Please!'

He stopped and whirled around to face her.

'*Que*?' he said angrily. 'What?'

She felt an insane desire to laugh at the stupidity of it all.

'Luis – I've been running after you all day and I'm tired of it. Actually, I'm just tired. Why are you doing this? Why are you being like this? It isn't fair!'

'I don't know what you mean.'

'Of course you do! What's wrong with you? What have I done?'

'Nothing. You have done nothing. Maybe it's what you *are*. That's all.'

'What am I? I don't understand you. What am I?'

'You were afraid. Embarrassed. Upset. You hadn't expected what you found there. They are my family, Margarita. I love them. I thought that you might understand. I could have kept it from you, but it would have been a lie, wouldn't it, *querida*?'

Even that term of endearment had an edge of mockery to it now.

'Kept *what* from me? I haven't the faintest idea what you're talking about!'

'Their poverty,' he said. 'Oh, Margarita!' He stopped, unhappily. This was all so irrational. And after all, what had she done? Nothing at all. 'I am whistling to you across the valley,' he said at last. 'Do you hear me?'

It was a plea for understanding, but she was so angry now that she didn't recognise it.

'I don't know what you mean,' she said. 'So they don't live in a castle. So what?'

She could hardly believe that he was blaming her. She had been simply overwhelmed by the size and volubility of his family.

'You know what I mean. It's not the sort of thing you are used to,' he said, stubbornly. 'And you showed it!'

She rose swiftly to her own defence.

'You were embarrassed,' she said defiantly. 'Ashamed and embarrassed.'

His anger changed abruptly to indignation.

'I? No. How can you say this?'

'I can say it because it's true. You gave me no chance, Luis. You were no help to me. You wouldn't translate. Or at least speak more slowly. You rushed me in there and you rushed me out again. We could have had a lot longer with them. How could you do that to me and then' – her voice rose querulously – 'just abandon me like that?'

'What do you mean, *abandon*?' he asked. 'When did I abandon you? When?'

'I mean you gave me no help,' was all she could say. 'I could have loved them.' She stopped, not knowing how to go on.

'You blame me?' He was genuinely surprised.

'You were ashamed of them. I don't know what the hell you expected of me. Did you think I wanted something from you? Something you couldn't give? Was that it?'

'They are not rich,' he said. 'They have some land and a great deal of pride but they are not rich.'

Pride. That was what lay at the heart of it. His pride.

'What in God's name does their money or lack of it have to do with *me*?' she asked furiously, but he rushed on with his own inexorable assumptions.

'So now, of course, now that you have seen the kind of man I am, you don't want me. Now that you have seen my family and how poor they are, you will suspect me.'

'What are you talking about?'

'All the time, I can see that you are afraid. That you do not trust me. But I'm a good man, a man of honour, and I can't bear it.'

'I know you are. I know.'

'Do you? No. I think Marie Carmen was right. You will say to yourself, "All he wants is to come to England. He thinks I'm rich. He wants to pursue me and take advantage of me." And that is all there is to it.'

The enormity of this suggestion, so far from the truth, took her breath away.

'Is that *really* what you think of me?' she asked. She found that it hurt her, a physical pain somewhere in the area of her heart. 'I don't know about a good man, but I'll tell you something. You're a foolish man. A very stupid one. Stupid and ignorant. How dare you! How dare you even think such a thing of me?'

He saw that there were tears in her eyes again.

'Oh, why do you make me *cry* so much?' she said, exasperated with herself as much as with him.

Then she turned around and walked away.

He watched her in amazement. Just once, at the bend in the road, she looked back. He stood exactly where she had left him. He thought that she was still crying, although she was too far away for him to see her properly. He was rooted to the spot. All the folly of the afternoon came over him. Dawning realisation of his own stupidity followed hard on the heels of surprise at her angry reaction. He had attributed to her a whole series of motives that had more to do with his own insecurities than with her perception of his family. Regret overwhelmed him and he watched her go with a sinking heart. In that moment, he knew that he loved her and thought that he had probably lost her for good.

CHAPTER TEN

I love you because I love you.
Nobody tells me what to do with my love.
I love you because I feel it
deep in my heart.

It was a whole week before she saw him again. Her sales technique seemed to take a turn for the worse.

'I thought you were getting better, Maggie,' said Stella. 'But you've been pathetic this week. What on earth's the matter with you? Have you had food poisoning?'

'Nothing's the matter,' she said. 'Nothing's wrong. I just can't seem to drum up a lot of enthusiasm. I'll try harder tomorrow.'

How could she begin to explain that she had quarrelled with a man she hardly knew over issues of honour and pride that she didn't understand. They had been out together only three times. She had seen him more often than that, watched his fingers moving on the strings of the guitar, heard him sing. But there had been only three dates, if dates they could be called, and two of those had been disastrous. Clearly, it wasn't meant to be.

She couldn't tell Stella any of this. Stella would think her very naive to have been so taken in by the charms of a Spanish musician. That was one of the pieces of advice they had been given on their short induction course, from a woman who had spent many years in property sales in Spain and Italy.

'The waiters are attractive, professional, and very flirtatious,' she had told them, sternly. 'If that's what you want too, fine. But don't have any illusions about *love*, will you? That's not what they're about at all.'

She hadn't even bothered to glance in Margaret's direction when she said this. Why should she? Margaret had been amused about it at the time, seeing herself as the person least likely to get involved with a twenty year old Spanish waiter. Well she hadn't. She had got involved with a thirty five year old Spanish musician instead, although you could hardly call it involved since they had done no more than kiss. And now she was wishing she hadn't.

She couldn't shake off her dejection. She went out with her companions from the office a couple of times, but it didn't help and she left after an hour or so.

At work, Conor watched her anxiously. 'You don't look very well, you know.'

'I'm fine. I'm a bit down, that's all. It's allowed, isn't it?'

Each morning and evening she walked along the beach, scanning cafes, hoping for a glimpse of Luis, but she was always disappointed. He seemed to have gone to ground. He hadn't told her which restaurant he cooked in, and she supposed she might have passed the place a dozen times without knowing that he was somewhere inside. She certainly knew the few places where he played, but she was reluctant to go into a strange bar all alone, and he only performed at La Paloma on Thursday nights. The property crowd would be going there as they always did. She tried to content herself and wait, but she wondered if she ought to go with them. It would be too humiliating if he was rude to her or worse, ignored her.

She lingered on the beach to watch dogs digging holes in the sand, the same kind of squash-faced dogs she had seen in Maria's kitchen. But she didn't want to think about Maria's kitchen. There were hotel exercise classes where people moved their arms lazily in time to shrieked commands from blonde giants in leotards. Further along, a slender man, wearing loose pants and top, did elegant Tai Chi with a group of acolytes trying, not very successfully, to follow his movements. She didn't see Luis. Sometimes she would catch a glimpse of a face in the crowd that was uncannily like his. After all, he had typical Canarian good looks. She was always disappointed. She realised that she was behaving irrationally, but she was as helpless to stop herself as any teenager. It was years since she had felt like this. There was even a sort of enjoyment in it, in the novelty of this kind of emotional distress. At least it made her feel alive. She decided that it was a crush. She would recover, but until then, there was nothing to do but go along with it and ride the waves of her own infatuation.

Meanwhile, she drank a lot more piña colada and wine than was good for her, so that she woke up in the early hours of the morning with a raging thirst and had to get up and sip bottled water or weak tea until she felt better. After work, she would sit on her balcony, pretending to read, but really she would be watching the crowds that came up from the beach.

There was no sign of him.

On the following Thursday, she went out with her colleagues.

'I take it we're off to La Paloma,' said Conor.

Niamh said, 'Yes, of course,' with a malicious or maybe just an amused glance in Margaret's direction. Conor and Niamh were a unit now, rarely seen outside working hours without each other, their limbs invariably locked together in the symbiosis of passion.

'There's a really nice singer at La Paloma, isn't there?' said Niamh.

'You mean Luis? Yes, I know,' Margaret said, with as much dignity as she could muster. 'I do know.'

'Did he ever ask you out again?' asked Conor. 'After you sprained your ankle that time, on that visit to Teide I mean.'

'Once or twice.'

'She's a bit of a dark horse, our Maggie,' remarked Niamh, and still Margaret didn't know whether she was being unkind or simply teasing. In an unguarded moment she had confessed to the younger girl that she liked Luis. They had been in the ladies' loo at work. Niamh had been applying make-up and Margaret had been spraying herself with cool water.

'Good for you,' Niamh had said, looking genuinely pleased, if a little surprised. 'Oh, good for you.'

It was plain that it had never crossed Conor's mind that there could be anything serious about Margaret's relationship with the musician.

'I'm not exactly ancient,' she was moved to say. 'It may seem that way when you're twenty but you'll be surprised how quickly it creeps up on you.'

The trouble was that she was used to being the young one. Her brother was four years older. At her primary school, she had been almost a year younger than the others. It hadn't done her a lot of good socially, but she hadn't been troubled by the work. She had gone to university at seventeen, and then she had met Alastair and married young too. Now, it was as though she had been under enchantment for years and had woken to find herself prematurely aged.

And yet here she was, walking towards the restaurant, and feeling that thirty-five wasn't old at all, wasn't remotely old enough to be able to deal with her emotions. She knew that if Luis wasn't there tonight she would find it difficult to hide her disappointment. She took a deep breath on the way in, told herself to keep calm. Nobody need know how she was feeling. To her relief and discomfort, she saw that he was in his usual place, perched on a stool, looking as relaxed as ever, cradling his guitar. She slipped quietly into a vacant seat, grateful that it was in a dimly lit corner of the bar, and accepted Conor's offer of a drink.

She found it very hard to pay attention to anything but Luis. She opted out of the heated 'shop' discussion going on at their table about the relative merits of various new developments as opposed to older apartment blocks. She concentrated on her own feelings, managing to watch Luis covertly, trying not to display too much obvious interest to the curious gaze of Niamh and Conor. Once more, she found his voice disturbing, as though her emotions were vibrating in tune with the notes.

Tonight he played a guitar solo from Argentina, so exciting and energetic that even the property crowd stopped talking so that they could listen. His hands moved from the strings to the body of the instrument and back again, almost violently, tapping out a strange rhythm. It was a passionate, angry, disturbing piece that drew enthusiastic applause from the holidaymakers. He followed it with a melancholy melody in waltz time: a Canarian *malagueña* or so he said, not the one most people knew, but the *malagueña del pais*, that he had come across in an old book, although she didn't think most of his audience cared very much.

She was sorry she had upset him, but she knew it wasn't her fault. She had done nothing wrong. He hadn't been fair to her. She felt the injustice of it warring with her attraction to him. The raw, physical quality of it had hit her in the pit of her stomach as soon as she saw him again, feelings that she had thought were long buried beneath the weight of a failed marriage. Now, when it seemed too late to do anything about it, she realised that she wanted this man more than she had ever wanted anyone in her life. Glad of the relative darkness of the bar, she was restless, shifting in her seat, queasy with a strange combination of attraction and revulsion.

She found herself talking and laughing far too much. She saw that her colleagues were looking at her in some surprise.

Make him notice me, she thought. Let him see that I'm here, at least.

Luis had finished his performance and, as on that first evening, she saw him sitting up at the bar, drinking a beer, talking to the barman. Margaret was shielded from his gaze by Niamh and Conor. She could see him without being seen. For a change he wore a suit, with a crisp white shirt and dark tie. She hadn't seen him so formally dressed. He looked very handsome and at the same time slightly dangerous. It gave him the air of a gigolo. His usual dress of jeans and T-shirts suited him better, made him seem younger. Trying to look at him objectively, she saw that here was one more reason why she had been afraid of him on Teide. It wasn't that he had done anything wrong. It was that he looked perilous. It was almost certainly an illusion, but if so, it was a powerful one.

The others were preparing to leave, talking about going on somewhere else, somewhere cheaper, for pizza.

'Are you sure you're OK, Maggie?' Conor whispered to her. 'The boss hasn't been getting at you at work, has she?'

'No, Stella's been fine.'

She seemed to spend most of her life telling people that she was fine when she wasn't. She wondered what they would do if she said, 'I'm very unhappy. Now what are you going to do about it?'

She stood up.

'You go on,' she said. 'I'll catch up with you in a minute. I have to go to the loo.'

'We'll wait for you.'

'No!' she said, with such emphasis that Conor raised his eyebrows in surprise. 'No. Don't wait for me. I'll only be a couple of minutes. You go on and I'll catch you up.'

Niamh took him by the arm. 'For Christ's sake, come on!' she said, without so much as a glance at Margaret. 'Are you thick or what? Just leave her alone. She'll catch us up in her own good time if she wants to.'

She pulled him through the door and out of the restaurant. Margaret felt grateful to Niamh, but relief was quickly followed by apprehension. What if Luis ignored her? In that case, you can just go home, she thought. But she knew that she would be disappointed and humiliated.

Thankfully, the stool next to him at the bar was vacant. People were starting to drift away. Soon, he would finish his drink and go too. He started his chef's work early, sometimes with marketing, often with food preparation, so he seldom kept late hours after he had been playing. She took a deep breath, gave herself no more time to hesitate and sat down next to him, holding onto the edge of the bar.

He was instantly aware of her, turning towards her with a start of surprise.

She forced a smile. 'Hello, Luis, how are you?'

Where she had half expected to meet rejection, she saw warmth and a sort of rueful relief.

'Margarita!' he said. '*Hola!*' He leaned over, took her by the shoulders and kissed her on both cheeks. '*Mi vida*. I didn't expect to see you.'

'I looked for you. I mean I looked for you in the town, but I never saw you. I wanted to speak to you. I was sorry, sorry we left things like that, anyway.'

He motioned to the barman. 'Let me get you a drink.'

'If you like.'

They waited in silence, until the barman moved away.

'I'm surprised you even wanted to see me again. *Yo era malo contigo!* I behaved so badly.' He seemed embarrassed. 'Have you been in here long?'

'All evening. I came with friends from work as usual. I was lurking in a corner.'

'I never saw you.' He sounded regretful. 'I never noticed. I was playing for you and I never saw you.'

'I figured you wouldn't want to see me.'

He took a drink of his beer.

'Why would you think that?' he asked.

She paused for a moment, pleased just to hear his voice, enjoying his proximity, the scent of him. The thought occurred to her that she had passed the point of no return. If he didn't return her affection, her recovery would be painful. Better to find out now. Better to begin the process immediately.

When had she let down all her defences, she wondered?

Had it been that first day on Teide when he had been so kind to her. She reached out her hand in an involuntary gesture and almost touched his wrist. It was what she had tried to do on the ferry, on the way back from La Gomera, only on that occasion he had rejected her. Now it was she who drew back, pulling away her hand.

'I'm sorry. I just wanted to apologise.'

'What for?' he asked. '*You* have done nothing wrong. Nothing at all.' He caught her hand briefly, squeezed her fingers. 'I should be apologising to you. I treated you badly. I was very rude. I was so ashamed of myself. I know you are not the kind of person I described to you. But I have met many people here who are suspicious of me. Suspicious of any friendship I might have to offer. They have an image, an idea of what I am like. I can't help it. But they refuse to see beyond it. To see me as I really am.'

He struck his breast with a clenched fist, a theatrical but oddly moving gesture. Then he laughed at his own self-dramatization. 'Do you understand me?'

'I think so. But perhaps I was wrong too. Perhaps I *was* a bit afraid of your family. Oh not afraid, that's the wrong word. But nervous, yes. It was all strange and different for me. You gave me so little time. We should have gone there in the morning, instead of the way we went, as though *you* were ashamed of them.'

'It must have seemed like that. I'm not ashamed of them, but I admit, I was afraid of the way you would see them. I was trying to see them through your eyes.'

'I don't think you know me well enough to be able to do that.'

'No. No. But I'm getting to know you better!'

She half expected Conor to come back looking for her and prayed that he wouldn't, but there was no sign of him, and she supposed that Niamh must have forbidden him to return.

'Have you finished for tonight?' she asked, although she knew that he had.

'*Sí*. Yes, I have.' He patted the guitar, perched on a seat beside him. 'I can go home now. But where are your friends?'

'They've gone home too. I told them not to wait for me.'

He really smiled then, a big happy grin. 'Good. I'm glad. So, will I walk you to your apartment?'

'If you want to.'

'And *quizas* we will try to save something of this friendship. OK?'

He got up and brushed his smart suit straight.

'Do you like me in this?' he asked her.

'Very smart.'

'*Sí*. I am very elegant. Too elegant perhaps.' He chuckled. 'I prefer my jeans, but sometimes my boss here, he likes me to look like this, so I oblige him. He bought the suit for me, so there is nothing I can do but wear it. He goes to Santa Cruz with me and he buys me this very fancy suit so sometimes I have to wear it.'

'You look very handsome in it.'

'I'm not sure. I think I look like a … like a *bravucón*. What is the word?'

'A bouncer? Well. Maybe. Just a bit.'

He carried his guitar in its case, but took her elbow very politely with the other hand and steered her out of the bar. Once they were in the sweet night-time street, quiet now after the blaze of the day, he captured her hand in his own again. He seemed to be restraining some great joy as, holding her hand very tightly and very close to his body, he walked with her towards her apartment.

CHAPTER ELEVEN

A Canary moves down
through your curls,
to drink water from your lips,
thinking that they are a spring.

Luis came into the flat, set down the guitar and took off his jacket and tie, opening the neck of his shirt with a sigh of relief. Then, while she made coffee, he walked around and looked at things: books, pictures, plants.

'It isn't very luxurious, I'm afraid.'

'No. But it's nice. Very nice, in fact. Better than the room where I sleep.'

'Where is your room?'

'In my friends' apartment. They own the restaurant where I work. They have a place over the business. And a beautiful house in the Oratava valley where they go when they want to get away from here. It's a good enough apartment but very hot and noisy. I don't think you'd like it. This is better. You see I'm always trying to save money for my restaurant.'

'I've got used to it here. It feels like home now. Well, most of the time.'

A refuge, she thought. For all that she sometimes felt lonely, it had become a refuge. 'It belongs to some family friends. They got a lump sum – you know, a sum of money from their pension – when they retired.

And they'd inherited some cash as well. They bought this. A long time ago. But of course now they can only come for ninety days at a time.'

'Ah yes. Your Brexit,' he said, grinning.

She pulled a face. 'Not mine. I didn't vote for it. Neither did most of Scotland. But we were dragged out of the EU whether we liked it or not. I was lucky to have other options. Anyway, their family use it as well, but they couldn't come this year. They were quite glad of the long let, I think.'

'There are many people who do that in Britain?' He sat down, stretching out his legs. He looked tired. Pale and tired under his tan. He worked long hours. He rubbed his eyes and sighed.

'Do what?' she asked.

'Buy apartments here and rent them out to holidaymakers.'

'Not so many now.'

She could see that he was verging on resentment again. He had said that he approved of tourism but she wondered just how much he approved of people who bought property here.

'You don't like the idea?' she said lightly.

He looked up and smiled at her. 'Ah, I don't know. I keep wondering how long before they start on La Gomera and then it will all be spoiled. Well, they have started of course. But if we had row upon row of villas everywhere, and tourists who liked to eat nothing but fish and chips – no, I wouldn't like that at all.'

'Or English breakfasts,' she added. 'The breakfast is compulsory.'

'*Por supuesto*. And when they meet they will complain about the awful *Españoles* and how it takes forever to get anything done. *Mañana*, you know. Until you begin to think that they plan to colonise the whole place. And I'll tell you something about *mañana*.'

'What?'

'It doesn't mean tomorrow.'

'What does it mean then?'

'It means not today.'

She smiled. 'Of course it does. But I thought you didn't mind the tourists. Aren't we good for your economy?'

'Well,' he relented. 'I don't mind the tourists. Much. Except for the horrible stag and hen parties. But sometimes I mind the colonists. And the hotels are just as bad. Have you ever seen them fighting over the sunbeds?'

'I have. And not just the English.'

'That's true,' he conceded. 'But you walk down the street here, every damn sign is in English. And then I think that if more of them came to La Gomera we would all be wealthier. We might not have to leave to make a living.'

He thought of the Cabellos's empty cottage and the sad abandoned photographs there.

'They do come to La Gomera. We saw that. That day we were there. The German ladies.'

'Yes. They travel around in coaches. But once large numbers of foreigners start to build and buy property, there is never very much left for us.'

'It's the same in Scotland you know. On the Isle of Skye, for instance. Rich incomers build big new holiday houses and local workers live in caravans because they can't find anywhere to stay.'

He frowned. 'I didn't know that happened.'

'Oh it does. They're everywhere. Motorhomes. You know, camper-vans clogging up all the roads. Roads that weren't meant for that kind of traffic. Leaving their rubbish behind them. Some of them bring so much stuff with them that they don't contribute much to the local economy at all.'

He sighed. 'Why are we talking about things like this? It isn't something we can ever solve, is it?'

'Have you heard of Robert Louis Stevenson?'

'Yes. The Scottish writer. He wrote Treasure Island, didn't he? I read it when I was at school. In Spanish of course.'

'There are no foreign lands, it is the traveller only who is foreign.'

'Did he say that?'

'I believe so.'

'Then he was right.'

She had been walking restlessly around the room, picking dead leaves off plants, straightening cushions, anything to keep herself occupied, to prevent her from doing the thing she most wanted to do, which was to sit down beside him, to feel him close.

'Why are you walking about like this?'

'I don't know.'

The truth was that the thought of kissing him, let alone anything more intimate, seemed impossible. But she could almost feel the strength of his desire for her radiating across the room, pulling her towards him. He patted the seat.

'*Tienes miedo*? Are you frightened again?'

'A bit.' But she sat down next to him. 'I don't know why. I'm all grown up.'

He put his arm gently around her, letting it lie along her shoulders. Then he kissed the top of her head.

'I think you're out of practice. Like when I haven't played for a long time. Don't worry.'

'I'm not worried.' She could feel her heart belying the statement, beginning to beat with a jerky, irregular rhythm and her breathing quickening with the familiar sensations of nervous panic. He took her empty coffee mug and put it down on the low table.

'Relax,' he said.

'I'm trying.'

'Listen. If you say to me now, stop, get up, put on your jacket and that horrible tie and get out of my apartment immediately, then that's what I'll do. You won't need to tell me again. And I won't mind. Well, not much, anyway.'

He was stroking her hair, gently, unhurriedly.

'I don't want you to go. I just don't know what I feel. It's been so long. So long since I was this close to anyone. The way I feel now confuses me.'

'And you think it doesn't confuse *me*?'

'I don't know. You don't look very confused to me, Luis.'

'Then we'll wait. There's no hurry. I have as much time as you want. As much time as you need. As I need.'

Why me? She still thought it, although she didn't voice the question for fear of insulting him, for fear of the evasive answer she might receive. Was she a challenge to him, bored with the young women who watched him play and flirted with him afterwards? Was that it? But how could she possibly ask him that?

As though reading her mind, he said 'I wish you would trust me, you know. I'm a good man. I said so and it's true.'

She didn't doubt it. But she doubted her ability to cope with it. She had been shocked by the ease with which Alastair had rejected her. For a while, it had made her question her own worth.

'Gaslighting,' her mother had said eventually, in exasperation. 'That's what he was doing to you, Maggie. Making you think everything was your fault.'

'Some of it was.'

'But most of it wasn't.'

It was easy enough to see that now, but still not easy to do anything about it. Perhaps she ought to begin by thinking more about Luis and less about herself. She had often noticed the obsessive self interest of the very shy. Once you were locked into it, it was hard to change that pattern.

Presently, she felt the irregular beating of her heart slowing and steadying. He seemed to feel it too because he stopped stroking her hair and they sat, close together, warm and comfortable for a long while. Then, he tilted her face towards him and kissed her on the lips.

When she responded, he kissed her cheeks, her eyelids, and her lips again, gently exploring her mouth with his tongue, arousing a hundred tiny sensations. When he stopped and sat back to look at her, she knew that she wanted him to go on.

He stood up and gently pulled her towards the bedroom. 'Come on,' he said. 'I think we should, don't you?'

'I don't know.'

'Trust me.'

All at once, her brain relinquished its grip on her body. Why not, she thought. I'm all grown up and I want to do this. So why not?

She lay down on the big, comfortable bed that almost filled the room, the bed that had always seemed so sadly empty, no matter how restful her sleep. With her willing help he took off her dress, sliding it over her head. He unfastened her bra and then delicately slid off her panties. But he hardly touched her until she lay on the cool sheet. He pulled the Indian cotton throw over her, smiled, said, 'One moment,' and then sat down on the bed and unhurriedly took off his shoes and socks. His feet were shapely and very brown. She sat up, forgetting to clutch the throw around her, and helped him with his shirt, peeling it off to display the brown arms beneath, gently touching his torso with its fine, dark hair.

He had a powerful, compact body. As he leaned over her, she could smell the bitter perfume of his skin, of his sweat. The night was hot. Her mouth watered with the desire to taste him. If she thought herself flawed, and at that time she did, she found Luis closer to her image of physical perfection than any man she had ever known. But perhaps she was simply captivated, and blind to his faults.

It surprised her in some detached part of her mind that she observed all this about him first, saw the whole man. She looked at him and he seemed pleased that she did. It aroused him, her sudden boldness.

'I love to look at you,' she said.

'Then let me look at you, too.'

She wanted to turn over, turn away from him, but he stopped her. 'There are no rules,' he said gently. 'Only what pleases you.'

He sat down beside her, then reached across to the bedside table and took up a bottle of suntan oil she had left there. He tipped a little into his hands and slowly, gently, began to massage her body, beginning with her arms. She felt the fingertips of his left hand calloused from the guitar, softened by the scented oil, sliding easily up and over her shoulders and then down on to her breasts. As he massaged he seemed to be paying attention to each part of her body in turn, looking at it as though memorising it. Down, down he moved on to her belly which had never contrived to be flat and smooth and taut, but he didn't seem to care, didn't even seem to notice.

'Oh my Margarita,' he said, 'You are such a – such a *woman!*'

Happiness flooded her and with it came full desire. He hesitated for a moment and then, taking more oil onto his palm, began at her feet and moved up her legs, slowly and carefully, until she felt herself growing wet and welcoming. She caught at his hand and pulled it closer.

'Oh my darling,' she said, impulsively.

'Do you love me? Do you?' he asked.

'Of course I do!'

'Just as well, *mi amor*,' he said, pulling her closer.

'Wait, wait,' she said, suddenly anxious. 'I never thought. Have you got anything? You know? Protection?'

'Hell no.' He sat back, dismayed. 'You're not – ?'

'On the pill? No. There was no need. Nobody in my life. Nobody in my bed, Luis.'

He shook his head ruefully. 'I'm dying here.'

'Me too.'

'No, no, no. *Momentito!*'

He slid off the bed, went through to the other room, came back carrying the guitar case.

'You're joking,' she said, laughter bubbling up inside her.

'I'm not joking. I'm not even sure they're still here.'

He opened the case, lifted up the guitar, rummaged inside, triumphantly slid out the small packets. 'Two,' he said. 'Just two.'

'You keep *condoms* in your guitar case?'

'Well, it makes a change from guns,' he said.

She stared at him for a moment, then started to splutter with laughter again.

'Desperado. Oh God! Luis! But why?'

She saw that he was blushing under his tan and that endeared him to her even more.

'Listen, Margarita, they were here for so long. So very long. I don't make a habit of this.'

'It doesn't matter.'

'But it matters to me, you know. It matters to me.' He was suddenly serious. 'I don't want you to think that I – screw around.' He half whispered it, disliking the word.

'I don't think that.'

'Good.'

'But I wonder if they have a use-by date.'

'I sure hope not.'

They started again. More slowly. More safely. He leaned over her and she saw his face, intent and serious above her, and felt his warm body encompassing her.

'I want you so much,' she said. 'So much!'

'Ah Margarita. *Ah, mi querida!*' He slipped magically into his own tongue and said the words of love and desire, '*Ah, mi niñita. Mi amor.* My heart's darling!' Then he slipped inside her, easily. Loving her, he relinquished control and let his body and his desire take him where it would.

She felt him let go. She called out to him and she felt him join her, so that they passed into the exquisite warm darkness together and then they were moving together, abandoned, moving to the peak of pleasure together.

'Margarita!' He cried out her name and she clung to him in an ecstasy of sensation, of love, of pleasure, until together they reached the crest of the wave, tumbled down and lay beached and gasping in each other's arms, on the crumpled bed, in the warm, dark night.

She must have slept and perhaps he did too, but when she opened her eyes, he was brushing her hair back from her face and gazing down at her. There was such tenderness in his brown eyes that she found herself shaking her head slightly as though denying the very possibility of it.

'Was it good?' he asked, still in his native tongue, still thinking in Spanish.

'Wonderful.'

'*No puedo hacerte el amor en Ingles*! I can't make love in English. Your language is much too cold for lovemaking. I must make love to you in Spanish or not at all.'

'Then you'd better make love to me in Spanish.'

He grinned. 'Now? I wish I were twenty again.'

'Soon.'

He stood up and walked through to the sitting room. She watched him, loving him so much that she felt lost apart from him. He poured a couple of glasses of wine and came back through, then got into bed beside her and put his arm around her, sighed, stretched, relaxed and drank.

'Listen,' he said. 'Do you want me to go home tonight?' He looked at his watch. 'What am I saying? It's not tonight at all. It's almost morning. Three o'clock already. But perhaps if people see me in the morning you'll be embarrassed. If you wish it, I'll go.'

'Do you *want* to go?'

'Me? Of course I don't want to go.'

'But you have work.'

'I don't care. I want to drink my wine and lie down here with you in my arms and go to sleep and wake up with you still in my arms. That's what I want to do, Margarita.'

She sighed with relief.

'That's what I want to do too,' she said. 'I think I might die if you went away just now.'

He laughed at her intensity. 'Would you? Then I can see that I must stay. Out of consideration for the *señorita* if nothing else.'

They finished their wine and kissed very gently. She yawned, half asleep already. She turned on her side and he switched off the bedside lamp and then lay down beside her. He put his arms around her and smoothed them once more down her body as though making an account of it for himself. They fitted together snugly in the warmth of the night, the sheet thrown over them, and soon they both slept. But all through her sleep she was aware of him, spooning into the shape of her.

She woke up wanting him, aroused to him, entirely of her own volition. She welcomed him in and quickly, very quickly, she came to a trembling climax, wrapping her legs around him. This time she was able to feel and see and enjoy his abandonment as he came, just a little later, with a cry almost of pain. He buried his face in her neck and pulled her so close to him that it hurt, hugging her harder and harder. At first she thought she must have misheard him, but when he repeated the words, she found that they had lodged in her heart as well as her head, taken root and begun to flower there. The words had blossomed in a matter of seconds into a single exotic bloom.

'I love you,' he said. 'I love you. Margarita, *quieres casarte conmigo*? Marry me. You must marry me or I can't bear it!'

CHAPTER TWELVE

Two hearts ill
with the same malady:
mine and my lover's.
Truly they must love each other.

The weekday morning routine in Fiona and Ian Sinclair's house seldom, if ever, varied. The radio alarm would come on at precisely seven o'clock: Radio 4 of course because they both liked to keep abreast of current affairs, however depressing. Fiona would get up first and go into the kitchen to make tea. She would take orange juice to ten year old Lottie, a glass of milk to eight year old Rory and a mug of strong tea to Ian. She would make sure that both children were wide awake, or at least claiming to be: Lottie in her bedroom, with its white furniture, much loved teddies that she would never outgrow and her Taylor Swift posters, Rory in his smaller den with football wallpaper, bunk beds in case a friend slept over and a row of toy cars and lorries garaged in the corner.

It gave Fiona a certain satisfaction to see the rooms so neatly arranged, though of late she had scented an air of rebellion. Lottie had begun to plaster her cupboard doors with pictures of horses and ponies, her latest passion. Now she was clamouring for riding lessons. Soon, thought Fiona, she would be asking for a pony. Rory, once a sweet, sturdy lad who had wanted only boxes of crayons and packs of playing cards, had started to ask for expensive gifts for his birthday and for Christmas: an iPad, the latest console with games that were much too old for him but which 'everyone' was playing. Fiona's friends had warned her about approaching adolescence but she hadn't expected it to begin quite so soon.

She sighed and plonked the milk down on his table, leaving the door open so that she could shout at him if necessary. Then she left Ian's tea beside him, or what she could see of him, which was a tuft of light brown hair, and went off to take her shower in peace in their tiny ensuite shower room. Soon the daily battle for the family bathroom would begin, with the children fighting to see who would get possession first, while the loser stood outside and complained about the unfairness of life. Actually, Rory wouldn't have minded not showering at all, but he still resented it when his sister got in there ahead of him, wailing that she took so long.

'The remedy is in your own hands, Rory,' his father always said. 'If you got up when mum woke you, you'd beat her to it every day.'

Fiona would sort out her hair, dress in the clothes she had carefully laid out the night before and then go down and make sour-dough toast for herself and dish out cereal in the kitchen, although it sometimes struck her that she did too much for all of them and they took her for granted. Still, she liked to think of herself as a supreme example of the organised working mother. By eight-thirty on the dot they were always ready to go out, Fiona driving the Polo and Ian taking the big Hyundai, dropping the children off at the nearby primary school on his way to the office. Ian worked for an accountancy firm in suburban Glasgow.

On this particular morning, however, things went badly awry. Fiona was towelling herself dry when she heard the landline phone in the hallway ringing. It rang for a long time before anyone answered it, though Fiona remained stubbornly in the shower room. This was her little bit of time to herself before the challenges of the day. Let Ian get up and answer it. Just as she could stand it no longer, she heard her husband get out of bed, gallop down the stairs and snatch up the receiver. Wrapped in her towel, she came out to listen.

'Yes?' he said. 'Yes?'

She opened the bedroom door a bit wider, the better to hear the conversation. Who on earth could be phoning them at this time in the morning? Scammers probably. If the mobile signal wasn't so bad here, they'd have done away with the landline years ago.

'Margaret!' she heard him say in some surprise.

She got dressed in a hurry, wondering why on earth Margaret would be phoning her brother. Why not just message him? Some imaginary emergency, no doubt. The silly woman was probably terminally homesick and had decided to see sense and come home at last. Well, Fiona had predicted it, although she would try hard not to say 'I told you so' when next she saw her sister-in-law. But the unspoken reproach would be there. It had been such a crazy scheme, the whole venture so stupidly out of character. Margaret was surely too old to be heading off to the sunshine. Too old, or not old enough. It was the kind of thing kids did during their gap years, or pensioners after retirement, not divorced women in their thirties. What Margaret had really needed to do, thought Fiona, was to stay comfortably in Glasgow, buying a nice little flat on the south side, with her mother and her family close by, so that they could support her as she readjusted to her single state. Flying south for the winter with the swallows had always seemed a crazy scheme, doomed to failure. It was a mistake to act on impulse, to go rushing off without carefully weighing up the pros and cons well in advance.

Tenerife, she thought scornfully. Whoever heard of anyone you knew actually *living* on Tenerife? It was a place where young, single teachers went searching for sunshine. Then they talked about it uproariously in the staffroom afterwards. Worse than that, it was a place where some of her less academically inclined students booked cheap holidays in huge hotels, missing their classes in the process.

Blackpool with sun. Or a volcanic wasteland. That was the way she envisaged it, although sometimes friends would challenge her, telling her that she was prejudiced. She and Ian and the children generally holidayed in some civilized country house hotel in Scotland or the Lakes, preferably with a golf course nearby and an activity club for the children. They would take bicycles and cycle, or Fiona would take the children off to various museums and country parks while Ian enjoyed his golf. They didn't have to cope with a foreign language and the risk of salmonella was minimal. Ian didn't like the heat much. Fiona had flown to Marbella once with a group of young colleagues, a long weekend involving a hen night, and it had been fun, a good laugh. But they had never left the hotel with its pools and bars. She had been rather glad of it if she was honest and Fiona was nothing if not honest, sometimes uncomfortably so.

She was suddenly aware of silence from the hallway. Ian had said nothing for some time. She wondered what Margaret was saying. She paused by the door, hairbrush in hand, to listen. At last, Ian spoke. His voice sounded strangely high-pitched.

'What did you say?' he asked. '*What*?' Then, a full octave higher, '*Married*?'

Fiona ran down the stairs. Ian was clutching the phone convulsively. His mouth was open as though he wanted to speak, but no sound came out. At last the words erupted into the small hallway.

'*What in God's name do you mean, married*?'

He had turned an unbecoming shade of puce. Fiona took the receiver from him. He made no protest but sat down on the upholstered seat at one end of the old fashioned telephone table and rested his head in his hands. He looked incongruous in his pyjamas, his designer glasses sliding down his nose.

'Margaret?' said Fiona briskly. 'Good morning!'

'Hello, Fiona.' Margaret sounded oddly defiant, not like herself at all.

'Did I hear right? Did Ian mention the word marriage? Is this a joke of some sort. If so, it's not very funny at this time in the morning!'

'Oh it's not a joke. I'm getting married again. I just thought you should know as soon as possible. Is Ian OK? He sounded very strange.'

'He's shocked and so am I. You can't possibly be thinking about getting married again. You've only just got divorced, Margaret!'

'A year. Almost a year. And we were separated for a long time before that. And Alastair's married again.'

'That's quite different.'

'Why is it different?'

'Well, he already –'

'Yes. He'd clearly been screwing around for ages. I know that.'

'Don't say things like that!' This didn't sound like Margaret at all.

'Why not? It's true, isn't it?'

Margaret was standing on the balcony of her apartment where the mobile signal was strongest. She didn't want to spend too long on the phone. Maybe it would have been better to have waited until she knew they had both gone out to work and left a message on their answering machine or gone online, but it seemed rude and she was already anxious about her family's reaction to her news. Luis was hovering in the background. When she had agreed to his proposal of marriage, she had surprised herself. It had seemed the right thing to do. The only thing to do. She hadn't been able to refuse him, but she hadn't really wanted to tell Ian and Fiona either. Her first impulse had been to go through with the ceremony without telling her family at home anything about it.

'Let's just get married and tell them afterwards,' she had said.

It was Luis who had persuaded her otherwise, Luis for whom such a thing was inconceivable.

'But you must tell them,' he said. 'Your brother and your mother. They may want to come to the wedding. Surely they will want to come to the wedding?'

'They won't. Well, I suppose mum might. But she's hardly ever flown anywhere except Dublin once in a while. And even Ian and Fiona don't much like travelling. All they'll try to do is persuade me that I shouldn't get married. That it's all a big mistake.'

'And will they succeed?'

'No, of course not.'

'Then phone them, please. I'll feel much better if you tell them. I think they have a right to know.'

'Listen,' said Fiona, trying to collect her scattered thoughts. Ian was mouthing questions at her. She shushed him and asked a few of her own.

'Who are you planning to marry? Can't it wait until you come home? This sounds crazy. Is this some kind of holiday romance, Maggie?'

'No it isn't and no, it can't wait.'

'Why not?' A terrible thought struck her. 'You're not *pregnant* are you?'

'Don't be daft. I just don't want to come home. I'm staying here. Luis and I are getting married here.'

'*Who* did you say?'

'Luis. He's Spanish.'

'What on earth do you mean?'

Margaret was suddenly angry. 'Fiona, is this a bad line or has the shock affected your hearing? Spanish. You know. The people who live here.'

'There's no need to be sarcastic,' said Fiona reproachfully.

She sat down next to her husband. 'She's marrying a Spaniard!'

Margaret heard her, and thought that her sister-in-law sounded as horrified as if she had said that she was marrying a Martian.

'Ask her what he does,' said Ian.

'He plays the guitar and sings,' said Margaret. 'And he cooks. He's a chef in a restaurant. A good one. But an even better musician. Listen, I want Ian to tell mum before I ring her. I don't want it to come as too much of a shock.'

'He plays the guitar,' Fiona relayed to Ian. 'And he's a chef. In a restaurant.'

Lottie came down the stairs, dressed but yawning hugely.

'Who plays the guitar, Mum? Who's that?'

'Never mind. Go and get your breakfast. I'll tell you in a minute.'

'Love to the kids,' said Margaret, brightly.

'No, listen,' said Fiona, hurriedly. 'Tell your mum what? Her daughter's marrying a Spaniard called Luis? She'll have a seizure!'

'I don't think so. I don't think mum's as delicate as all that, Fiona.'

'But Luis what? What's his name. Where is he from?'

'Luis Herrera Garcia.' Margaret loved saying his name. 'And he's from an island called La Gomera. And I love him to bits.'

Herrera was his paternal surname, he had told her, and Garcia was his mother's name. After their marriage Margaret could, if she wished, add his name to her own, assuming the rather grand title of Margarita Sinclair de Herrera Garcia. Or she could more simply be Señora de Herrera Garcia. Although if she wanted to keep her own name, that was fine by Luis as well.

'But if we have children,' he said, 'they will be Herrera Sinclair.'

They had been sitting over breakfast when they had this conversation, croissants from the bakery down the street, freshly squeezed orange juice, coffee.

After a pause, Luis asked, 'Was it true?'

'What?'

'What you told me about children. About not wanting them.'

'I never said I didn't want them. Well, only when I was quite young. Alastair said he never wanted children. I changed my mind but he wouldn't. Or so he said. But then his new wife was pregnant when I last saw her so perhaps he just didn't want *our* children.'

'That still hurts you.' He reached over the table and took her hand. It was a statement rather than a question.

'Not really. Not about Alastair anyway. But I would have liked a child. It seemed very unfair of him. I resented it. It's quite hard to get rid of that feeling.'

'I've always liked children. I can't imagine a house without them. I think we treat children quite differently here.'

'You spoil them, you mean!' But she was smiling.

'Oh I have never understood this word spoil,' he said gravely. 'We just love them. That's all. Sometimes when I was in London, I felt that you British saw children as a kind of inconvenience. Here we like to be with our children. We don't just love them. We like them as well. And we are not afraid to say so, either.'

He was right, of course. And it was one more thing about him that she loved.

'His name is Luis Herrera Garcia,' Fiona whispered to Ian.

'My God,' he moaned. 'He sounds like a football player.'

'That would be OK,' Fiona hissed. 'At least he'd be rich.'

'Ask her when the wedding is.'

'Soon,' said Margaret, who could hear him. 'At Easter. I'll send you an invitation. You can fly out for it if you like. He's very nice. I think you'll like him. I know mum will.'

Fiona had got over her initial surprise and had moved into what she liked to think of as 'crisis mode'. She spoke very quietly and calmly, the way she tackled recalcitrant teens when she was teaching at the college.

'Maggie,' she said, 'I do think this is a bad idea you know. I mean where's the hurry? He may be very nice but you can hardly claim to know him well. And you know what they say about marrying in haste.'

'I know all about repenting at leisure, Fiona. I thought long and hard about marrying Alastair and look where that got me.'

'But I don't see what the hurry is. Why can't you wait and think it over? Or come home and talk about it? What's the matter with you? You don't sound at all like yourself. You sound quite different.'

Margaret laughed. 'Oh, I *am* different.'

'What has he done to you?'

'Captivated me. Enchanted me!'

'Maggie, are you sure you haven't had a breakdown of some sort? Perhaps you ought to see a doctor.'

'I don't need a doctor. There's nothing wrong with me.'

'Well at least give yourself some time to think about it. It's such a big step to take.'

'Look, Fiona. I don't want to think it over. I've always thought things over. I just want to get married. I've never been so sure about anything in my life so that's what I'm going to do. I must go now. I'll message you from work. Explain all about it. Love to Ian and the kids. And love to mum, too!'

Margaret ended the call abruptly. Fiona was left staring at an uncommunicative receiver. Slowly she replaced it and looked at her husband.

'She sounded serious. I think she's actually going to go ahead and marry this person. I really think she means to do it.'

'That was the impression I got,' said Ian. 'She's completely off her head. She can't possibly have known him for more than a few weeks. She messages you, doesn't she? Has she ever mentioned him?'

'No. She's on Facebook but she's never said anything about a man at all. No pictures. Nothing.'

'There's something quite sinister about it. Don't you think so? I wonder what he's done to her? How could he make her behave so out of character? Is it one of those romance scams you hear about?'

'It could be but they're usually online. Or long distance. I suppose it was love at first sight,' said Fiona with more than a touch of wistfulness. 'If you can believe in such a thing. But you're right. The sun has turned her head. She's clearly fallen for him hook, line and sinker. The first man to show any interest in her for years.'

'I suppose so.'

'He's probably after her money.'

'She doesn't have much money,' said Ian.

'Of course she does. She has money stashed away from the sale of the flat. She got half. Even after they'd paid off the mortgage there was quite a bit left. You should know. You helped with the conveyancing.'

'That's true, right enough. I suppose she *has* got a bit of money. As far as this man is concerned anyway. He may think she's a rich divorcee. But how can he possibly know what she has?'

'She's probably told him. You know what she's like. I suppose it makes her a catch in his eyes. You see this kind of thing on the television, don't you? Women being conned by foreigners.'

'But they don't seem to be planning to come over here to live.'

'They don't have to. Not yet. She probably couldn't bring him anyway, although I suppose they could go to Ireland. No, you mark my words, he's after her money. He'll marry her in haste and that gives him a right to her cash. Dear God, he could even be a potential murderer!'

'Surely not.' This was a bridge too far even for Ian. 'I think you've been watching too many TV dramas.'

'But these kind of things do happen, Ian. I know they don't happen very often. But they happen from time to time, so why not to your sister?'

'I suppose it's possible.'

'There's a lot of hostility towards tourists there you know. I've read about it.'

'I think it was exaggerated,' said Ian, mildly. 'Besides – she's not a tourist. She's working there.'

'Yes but selling flats to incomers.'

'All the same, I don't think our Margaret's the type to invite hostility, do you? I think they mean the stag parties. Drunken young men and women.'

'But she's quite naive, you know. One of life's victims.'

Ian demurred. 'She's quite pretty. And she was always brighter than Alastair.'

'This Luis is probably attractive, paid attention to her. No man has paid attention to her for years. She would believe anything he said. And there are a lot of predators out there. Oh God, Ian, what are we going to do?'

'I don't know. What a mess.'

Rory stood in front of them, wide-eyed, half dressed. 'What's wrong?' he asked. 'Was that Aunty Maggie?'

'Yes, son. She's having a spot of bother,' said Ian. 'Nothing you need worry about.'

'What kind of bother?'

'Nothing important. We hope she might be coming home soon. That would be nice, wouldn't it? Go and put the rest of your clothes on.'

Rory headed back upstairs. 'It would be OK. But I'd rather go and see her in Tenerife.'

'Who's Luis Herrera Garcia?' asked Lottie from the kitchen. 'Has Aunty Maggie got a boyfriend?'

'Just a friend,' said Ian. 'And you shouldn't have been listening.'

'You were both shouting. We heard. Is her boyfriend Spanish then?'

'That's right.'

'Melissa's big sister met a Spaniard when they went on holiday to Ibiza.' Lottie gave the word its full, exotic value, rather as though it were synonymous with 'pirate'. Ian had a sudden and irrational vision of Blackbeard, buried treasure, doubloons.

'And?' he said.

'She went clubbing with him every night and he wrote to her and then one day the doorbell rang and there he was. He said he was going to try to get a job in Glasgow and could he stay with them. Melissa's dad was raging. And Melissa's sister was mortified because she was going out with Donny Frazer's big brother by that time and she didn't fancy the Spaniard any more.'

'Oh God,' said Ian, dramatically. 'What on earth are we going to do?'

Fiona made another pot of tea. She felt oddly elated. Sometimes, contented as she was with her husband and children, she had the feeling that life was a little dull. Here, at last, was something that would provide food for excited speculation for a long time to come. They would have to tell Annie, of course, but Fiona had a strange idea that her mother-in-law wouldn't be as shocked as they were. Annie was unpredictable. Fiona blamed her Irish blood. Ian and his late father had been very much alike, rather conservative and careful, but Annie had an adventurous streak. It showed up in small ways. The evening classes Annie chose to do were always slightly odd and random: philosophy, aromatherapy and yoga for instance. She might even approve of her daughter's remarriage. Tell them not to interfere.

Surely, Fiona thought, some more direct action was called for. Surely they ought to make some effort to save Margaret from her own folly.

'Do you think,' said Ian, 'That we ought to get Alastair to phone her or write to her or something?'

'*Alastair*? Oh, I don't think so.'

Sometimes, Fiona thought, men could be quite astoundingly obtuse.

'I just thought he might talk some sense into her.'

'Why on earth would you think that? He's not exactly flavour of the month with her.'

'I thought they managed to sort things out quite amicably in the end.'

'Well they did, but I don't think Alastair's ever going to be able to persuade her not to remarry. Do you?'

'Well. No. I suppose not.'

'Quite the opposite.'

'I was just thinking of the money. I mean he was fairly generous. And he wouldn't want to see it all go to a foreigner, would he?'

'I don't know if he was that generous. He caused the split, didn't he? He's got a new wife. And a baby on the way. He only gave her her due. She'd contributed more than enough to that flat.'

'I suppose so.'

Fiona wasn't usually so defensive of Margaret but she had been shocked by Alastair's behaviour. She had always liked him, admired him even. He had rocked the security of her world and she had never quite forgiven him for it. All the same, she was genuinely worried about her sister-in-law. Her vulnerability. Surely they ought to make an effort to save Margaret from the consequences of her own folly.

'Why don't we go to Tenerife?' she asked suddenly, pausing in the act of spreading sunflower margarine on a piece of toast.

'To Tenerife?' Ian looked horrified. 'But I've got a liquidation and two creditors' meetings this week.'

'Well, we could go for a long weekend. We could maybe go on Friday or Saturday and come back on Wednesday. I expect we could get a flight from Glasgow. You could go online, see what you can find.'

'But what about you? What about college?'

'This is a family emergency. I'll take the time off. I'll say she's ill. She is, sort of, when you think about it. She must be.'

'Should we book a hotel?' asked Ian.

'We don't need to. That apartment sleeps four. There's a bedroom and a double sofa bed in the sitting room. I remember her saying that when she borrowed it. Remember? We said we might go down there and stay with her.'

Ian frowned. 'I don't fancy that. Besides, this man might have moved in with her. It would be so embarrassing.'

'I expect he *has* moved in. But maybe that's why we should stay with her. Find out exactly what the situation is. And it would only be for a few nights.'

'What about the kids?'

'They could stay with your mum, couldn't they?' said Fiona. 'Or she could come here for a few days.'

Her own parents lived in Perth. She didn't see very much of them, although they paid a duty visit two or three times a year.

'But I want to go to Tenerife as well,' said Lottie, pulling a face.

'So do I,' echoed Rory.

'Well you can't. Not this time. You've got school.'

'So've you got school,' said Rory, defiantly. 'Well, college.'

'I know. But this is an emergency.'

'You said there was nothing to worry about. Now you're saying it's an emergency,' Lottie pointed out, finishing her cereal and starting to sort out her school bag.

'There's nothing for you kids to worry about. It isn't that kind of emergency. Nobody died or anything.'

'I should hope not!' Ian looked askance.

'But I think we need to have a serious chat with Maggie. And the only way we can find out what's really going on is to be there. We can't do it online or on the phone.'

'I suppose not,' said Ian, doubtfully.

'At least we ought to check this person out. See what he's like.'

'What person?' asked Rory.

'The person Aunty Maggie's going to marry, silly,' said Lottie in great exasperation.

'Oh. Is she going to get married again? Like Alastair?'

'We don't know yet, Rory,' said Fiona carefully. 'We'll see. It may just be a joke. Or a big mistake. Who knows. But we have to go and see for ourselves.' She looked across at Ian. 'We do, don't we?'

Ian sighed. He knew when he was beaten. 'Do you want me to sort it out? Do you know where the passports are?'

The passports were stored away carefully in a documents folder, useful for the internal flights Ian in particular sometimes had to make.

'I'll sort it all out,' said Fiona, unwilling to trust him to do it. 'I have a free period this morning. I'll see what I can find in the way of flights.'

'You make the arrangements and I'll take the time off. Then we'd better let Maggie know what we're doing.'

'I suppose so.'

'You weren't thinking of just surprising her, were you?' Ian blenched. He was all for a quiet life.

'Well, it had crossed my mind.'

'I'm not sure that's a good idea.'

'Perhaps not. I suppose we'd better tell her we're coming.'

'I'm not even sure we should be rushing down there.'

'We must. It's our duty to protect her. That's what families are for, Ian.'

I suppose you're right, Fiona. You usually are.'

CHAPTER THIRTEEN

Early this morning, tea was brought to us, and later we had what is here called breakfast. Soup with bread floating in it, fried eggs, rice, beefsteak, raw onions and parsley, fried potatoes, banana fritters, roast fowl and potatoes, wine, peaches, pears, preserved peaches, cakes, coffee, appeared to us poor wanderers, accustomed to scanty quantities and great appetites, a sumptuous repast.

Olivia M Stone, 1887

On Friday morning of that same week, Annie arrived in a taxi, and Ian and Fiona took the same black cab to the airport and flew out to Tenerife on what they considered to be a rescue mission, a last ditch attempt to snatch Margaret from the clutches of wicked Luis Herrera Garcia. In Ian's mind, Luis had begun to assume some of the qualities of a pantomime villain. Annie Sinclair had, as Fiona had predicted, been no help at all, other than by agreeing to look after the children. After the initial surprise at the suddenness of it, the news seemed to have positively cheered her up. Ian could see that she was faking a sort of polite concern when really she found the whole thing exciting. 'She sounds so happy! Isn't it wonderful?' was all she would say. And when she found out that Ian and Fiona were planning to go to Tenerife, she said, 'Just be careful, won't you? Don't spoil things for her. But then I don't think you could, really, do you?'

As soon as she heard the news, given gravely by Ian, as though reporting a death, she had gone online to speak to her daughter. Margaret was positively overflowing with joy. It had been impossible to remain unmoved by the change in her, the happiness, the excitement. This was her only daughter, she loved her dearly and Margaret's depression had been a constant source of worry for the past months. Perhaps Annie should have shared Fiona's suspicions, but she couldn't. Margaret's delight was too infectious.

'She seems absolutely fine to me,' she repeated.

On the day Margaret dropped her bombshell, Fiona had organised a 'family meeting' with tea and cake. How like Fiona to want to formalize things, make them seem more important than they really were, thought Annie, realising that the family meeting would have been helped by the application of a few glasses of wine. Rioja, preferably .

'I wonder what he's like? He sounds lovely. He seems to have swept her completely off her feet!' she said, enthusiastically.

'I can only imagine.' Fiona shuddered delicately over a Danish pastry, thinking that Annie read far too many romantic novels.

'Can you, though?' asked Annie. 'I mean I can't. I haven't a notion. I haven't got the foggiest idea about the kind of man who would make our Margaret do such a thing.'

'Well, exactly. It's completely out of character. It's like when somebody's brainwashed into joining a cult.'

'Oh, I wouldn't go so far as to say that. But he must be really special. I just hope she's doing the right thing for her, that's all.'

'That's what we're afraid of, mum. That she might not be doing the right thing,' said Ian, plaintively.

'She's a grown woman. I mean she may be your little sister, but she's all grown up. And not stupid. She has to make her own decisions.'

'Mistakes, you mean. They could well be mistakes. And she might do something she would regret for the rest of her life. Marrying a foreigner, somebody she hardly knows. I think we should go out there and see what we can do,' said Fiona.

'And do you think it's going to make any difference to her?'

'We might be able to make her see reason.'

'Reason? Is that what you call it? I don't know so much.' Annie helped herself to another piece of cake, poured out more tea. 'You know, she's never really listened to you or her brother before. I don't see why she should begin now, do you?'

This was not, thought Fiona, the appropriate maternal attitude. She tried to imagine herself in this situation with Lottie, many years down the line, but failed miserably. It simply wouldn't happen. Her daughter would be much too sensible. She would see to that. But ever since the death of Ian's father, five years earlier, Annie had begun to show signs of an eccentricity that Fiona had never previously suspected her mother-in-law of possessing. It was worrying. Sometimes she feared for Annie's mental health. She hoped that similar tendencies would not become apparent in Ian as the years went by. Or would they, she wondered suddenly, make life more interesting? As usual, she was torn between her desire for safety and a streak of romance, of adventure, that seemed to want to make itself felt every now and then. It could have been summed up in one sentence. She wanted things to happen, but preferably not to herself.

Ian and Fiona arrived at Margaret's apartment, hot and tired and angrily convinced that the taxi driver had fiddled them out of a few Euros. Ian wore dark trousers, a shirt and tie and highly polished black shoes. He had been to work for a few hours that morning. Fiona was smart, in a linen suit.

'I take it it's quite cold at home,' said Margaret, hugging them.

She looked different, Fiona thought, with a twinge of envy. All these weeks she had carried in her mind the image of Margaret as she had been when she left Glasgow: pale, unwell, looking older than her years in beige clothes, a baggy sweater, a shapeless raincoat. Fiona prided herself on dressing well. She had generally thought of Margaret as a plump, dowdy, chaotic sort of person. Looking at her now, Fiona saw that she was still a little plump but no longer dowdy.

You would never call Margaret smart or elegant. She was wearing an Indian cotton skirt, a pretty white lace top and sandals. To her horror, Fiona realised that her sister-in-law was wearing no bra. Fiona herself always wore a bra, even though she could easily pass the pencil test. If you could hold a pencil between breast and chest you were supposed to be too big to go without a bra. Fiona couldn't. Margaret could probably hold a whole case of pencils but there she was with her nipples very faintly visible beneath the lace. And yet, thought Fiona, there was something quite different about her. Her hair was much longer and less disciplined than it had been in Glasgow, bleached blonde at the tips by the sunshine, and it suited her. She wasn't deeply suntanned but her legs were golden against the pale green of the skirt and there was a faint, healthy flush of sunlight about her cheeks. She wore scent. She smelled of – what was it? Something spicy and citrussy and flowery at the same time.

'You smell nice,' Fiona said. It was all she could think of to say, wanting to be friendly, wanting to get the tone of the conversation right.

'It's a really old Spanish scent. *Embrujo de Sevilla*. Enchantment of Seville. Luis found it for me! Heaven knows where. It's my favourite perfume at the moment.'

There was a kind of bloom about her. She looked voluptuous and – good Lord, thought Fiona – she looks sexy.

Was it the island? Or was it the new man in her life?

She glanced across at Ian, wondering if he had noticed the change in his sister, but he seemed too preoccupied with his own discomfort in the heat. Perhaps men didn't really notice things like that. Or not where their sisters were concerned, anyway.

All of Margaret's life, Ian had irritated her with his precision, with his measured pronouncements, with his careful behaviour. He had always liked to have a routine, even as a small boy, and he would stick to it through thick and thin. His children, too, had routines and were encouraged to stick to them. Between Fiona and Ian, they didn't stand a chance. They had both slept the night through by six months and been completely potty trained by eighteen months. Ian had carefully monitored their television viewing and the computer games they were allowed to play. Which was, thought Margaret, all very laudable. But still, it irritated her. Ian didn't much approve of fantasy and Fiona went along with him, although Margaret had never quite been able to work out whether her sister-in-law agreed with him in this respect or not. Even so, things had changed when the kids went to school. It was bound to happen. Other influences took over. In a sincere effort to counteract them, Ian had set up a model railway in the little downstairs study. He played with it far more than the kids did. Lottie had been briefly interested. Rory had to be persuaded to play with it, although he was happy to go to model railway shows with his dad. When Margaret argued that this hobby too was all fantasy and none the worse for it, Ian denied it. Railways were real, weren't they?

'Well, what about spaceships?' asked Margaret.

'Alright then. I'll give you spaceships. But not monsters. And not extra terrestrial forces and battlestars and other rubbish.'

'But how do you know that it's rubbish?'

Ian always lead her into such extremes of defiance. It struck her that she might have defended the flat earth theory if she had been arguing with Ian about it.

'Oh, don't be so silly, Maggie. You'll be telling me you believe in fairies next.'

'I'm not saying I don't. Fairies, goblins, dragons and unicorns too. I certainly believe in magic.'

All her life, he had said to her, 'Don't be daft, Maggie,' as, predictably, he said it now.

'Don't be daft. How can you even think of marrying a complete stranger.'

'This isn't a good beginning, Ian.'

'Don't be daft,' he repeated.

'You're the one who's being daft. And he isn't a complete stranger. If he was, I wouldn't be daft enough to marry him, would I?'

'You must come home with us. We've come to take you home.'

He sounded so much like the outraged Victorian brother of a young woman on the point of eloping with an unsuitable admirer that she began to laugh at him. She turned to Fiona.

'What is he like, Fee?'

Fiona was taken aback. It wasn't like Margaret to laugh at her brother. Usually she took Ian almost too seriously, even when he was teasing her, even though she generally ignored his advice. She had heard Ian telling his sister not to be daft with a sinking heart. She knew from experience how such arguments usually ended, with a defiant Margaret and a disgruntled Ian. But laughing in his face like this? Besides, she couldn't help agreeing with her husband. Margaret was being extremely silly, no doubt about it.

'Margaret,' she said. 'This isn't like you at all, you know?'

'Well I'm very sorry if you're offended, but I can't help laughing. What do you mean, you're going to take me home? Are you mad?'

'No. But ...'

'But you think I am? Do you think the sun has turned my head? Is that it?'

'No,' said Ian. 'But something has.'

I've told you, I'm not coming home to Scotland. This is going to be my home from now on, I hope. I'm getting married. I'm not mad, I'm not deluded and there's nothing you can do about it.'

'Oh, Maggie ...'

'Listen, why don't you have a shower? Get changed. Have a drink. You'll feel much better, you know. Much more comfortable. You look so hot. Luis is coming round for supper. He works in a restaurant during the day, but he'll be here in a little while. And you have to promise to be nice to him.'

They did as they were told meekly enough and changed into more suitable clothes, Fiona into a flowery maxi dress that made her look younger and prettier, Ian into golf trousers and a smart polo shirt. Margaret had always had an unreasonable aversion to Ian's golfing clothes, the trousers that, no matter how well tailored, flapped inexorably about his spindly legs, the absolute smoothness of the sweaters and shirts, the acid, often clashing colours. But at least this was better than his suit.

She poured drinks and they sat on the edges of their seats, waiting apprehensively for Luis.

'He's working tonight as well,' said Margaret. 'He plays the guitar in one of the restaurants. But he's promised to come here first. I've bought a cooked chicken. Lots of salad and fruit. I thought we could eat here tonight. Maybe we'll go out tomorrow, though.'

'So what does he do? This Luis.'

'I've told you. He's a chef. And he plays the guitar and sings. He's very good at it. Especially his playing. That's what he loves best, I think. He's saving up for something. There's a project.'

Ian pricked up his ears at that. Perhaps Fiona had been right to be suspicious of the man's motives.

'What kind of project?'

'I think I'll let him tell you about that himself.'

They sat on the balcony in the sun. Margaret had opened a bottle of gin, hoping that alcohol might ease the obvious tension.

'This is nice, isn't it?' she said. 'I try not to drink in the day, but it's a good excuse. Having my family here. How's mum?'

'She's very well.' Fiona took a gulp of her drink. Dutch courage, she thought. 'Is he actually living here?' she asked.

'He has a room in his friend's apartment in the town. But he stays here as well. Sometimes. We haven't been together all that long, you know.'

'No. It was all very sudden, wasn't it?'

They drank and made small talk. Once, after Ian had gone indoors to the loo, Fiona followed him on the pretext of finding her sun hat, and they had a whispered conversation. What were they to do? Everything seemed so normal, so ordinary, and Margaret seemed so happy.

'Let's wait and see what he's like,' said Ian. 'Have another gin.'

'We'll be drunk.'

'It seems like quite a good idea right now.'

Eventually, they heard a key turn in the lock and Luis came into the room. Margaret watched him and her relatives, Luis defiant but determined to be charming, her brother and his wife polite but deeply suspicious all the same. And embarrassed. They seemed very embarrassed. She thought that Luis was not what they had expected. But what had they expected? A waiter perhaps? Don Juan in jeans? Luis had changed out of his chef's whites into a blue T-shirt and denim shorts. He looked sunny and handsome and younger than his years. He came in and shook hands all round.

Fiona found her sense of superiority evaporating in the face of his courtesy, his command of English, his charm. How nice he is, she thought. Then he embarrassed her by kissing her on both cheeks. But she would have expected him to be charming. That was always the way of it. How else would he have swept Margaret off her feet like this? How else would he have persuaded her to such folly? Charming foreign rogue deceives unsuspecting woman into marriage. It was the stuff of a dozen television shows and podcasts. The regrets always came later when the poor woman was abandoned, her life savings gone and her lover with them. All the same, Fiona couldn't keep her eyes off Luis. Beneath her conventional exterior, there lurked an accumulation of untapped fantasy. Maybe it would all end in tears, but right at this moment, she couldn't help envying Margaret.

When they were settled on the balcony again, with more drinks, she kicked Ian under the table. Best get it over and done with.

'My sister tells me you and she are thinking of getting married,' Ian said, clutching his glass.

'Oh, we're not just thinking,' said Luis. 'We *are* getting married. In a few weeks in fact. Isn't that right?'

He smiled at Margaret, showing perfect white teeth, and she nodded, happily.

'Weeks?' Ian blenched.

'Why wait? We know our own minds. We thought you might like to come. But can you stay here so long?'

'No, no. We have to go back early next week. We both have work. And the children. I'm an accountant and Fiona teaches. Didn't Maggie tell you?'

'You did say, didn't you, Margarita?' Luis turned to her, uneasily aware of the way this pair seemed to be sidelining her. 'But I thought you might have changed your minds.'

'No. It isn't possible. And I'm not sure we could come back here in time. For the wedding, I mean.'

'A pity,' said Luis, who didn't think it was a pity at all. He had been very anxious to meet Margaret's relatives until he saw them: a fussily overdressed man exuding hostility and a woman wearing too much make-up and too much jewellery. Fiona kept glancing covertly at him as though she couldn't quite believe what she was seeing. He caught her looking at him, even while she was nodding vigorously at everything her husband said, and interrupting him with frequent comments of her own. He saw that they were, to all intents and purposes, ignoring his Margarita, engaging with him instead, trying to pretend that what she said and thought didn't matter.

Had this been the way of it all her life, he wondered, with sudden insight? Was this why she was so lacking in self assurance? Had nobody told her, as his mother had so often told him, that she could do anything she wanted if she worked hard enough? His parents and his sisters had always had faith in him, always thought him talented, capable of just about anything he set his mind to as long as he was prepared to work hard. That was the key. Commitment. He had done the same for his sisters himself, praising them, rejoicing in their triumphs, commiserating with their set-backs. It hadn't been wholly true of course. You couldn't do anything you wanted – nobody ever could. But life and experience taught you that harsh truth soon enough. There were plenty of lessons to be learned out in the uncaring world, without your family adding to them. Luis didn't subscribe to the doctrine of tough love at all. Nobody in his family did. There were times in life when only the knowledge that your family had faith in you could buoy you up enough to keep you from sinking. Without that resilience, you would be lost. Maybe Margaret's family had never instilled such confidence in her.

He could barely bring himself to be polite to them, though for Margaret's sake he tried very hard. As he was going through to get more lemon and tonic, he stood behind her briefly and put his hands on her shoulders. She leaned back against him, then reached up and touched his hands. He pulled her hair back, stroking it between his fingers. He could feel her responding to him, much as the guitar responded to his touch. She turned slightly and he bent over and kissed her on the lips.

Ian and Fiona slept in Margaret's double bed for the duration of their stay. On the first night, Luis went back to his room in his friend's apartment. It seemed more tactful that way and he thought it might be better to give her some time alone with her relatives. Then they could talk about him in peace. He had a few misgivings about this. He knew they were intent on making her change her mind, but he didn't think they had a hope in hell of succeeding. All the same, he woke up in the early hours of the morning, wondering 'what if?' What if they managed to persuade her that his intentions were not good, that he was after her money? He wasn't even sure that she had any money. They hadn't talked about it. He knew that her job didn't pay particularly well, and she didn't even earn much in the way of commission. They had talked about the divorce, but not about money. Why should they? It didn't matter. He drank some water, read a little, and then messaged her. 'Are you OK? *Te extraño*. I miss you.'

She replied so instantly that he thought she must have been lying awake as well. 'I'm missing you too. Wish you were here. Love you. xxx'

'Love you too,' he told her.

In the morning, his worries seemed foolish, but he still couldn't bring himself to like Ian and Fiona very much. They seemed impossibly inhibited to him: the kind of people who would throw cold water on every suggestion.

The following night, Saturday, tired and disturbed, he asked if he could stay. Margaret didn't argue. His absence had given Fiona in particular the chance to question her closely, much too closely, about Luis and his family. It wasn't that she was uncomfortable or ashamed – she knew that now – but she felt indignant at having to explain herself and her feelings to anyone, least of all Fiona.

She was relieved when Fiona and Ian, exhausted by the un-accustomed heat, went to bed early. She had insisted on them taking the bedroom. She and Luis opened up the couch, made the bed, undressed and crept in, feeling very much inclined to giggle.

'It's like being a boy again!' said Luis. 'It feels ...' He hesitated, searching for the right word.

'Illicit,' said Margaret. 'It's quite exciting, really!'

'They're quiet aren't they?'

'They are. Do you think they're whispering about us?'

'Maybe.' He looked down at her. 'Are you happy?' He often asked this, as though seeking to reassure himself.

'I'm very happy. But – you don't like them much, do you.' Margaret realised that she was whispering herself, but what else could she do?

'Not much, no. I'm sorry, *querida*. I'll try.'

They were in each others arms, pressed close, desperate to make love. She could feel the warmth of his breath against her cheek.

'I wish you could like them.'

'But they don't seem to like me much, do they?'

'Give them time. They will. But even if they don't ...'

'What?'

'It's their loss, my darling. Their loss.'

Nevertheless, Margaret disliked the slight hostility between her lover and her brother. She could laugh at Ian but she found to her consternation that she didn't like it when Luis disparaged him.

'Don't do it,' she said, when they were briefly alone again. It was Sunday evening. Ian and Fiona would be going back to Scotland on Tuesday, so Margaret had taken Monday off work. They had booked a coach trip to Teide, just the three of them, a family outing, Fiona called it. Today, though, Luis had offered to make something for their supper: prawns and other seafood, cooked in garlic and olive oil, with a big platter of salad and fresh bread. Fiona and Ian had gone out for a walk. The apartment was too small to hold them all, especially Luis, whose personality sometimes seemed far too large to be contained within these white walls. Luis was playing later on. He was planning to cook and then leave them to eat together. He never ate much before a performance, contenting himself with a bread roll with tomato and olive oil, or a piece of tortilla and some fruit. They would be joining him in the restaurant where Margaret had first seen and heard him performing.

'Don't do it!' she said again. He was washing salad leaves in bottled water, opening a jar of olives and a tin of oily anchovies, crushing garlic, sniffing at the pungent, appetising smell of it on his fingers. She loved to watch him working with food like this. There was something sexy about it, something that fairly took her breath away. Food and sex. Wine and sex. All of it magical. She felt dizzy with desire and had to shake herself, move away from him.

'What?' he said, preoccupied with his cooking. 'What am I not to do?'

'I was distracted.'

'*Que?*'

'I was distracted by you. I want you so much!'

He shook his head. '*Querida, querida*, we have no time. *Te quiero. Siempre.* But they'll be back any moment.'

'I know.'

'With more wine. Looking for *gambas*. And *ajillo*.'

'Good thing you're not eating the *ajillo*. If you're singing I mean.'

'True. Garlic scented song.' He chuckled.

'But you mustn't laugh at them. They mean well, you know. They can't help the way they are. I used to be a bit like that, used to fit in with them. Before I met you.'

'Sure you did.' He looked sceptical. Turned around, popped an olive into her mouth. She sucked at his fingers. Feeling worse, better, desperate. She touched him.

'Oh, Jesus, Margarita, don't do that to me. Not right now. Please, not right now. You're killing me.'

But he opened his arms and she moved into them. He held his hands away from her, like a surgeon preparing for an operation. 'My hands are oily!'

She pressed herself close to him. 'We can do without hands.' He bent and kissed her, tasting olives on her tongue.

'Can I sleep here again tonight?' he asked.

'I think so. Yes. Of course you can. You must.'

'We're grown up people. It's allowed.'

'I suppose so. But we'll have to be quiet, won't we?'

'I can be quiet. Can you?'

'I can try.'

He sighed, moved away from her and went back to his cooking.

'I can't help laughing at your brother,' he said. 'He is very funny, coming storming over here to carry you home to Scotland. Away from the terrible gigolo. The terrible Don Juan. That's certainly the way he sees me, isn't it? But he's afraid to make a scene and storm and shout and offer to fight me. I wouldn't mind a fight. We might be friends afterwards. We might respect each other.'

'If you didn't kill each other first.'

'And as for your sister-in-law, Fee-ona. She's so jealous that one.'

'Jealous of me? Never.'

'Oh yes! She likes to organise other people's lives and she can't bear it when they don't fall in with her plans.'

'Luis,' she said, trying to be patient with him. 'We don't usually do things like fighting over a sister. Well, not in Newton Mearns anyway. I'm sure it goes on in some parts of Scotland, but we're very civilised in our suburb and keep it all bottled up inside.'

'Idiots,' he said, succinctly, scattering olives and anchovies over his decorative salad.

'Do you know, I don't think they like anchovies much.'

'I like anchovies. Very much. That strong taste, like –' He started to laugh. She shook her head, seized by desire for him all over again.

'Don't say it. You're incorrigible!'

'What's incorrigible? What is this?'

'Incurable. Hopeless. I love you.'

He kissed her, running his hand down her back, forgetting about the oil and the garlic, pulling her against him.

'And I love you. And anchovies. I love both.'

'Shsh. But I still don't think my brother likes them.'

'I can't imagine he does. Poor Fee-ona.'

'Don't! You'll spoil his salad.'

'Tough. He can pick them off.'

'Luis, you have to be nice. For my sake. Just be nice to him. It's only for a couple of days. They'll be gone soon and we'll be married. And then you won't have to worry about them any more.'

'Then they'll be family and I'll worry about them even more.'

'Be nice!'

'I am nice. I'm always nice.'

'No you're not.'

'Well, I'll try. For you.'

He did try, very hard, but it seemed that total capitulation was beyond him, for occasionally she would see that he couldn't help taunting Ian. Margaret would notice a scornful twist to his mouth and she didn't like it. It rang alarm bells deep inside her, alarms that were drowned out by the loud waterfall roaring of her love for him.

CHAPTER FOURTEEN

Lorenzo lies quietly outside, his head alone in sight, like a faithful watchdog;
the last malagueña of the homeward bound goatherd has died on the dark
hillside; whilst the contented crunching of oats by the horses and the piping
treble of the grasshoppers only break the profound stillness upon which
the moon and the stars look down.

Olivia M Stone, 1887

Ian and Fiona had come predisposed to dislike the island, to find faults and inconveniences everywhere, and that was what they saw. All their preconceptions were confirmed by experience, even though they were only there for a few days. Fiona came out in a severe prickly heat rash and Margaret had to take her to the pharmacy to get some soothing cream. Ian had an upset stomach and blamed Luis's cooking.

'Did you use tap water to clean your teeth?' his sister asked him.

'Yes. I did.'

'Then that may be your problem. It's not exactly dangerous, but your stomach just isn't used to it. That's why there's bottled water in the bathroom.'

'I never thought about it. How appalling.'

'The locals are OK. Luis is OK. They're used to it. We aren't. Not when we first get here. I'm still adjusting. Actually, the water on his home island is excellent. Pure and sweet. You can drink that.'

They looked for squalor everywhere and consequently they found it, found the squashed cockroaches on the pavements, found the bad smells wafting out of overheated drains, found the drunks, although since these were generally young English or Scots men and women, never Spanish, Luis argued, quite reasonably, that they were more Ian and Fiona's responsibility than his own.

'You supply them with the stuff!' said Ian, tetchily. 'That's what they come here for I think. All these groups of young men. And the girls are just as bad. Hen nights.'

'We would much rather they didn't,' said Luis. 'You know, we would much rather have civilized tourists. Not people who think they own the place and abuse us and our hospitality. That's why you'll see the graffiti here and there. And I'll tell you why you don't see many drunk Spaniards here – we know how to drink. It's not considered manly to get drunk. I've never understood the way you Brits think. We love to drink, but it's always considered the mark of a man that he doesn't get drunk, doesn't look drunk, doesn't behave like a crazy guy.'

Ian sighed. There was some truth in it and he didn't know how to respond. They were sitting on the balcony of Margaret's flat, watching people sitting beside the pool or wandering past. The sun was over the yardarm, as Ian always termed it – not that it seemed to make much difference here – and they were drinking chilled white Rioja.

'You know,' said Luis, glancing at Fiona, 'I think you should take off that gold jewellery.'

Fiona wore a chunky bangle and several gold chains.

'Why?' she asked him, indignantly.

'Because you make yourself a target for robbers, that's why. *Bandidos*, thieves, muggers. You know that Spain has one of the highest crime rates in Europe, but it is mostly theft from foolish tourists like yourself. Nothing more serious.'

'Oh, God,' said Fiona dramatically. 'This is a terrible place.'

'Why? Are there not also thieves in Glasgow?'

'Well, yes. Thieves and muggers there too.'

'Luis is exaggerating a bit,' said Margaret mildly. 'There are thieves and you'd be better not to wear expensive stuff in the town. But it isn't all that dangerous, not if you're careful.'

Luis grinned, wickedly. She would have kicked him, if she had been sitting closer to him.

Fiona took off her jewellery. Her nose had begun to peel. She didn't like the glaring sunlight of the islands. It made her feel uncomfortable in all kinds of ways, even within her own body. She couldn't sleep at nights for the itching of her overheated skin. How could Margaret think of living in this place?

She came back and sat down again. Margaret had refilled her glass, hoping that wine would soothe her indignation.

'Where do you plan to live if you get married?' Fiona asked, abruptly. Ian frowned at her.

If Margaret noticed the use of the 'if' word, she didn't remark on it and it seemed to have passed Luis by. He had set the table and he was getting ready to go out.

'I must go now,' he said. 'You'll come down later?'

'We certainly will.' Margaret went over and kissed him, a friendly peck that turned into a long, lingering kiss by the door, where Ian and Fiona couldn't see them. He pulled her close, hugged her tight, lifted her just about off her feet. Then he picked up his guitar and left.

Over the food – Margaret had been right and they picked the anchovies and the olives carefully off their salad but managed to eat the artichoke hearts – Ian said again, 'So where will you live. With him? He doesn't have a proper house, does he? You can't stay here. This was just lent to you, this apartment. Bill and Jess will want it back. I don't think they intended it to be let to a married couple.'

'Have you been speaking to them? Have you been going behind my back, Ian?'

Ian looked uncomfortable. Fiona had made him phone the owners of the apartment. They had wondered if anything could be done to deter Margaret. Perhaps if her Spanish lover knew that she didn't own the flat, that she might be told to leave at any moment, then he would be less enthusiastic. In the event, Bill and Jess had politely told Ian to mind his own business. Not that they had used those words, but it amounted to the same thing. They had already had a long and friendly conversation with Margaret. The let was still a temporary one but they were happy for the couple to stay on for a while. Margaret had plans for the future and if Ian didn't know about them, then he had better ask her, hadn't he?

'I spoke to Jess. We'll keep this place on for a few months longer. They don't mind. I'm paying regularly. And you know what it's like out here just now. I think they're glad to have a nice tenant like me and they certainly don't want to do holiday lets. The market isn't what it was. I should know that. There's a real push on to help local people find homes. As it should be.'

'So where will you be living? '

'Luis's home. La Gomera.'

'La Gomera?'

'I told you. That's where he's from.'

'I know, but – '

'It's the island you can see out there. It's quite different from Tenerife, you know. It's very beautiful. Not that I don't like it here too. But I must say, I like La Gomera better.'

'It can't be all that different, can it?'

'You'll have to come and see. Once we're settled there. Won't you?'

'But what will you *do* there?' Ian seemed dismayed. Goodness knows what he was expecting.

Margaret smiled. She was enjoying winding them up.

'We have plans. All kinds of interesting plans. I'll tell you about them soon.'

Later that night, they walked down to the restaurant, found a table and listened to Luis playing. Ian watched the man with a certain veiled respect. The performance surprised him. There was something dark, mysterious, moving about it. It was many years since Ian had hero-worshipped one of his own sex, and even then it had been from a respectful distance. He had been in the first year of his secondary school, small for his age, clumsy and bespectacled, and the boy in question had been captain of the school football team, self-confident, good looking and cheerful to boot. He had, on more than one occasion, been unexpectedly kind to little Ian Sinclair. There had been nothing sexual in the admiration: it was imitative, based on the knowledge that this was who and what he would like to be, combined with the appreciation of something casual and confident about his hero, something which he, Ian, knew he could never achieve, never even aspire to. Now, looking at Luis, watching his skill on the guitar, he felt a pang of the same regretful admiration. It must be nice to be like that, he thought, ingenuously. At the same time, and perhaps because he was more sensitive than his wife, he became aware of something else. He saw and appreciated, as his wife never would, how kind this man was to his sister. He saw a bond of real affection between them that seemed to be almost separate from the more obvious physical attraction. Luis treated Margaret with a courtesy and consideration that surprised and reassured Ian. They already behaved like close friends. As though they shared thoughts, as well as a bed.

The following day, Margaret, Ian and Fiona took a coach tour to Teide with a mixed group of British tourists.

'Have you been here before?' asked Ian, impressed with the landscape in spite of himself.

Margaret thought about that first visit with Luis. She smiled.

'Oh yes. I've been here before. It was ... well, it was our first date, I suppose. Although I don't think either of us intended it as a date. It was just an excursion. I'd complained that I'd never been to see Teide at close quarters, not even with Alastair, that time when we came here years ago. Luis brought me up here.'

They were sitting outside the same cafe, high up on the mountain, near the cable car. Fiona had gone to the Ladies.

'And the rest is history,' said Ian with a sigh.

'Yes. The rest is history. Or it soon will be.'

'Are you absolutely sure you're doing the right thing,' he asked, doubtfully, sipping his beer.

'I've never been more sure of anything in my life.'

As she said it, she realised that it was the truth. She was certain of it, certain of Luis.

'Fiona's worried about you.'

'When was she ever not? But what did you expect to be able to do? Drag me home, kicking and screaming?'

'Me?'

'Well it isn't exactly your style. But you have been behaving a bit like an outraged brother in a melodrama. More like a Spaniard than a Scot, in fact.'

'I know. I'm sorry. But it's all been so sudden. So unexpected.'

'I'm sure I'm doing the right thing.'

'I can see that. Anyway, you know where we are if you need us.'

'I do, Ian.'

She leaned over and kissed him, a peck on the cheek. Fiona came back, frowning at the intimacy of the gesture. She had been prompting her husband to 'have words' with his sister, but she doubted if they had been the right words. Ian was too easily persuaded. All the same she had a plan. It would have to be put into effect tonight, because they would be leaving tomorrow and by then it would be too late.

Ian screwed his courage to the sticking place. Fiona had been nipping his ear for what seemed like hours, spoiling the trip to Teide, bombarding him with plans and proposals. He wondered why she cared so much, but he couldn't withstand her when she was in this mood. He simply had to go along with her suggestions, however inadvisable they might seem. And they were inadvisable, he was sure of it. He found himself, rather unexpectedly, hoping that he was right and Fiona was wrong. The thought gave him a thrill of excitement.

Later that day, when Fiona had carried Margaret off to do some last minute shopping, gifts for the children and for Margaret's mother, he brought out a couple of cold beers and sat down with Luis on the balcony.

'So,' said Luis, aware that Ian was looking embarrassed. 'Have you enjoyed your visit to Tenerife?'

'It's been good. Yes. Very nice.'

'Really?' Luis grinned. He could see that Ian was gathering himself together to say something. He had intercepted a keen glance between Fiona and Ian just before the women left. He didn't know what was coming, but he knew that Ian had something important to say. Nothing good, he suspected. Nothing helpful or congratulatory. It was clear that Fiona intended to meddle and for the moment, her chosen instrument was her husband.

'Luis,' said Ian. He always mispronounced the name. Lewis. The way it would be in Scotland. It irritated Luis, but he let it go. He would do almost anything to please his Margarita and he knew that she wouldn't want him to have any kind of row with her brother. She clearly loved Ian, so he would have to find patience in himself. Not one of his cardinal qualities.

'Yes, Ian?'

'Listen to me. I have to ask this, you know. I have to ask this before we go. I have to ask about you and my sister.'

'*Por dios!*' said Luis, leaning forward. Ian sat back in his chair. The man's intense energy alarmed him. Where would the lightning strike next?

'No, no. Just listen to me for a moment. Please. I'm not sure quite how to say this, but ...' Ian hesitated again.

Luis almost lost his temper. Controlled himself with an effort.

'Why don't you just say it anyway? You don't approve of me. You don't approve of your sister marrying a foreigner. Is that it?'

'Not exactly, no. We've nothing against foreigners, as such.'

'I'm glad to hear it. Xenophobia isn't nice, Ian. Even though your tabloid newspapers seem to be full of it.'

'I don't read them. I don't like them.' Ian was momentarily distracted. Was he being xenophobic? 'I'm just worried. We all are. We're worried at the speed of this. We, well, we want to know why. We need to know why. Why would you want to *marry* her in such a hurry? I mean, you could date, maybe even live together. Get to know each other better before making such a huge commitment. But marriage? Why marriage?'

Luis shrugged. 'Why *not* marriage? Why did *you* get married, Ian?'

The question, bluntly put, brought him up short.

'I was very fond of Fiona. I suppose I loved her. It seemed the next logical step. But you hardly know Maggie. You know nothing about her.'

'I know she doesn't like to be called Maggie. Or Mags.'

Ian frowned, distracted again. 'Doesn't she? She's never said.'

'Did you ask her? I call her Margarita. Like the flower.'

'But you know nothing about her. She's had a hard time these past few years, and we wouldn't want her to be hurt all over again.'

'And you think that's what I'll do? Hurt her all over again?'

'No. Yes. Maybe. Luis, what do you want from her? Is there anything we can do? Anything we can give you that would change things? That would make a difference? You know what I mean?'

Luis was silent for a moment. It was hard to understand sometimes when the words were spoken in a foreign language. Hard to catch up. But suddenly he knew exactly what Ian meant.

'You mean,' he said, slowly, 'You mean, you think I want Margarita for her money? Does she have money?'

'A little. You must know she has a little. It might seem like a lot to you. They sold a flat in Glasgow. She got half. After the mortgage was paid off. Half of what was left.'

Luis shook his head. He remembered that first visit to La Gomera. How he had made assumptions about her and what she must be thinking. He had been wrong on that occasion. She hadn't thought anything of the sort. She had just been overwhelmed. But that was what Ian and Fiona were doing now, assuming that he was some unscrupulous bastard who only wanted this woman for her money, a meal ticket, a prize. They were more or less offering to pay him off.

He got up abruptly and went into the living room, punching one clenched fist into the other palm, wanting to react physically, to wipe the ingratiating smile off the man's face. He took several deep breaths, thinking of Margarita, her innocence, her extraordinary passion for him. What did these people matter? Why should they spoil anything for him? For them. He had almost ruined things once before and he wasn't about to let it happen all over again.

He heard the door open and the two women came back, laughing over their purchases that included a woolly bull, a fan and castanets for the children.

'What's the matter?' asked Margaret, aware that Luis was controlling himself with an effort. Ian was still on the balcony, Fiona in the bathroom.

He shook his head, muttered, 'Your brother thinks I want you for your money.'

'What money? I have a bit, but it isn't exactly a fortune.'

'Nevertheless ...'

'You must have misunderstood. You do sometimes, you know, Luis. He didn't say that, did he?'

'Not in those exact words. But he asked me what they could do, if there was anything they could *give* me to make me change my mind about you. I expected him to pull out his wallet and try to buy me off. It is *insostenible*, Margarita!'

'Hush.' She did the only thing possible to quieten him, kissing him full on the lips. He struggled free.

'But if your family think that, then maybe other people will think that too. It is terrible!'

She kissed him again, felt him respond, felt him soften, whispered, 'Who cares? I know the truth, and you know the truth. I love you. You love me. What else matters?'

'Nothing, I suppose.'

'Exactly. Now come on. Let's be polite. It's only for one more night. Then we can be rid of them and get on with the rest of our lives.'

Luis was very relieved when Ian had gone. He laughed about him, mocked his too precise mannerisms, and Margaret laughed too at first but then became quiet. More sensitive to her feelings than she knew, Luis saw immediately that he had gone too far.

'I'm sorry. But he is both rude and funny. I know I shouldn't make a joke of him but I can't bear the way they insult me and the way they discount you all the time. They think you don't matter. They have the wrong idea about you. I hate it.'

'You wouldn't like it if I made fun of Cristina.'

'I would not. But she is not the same.'

'No. She isn't. But it's still hard. He's my brother. He may act like an idiot sometimes. Usually because Fiona has told him to do something against his better judgement. But I love him. Sauce for the goose.'

'What is this, sauce for the goose?'

She explained the expression to him and he repeated it, as pleased as a child with a new toy. She found herself laughing at his obvious delight in the words. In their mutual teasing the past few days were forgotten.

On the plane and much to Fiona's indignation, Ian refused point-blank to talk about Luis and the forthcoming marriage. He had changed back into his more formal clothes and taken papers out of his briefcase.

'What do we tell your mother?' she demanded.

'We tell her that he seems like a nice man. That's all we can do, Fiona.'

'But you surely don't believe that, do you?'

He sighed. He wished she would leave him alone. She was like a dog with a particularly juicy bone, intent on carrying it reverently about so that she could worry it now and then or bury it and dig it up again. She had always been like this but it had never upset him as much as now.

'Fiona,' he said. 'Do you mind? I've got work to do. Can't we just forget about Margaret and Luis for the moment?'

'If you like.' He could tell from the sudden freeze in her voice that he had upset her. Tough, he thought, with uncharacteristic defiance. She'll just have to stay upset. Perhaps a touch of Luis's *machismo* had rubbed off on him. The thought made him smile. Very unlikely. They were flying over the island. He looked down, fascinated by the vision of mountains and villages he had not seen nor even enquired about, content to walk the dusty streets of Los Cristianos, disapproving of all he saw. He thought about the people living in them, leading lives of which he took no thought, people whose preoccupations were entirely different from his own. Or maybe not so very dissimilar. Then he thought about them speaking another language which perhaps shaped their thoughts in a different way so that maybe they saw the world differently too. This was such an unaccustomed leap of the imagination for Ian that it frightened him and he turned back to his familiar balance sheets with relief. When he looked again, the island had gone, and they were flying in a cold blue sky over a floor of impenetrable white cloud.

CHAPTER FIFTEEN

The men in Gomera are very fine; they have open countenances and lithe,
active, muscular figures. The latter are shown off to advantage by the white
shirts and trousers tucked up to above the knee or hanging loose just below it
and a girdle or sash round the waist.

Olivia M Stone, 1887

With a little more than a week to go before the wedding, Margaret and
Luis took a couple of days off work and went over to La Gomera again,
this time to stay overnight. Luis was in a very nervous frame of mind.
He, no less than Margaret, had been swept along by the power of his
own feelings to a point where nothing but marriage would do for him.
There was a certainty about his love for her, a rightness that he had
never known before. Having almost let her slip through his fingers
once, he was determined not to let her go, and he was pathetically
anxious that this visit to his family should be better than the first.

Even so, his meeting with Fiona and Ian had brought him face to
face with the cultural abyss that lay between them. He wondered what
Margaret's mother was like. He was forced to face the fact that their
marriage would involve all the compromises necessary between two
very different families. True, the geographical distance between the
two sets of relatives would ease matters, but his realisation of just how
much he disliked Fiona and Ian cast a shadow over his relationship
with Margaret. How could a brother and sister be so very different,
he wondered. He compared that relationship with his own love for

his sisters. Then, other doubts would begin to creep into his mind and when he was away from Margaret, he would begin to wonder just how well he really knew her. It was confusing and distressing.

From time to time, he found himself thinking about Emelina, the girl from Barcelona, about his desperate desire for marriage back then, and her subsequent desertion of him, and he would wonder if he should have learned his lesson the first time round, forgetting that the one sure lesson to be learned from history, even from our personal history, is that a situation never presents itself in the same way twice. But the instant his Margarita walked into a room, the instant she smiled at him, he knew that he was doing the right thing. He knew that there would be no betrayal and that he would just have to learn to tolerate her family as best he could.

They arrived at the house in the middle of the morning. It was full of the scents of baking and fresh coffee and Luis thought how much he had always liked this room. When he was away, it was this open plan living kitchen he remembered with nostalgia. He could picture Cristina and himself doing their homework together, side by side at the table, and the variously muted or hilarious conversations of women going on around them. In his memory it was always the women he could hear, talking of who was in love with whom, who had fallen out, talking of pregnancy and childbirth and the failings of menfolk in general.

Luis saw his mother sitting at this same table, watching Margaret, assessing her as well as she could on such short acquaintance. Each time he saw her, he worried about the fact that she was growing older. She looked well and very youthful, in a button-through cotton dress and an old straw hat that she always wore whenever she went out into the full glare of the sun. But there was no denying that she had grey hairs here and there, that her skin was more delicate, with a few wrinkles, as beautiful and precise as the lines on a fallen leaf. He was probably the only one who noticed this because, unlike his sisters, he didn't see her every day. He worried about her. He wanted to hug her close. He remembered lying in bed as a child and praying to the Holy Virgin not to let his parents die for a thousand years. He had believed then that some magical age would come to him when he would be able to cope with anything, even the loss of his parents. Even when he had been in his teens, he had dreamed of some future date when he would be self-confident and capable. To some extent that time had come, but the disappointment was that it was just as difficult to cope with life. The only thing that changed was your ability to dissemble. To hide your disappointment, or at least to come to terms with your grief or despair.

His father's death had taught him that. He remembered the ache of loss, the rawness of the pain. Since then he had lost count of the number of times he had wanted to ask him for advice, wanted a hug from those strong arms. The older he grew, the more he loved his mother, knowing that when she was gone, he would somehow move up to the front line. He had felt it after his father's death too, felt as though he were suddenly the head of the household, even though he was seldom at home, even though his brother-in-law was there. He couldn't say any of this to Maria. She would laugh at him, tell him she was still young, tell him not to think of dispatching her too soon. She had said it more than once. 'I don't plan on going anywhere just yet, *mi hijo!*'

Maybe this was why he had proposed marriage to Margaret so suddenly, preparing to assume the mantle of parenthood himself. He didn't think about it in so many words but he found himself brought up short by the pang of seeing his mother's smiling face, her glasses perched on the end of her nose. Like an unalterable image contained deep within another, like the painting not yet obscured beneath the patina of years, he saw in his mother the grave, glad girl his father had loved and married all those years ago.

To Luis's relief, Cristina seemed to be delighted with Margaret.

They had always been so close that he had been dubious about her reaction, but on this second visit she embraced the incomer, kissed her and subjected her to a barrage of questions and comments in English.

'Welcome!' she said. 'Welcome to La Gomera. I can't tell you how exciting all this is. And how glad we are to have you here, Margarita. Oh but I hope you like it. I hope you like us.'

'How could I help but like you all! You make me so welcome.'

'If Luis loves you, then so do we.'

Maybe if Cristina had arrived home earlier during their last visit things might have gone better, thought Luis. Tactfully, Isabel and Juan had taken the children out for the day, to give Maria and Cristina time to get to know Margaret better. Luis had brought the car over on the ferry so that he could show her more of the island. They ate a lunch of bread, cheese and salad and in the afternoon, Luis took them to visit his old school friend, Antonio.

He had known Toni since they had begun school together. They had fought like two small dogs in the dust and had to be separated, bleeding and angry. He couldn't remember what that first fight had been about: some real or imagined insult presumably. He couldn't remember who had won, because they had been rudely pulled apart before a victory could fall to either side. After that, though, they had become inseparable, sitting together in class, defending each other against all comers, and spending their free time roaming the country-side, together with a small gang of boys who were content to follow Luis and Toni as their undisputed leaders.

Luis had been a tall child, slender as a vine pole, but with a natural grace that pre-empted mockery. Only during his teens had his body begun to fill out, making him into a more formidable young man. He wasn't, and never had been, aggressive by nature. What he had, though, was an explosive temper and injustice in particular could rouse a volcano in him. Occasionally, where provocation was extreme, his instincts still got the better of him.

Antonio had been a small, sturdy boy and now he was a small, sturdy man. In their youth, Luis had provided most of the brains and Toni most of the brawn. They had been a formidable combination and had been chased away from many an orchard, heavy with luscious oranges or apricots or their favourite mulberries that fell on the ground when fully ripe. After all, it would be a waste to leave them. Luis remembered irate smallholders shaking their fists and shouting, 'I know you two and your fathers are going to hear all about this!' and dogs, snapping and snarling at their bare heels. It was a matter of debate which deterrent was more effective: the immediate one of sharp white teeth or the awful consequences of misbehaviour reported at home. They had been daring boys, egging each other on to greater sins, but both threats acted as an effective curb on their more serious misdemeanours. Now, when Luis thought of some of the trespasses they had committed all those years ago, he felt ashamed of himself. But only a little, because the memory still made him smile.

His friendship with Toni was of the most enduring kind. When he came home to the island, he and Antonio would always meet and drink wine or beer. They would reminisce about the old days and commiserate with or congratulate each other about whatever was happening in their lives. Antonio claimed that he had always known that Luis had a musical future. 'The loudest voice in the class,' he would say with a grin, but when Luis used to play the guitar, even as a boy, the other children would listen with interest and even respect. They knew that his Uncle Paco was a fine musician.

As a young man, Paco had played the *timplillo*, a small guitar, native to the island, which was all he could afford back then, and had improvised songs to his sweethearts, the last of whom, Carmen, he had married. Carmen's father had been a well-to-do farmer, known locally as *El Panzudo*, the Paunchy Man. He was generous as well as paunchy, and he had bought for his daughter and son-in-law an old and beautiful but very run-down *finca*, bordering on his own property. With great enthusiasm and energy, Paco and Carmen had built the place up into an excellent little restaurant. Carmen had been a good manager. She had learned the skills from her father and from her mother, who had helped *El Panzudo* to manage his farm. The restaurant was very successful, especially once tourists began to visit La Gomera in greater numbers.

Unlike Luis, Antonio had always been more or less content with life on the island and, apart from a couple of years spent working in Santa Cruz de Tenerife, in a fish factory, had passed most of his life to date there. It gave him a clear if slightly restricted view of life that Luis, his own perspective clouded and confusingly extended by travel, half admired, half rejected. If it was true that travel broadened the mind, it was also true that it blurred your vision. There were no certainties for Luis any more. After that small interval, Antonio had come back to work in his cousin's *gofio* mill, toasting the mixed wheat and maize brought in bags from a multitude of small farms and grinding it into the tasty flour that had been the mainstay of the old *Gomeros*.

Toni had married young and was now the father of six children: three boys and three girls. Toni's wife, Conchita, as well as looking after the children and the gardening, did the books for the business and kept bees, a skill that earned her a respect approaching mystique in Luis's mind. He had always had half a mind to try beekeeping himself, but it had assumed the properties of a ritual for him, hedged about with custom and belief. One day, he thought, when I have some land of my own, then I'll do it. One day, when we have the restaurant. That will be the right time. He knew that there were hives at *La Manzana Dorada*. Carmen kept bees too.

Antonio was at work when they arrived. The women sat outside, around a wooden table surrounded by as many varieties of flowering plants as Conchita had been able to cram into all kinds of unlikely containers. Even old pots and pans and jars had been pressed into service. The effect was dazzling and eccentric and beautiful. Conchita spoke a little English; Margaret was struggling bravely with her Spanish, which was improving, but not quite up to this kind of speed. Maria was listening quietly and Cristina was translating with gusto. Her English was certainly as good as her brother's these days. Perhaps she had been practising. They were, thought Luis, enjoying each other's company enormously, and he marvelled at how easily women became intimate, even in a foreign language, speaking about topics it would take men years of careful acquaintance to broach with one another.

Luis, knowing when he wasn't wanted, walked down to the mill and found Antonio hard at work in his blue overalls and white cap, hot and dusty amid the *gofio*. The smell was richly familiar and comforting. It sent his head spinning back in time. He had come here for the first time with his father, when Antonio's cousin had run the mill, roasting the grain in big pans over a fire, stirring all the time so that it shouldn't burn. It had seemed enormous and dangerous to him, but he must have been very small then because it had shrunk to normality now. Back then, Eduardo and Luis had brought their own blend of maize, barley and wheat. The blending was important and each family kept to its own recipe, bringing the results in marked bags to be toasted and ground at the mill.

Today, Antonio hugged his friend, took a break and walked out with Luis to sit on a bench and breathe cooler air.

'I'm so glad to see you,' said Toni. 'Not that we *do* see much of you these days. More attractions elsewhere, I suppose. I hear you're taking the plunge at last.'

'I am!'

'Not before time, Luis. I'd almost given up on you.'

'I just took my time. Nothing wrong with that. And she was worth the wait. But I'm working hard as well. You know how it is. I have my sights set on *La Manzana Dorada*.'

'And what if you have to brave the dragon to find it?'

'Oh, Toni, I've already done that. You should see her sister-in-law!'

'A dragon? I thought that would be the mother.'

'No, no. I've never met her mother. Not yet anyway. She assures me her mother's a very nice woman and who am I to argue? I love her, so why not her mother? But the sister-in-law is a piece of work.'

Luis looked at his friend's warm, open face. Antonio lit a cigarette and offered one to Luis but he shook his head. 'I gave up.'

'So you did. And so should I.'

Antonio's hair was just beginning to recede at the temples and there was a sprinkling of grey in it, more than in Luis's own curls. Toni pulled out a handkerchief and wiped his sweaty face, then puffed contentedly on his cigarette.

'Don't you miss them? The cigarettes?'

'A bit. Not much. Far too expensive. Besides, I'm saving.'

Toni was very dark, darker even than Luis, and there was already a blue shadow of growth on his chin and upper lip. When he smiled, he pursed his lips, turning them down and tightening them at the corners, giving his face a good-humoured, quizzical look.

'What's she like?' he asked. 'Your – Margarita, is it?'

'Margarita. She's Scottish. She's nice.'

'Does she speak Spanish?'

'No. Well, a little. She's doing her best to learn more. I think she'll get there eventually.'

'Have you known her long?' asked Toni.

'No.' Luis grinned sheepishly. He seemed reluctant to talk about his forthcoming marriage all of a sudden, and yet he had come here yearning to confide in someone, not his sister or mother, but another man. Antonio had seemed the obvious choice.

'No. Not very long. It all happened very quickly. But you'll like her.'

It sounded almost like a plea rather than a promise.

'And where are you going to live? Is she rich? Will you live in Scotland?'

'No, no. God forbid! Here. Paco's place. The restaurant. When we can afford to move. We'll stay at Cristianos for the rest of the year. She's renting a holiday apartment from friends of her family and I'm spending half my free time there anyway. We can keep it for the next few months. You know I've been living with Ramon, but I'll move out. Well, to tell you the truth I already have more or less moved out. You know how it is? You leave a toothbrush and then a few clothes and before you know it ... '

'Well I don't know,' said Toni. 'You know Conchi's dad. There was no way there was any funny business going on until we were well and truly married. But then we were both very young.'

'Margarita has already been married and divorced. I don't think it was a very happy marriage.'

'At least you didn't make that mistake with ... '

'Emelina? No. But I would have, if she'd said yes at the time.'

'Always impulsive, eh, Luis?'

'I suppose so.'

'And how does she feel about living here? About moving here. When you get the restaurant?' A bee buzzed into Toni's face. He brushed it gently aside with a big brown paw.

'I think she's looking forward to it.'

'You don't sound very sure. Has she even *seen* the restaurant?'

'Not yet.'

'Are you going today?'

'Not today. But tomorrow. I think we'll go tomorrow. I want to take her there when it's just the two of us. Not with other people. Not even with my sister and my mum. It's difficult.'

'The language thing? You speak pretty good English, so I'm told.'

'I speak it but I don't think it.'

'What do you mean?'

Plainly it meant nothing to Antonio. Luis wasn't totally sure what it meant himself, except that different tongues meant different minds. Or did they? Weren't basic human impulses much the same everywhere? However could you know? He said nothing, not knowing how to continue.

'What's the matter, Luis?' asked his friend. 'Is something wrong?'

'Why do you ask?'

'You don't have the air of a man who's overjoyed with life. So tell me about it. Do you think you've made a mistake?'

Luis shook his head. 'No. No, I'm sure I haven't. That's the one thing I'm sure about.'

'What, then?'

Luis got up and walked about, hands tucked into the pockets of his jeans, shoes scuffing at the dusty ground. He found that he didn't want to look his friend full in the face. Antonio finished his cigarette calmly until Luis came and sat down again, leaning forward on the bench.

'I was certain I wanted to marry her, Toni. In fact it just came out before I could stop myself. I thought I would die if she didn't marry me.'

'Well that's usually what happens, isn't it?'

'I wouldn't know. All I knew was the thought of *not* marrying her – of her maybe going back to Scotland – I couldn't stand it. Still can't.'

'So, what's wrong with that?'

'I met her brother and her sister-in-law. They came here to see us.'

'As you said. The dragon lady. But wasn't it nice of them to want to meet you?'

'Not really. That wasn't why they came. I think they were hoping to stop the wedding.'

'No!'

'Yes. And it's understandable in a way. If Cristina went off to England or somewhere and then phoned and told me that she was planning to get married next week, I'd be going demented.'

'I know you would. I can just picture it. So, when they met you? What then? Did you make them change their minds or did you just get angry?'

'I don't know how they felt. That's half the problem, I suppose. We didn't get on. Her brother's maybe not so bad.'

'But he does as he's told?'

'By his wife. Fee-ona.' He shook his head. 'I can't begin to tell you what I think about Fiona.'

'Not much, apparently.'

'No. Not much.'

'But you are marrying your Margarita. Not her family.'

Luis shook his head. 'You marry the family as well. You must know that.'

Antonio pursed his lips. 'You know how I've never got on with Conchita's brother?'

'Well I didn't know that. Not really. I mean you don't socialize with them much.'

Antonio frowned. 'I've never said this to you before. It's better to keep such things in the family. Well, it isn't better. That's a lie. But you do. Whenever he gets drunk he gives Modesta a beating. I hate it, just hate it, but she won't leave him. I can't stand men who abuse women. Can't stand a man who even raises his hand to a woman. It never happened in my family. Never.'

'I had no idea.'

'They keep it well hidden. There have been occasions when we've almost come to blows about it, him and me I mean. I keep wanting to teach him a lesson, let him know what it feels like. He's a coward. I know I could fell him with one punch. Conchi says I just have to control myself, but it's hard. She says I'll only make things worse, because Modesta will never leave the bastard and it's true.'

'Where would they go?'

'They could come here and welcome. I've suggested it more than once. We have plenty of room and so many kids ourselves that two more are not going to make a difference.'

Antonio and his family lived in the old mill house, a shabby but comfortable warren of a place. Luis could well imagine that two more kids wouldn't make any difference.

'But she won't leave him?' he asked.

'No way. She comes here for a day or two and we try to persuade her, but she always goes back. We called the police once. They charged him but it made no difference. He comes whining round the door and she goes back. She loves him and she thinks he'll change. He won't. Pigs will fly first. Or not unless he gives up the drink, which I suppose might happen if he makes himself sick enough. Either that or he'll die first. Which would be no great loss.'

'I knew he had a bit of a problem with alcohol. But I didn't know the rest!'

'Nobody does. Modesta covers for him all the time. Let him drink himself to death, I say. And quickly. But the whole point of this story isn't to slag off Diego. Though I'd be quite happy to go on doing that all afternoon. No, the thing is, it hasn't affected me and Conchi too much. We have the odd tiff over him. He is her brother after all and she remembers when he was just a little lad, before he started drinking. Most of the time we try not to even think about it. Sometimes we have to. Too bad. We cope with it. It's something that happens in all families, isn't it? I mean there's always a black sheep of some kind.'

'You knew Conchi so well before you were married.'

'That's true. She knew what she was letting herself in for. And so did I. But there are always things you don't know. Even after all this time there are still things I don't know about her. She can still surprise me.'

Luis nodded. 'I suppose you're right.'

'I can't speak for you, can I? I haven't met your Margarita.'

'Come and meet her now. I've brought Cristina too, to help with the translation. And my mum.'

'I love your mum.'

'Can you stop work?'

'I don't see why not.' He stood up. 'For what it's worth, Luis, I think it's time you were married. Seriously.'

'You sound just like my mother.'

'And I'm pretty sure you wouldn't have asked her if she wasn't right for you.'

'Wouldn't I?'

'Not the Luis I know.'

'I asked Emelina. Didn't I?'

'But you knew she would say no,' said Antonio. 'I think you knew that this one would say yes.'

Later that afternoon, just as it was growing dark, they drove back to San Sebastian. The visit had gone well. Conchita had fed them on fresh bread, olives, tomatoes, and home made soft cheese. They had drunk a fruity red wine. Then she had brought out a plate of crispy home made doughnuts. They had lingered outside for a long time, chatting, laughing. Sometimes Luis would translate for Margaret and sometimes Cristina would translate, and gradually Margaret had relaxed enough to join in, in Spanish, shyly at first but with steadily growing confidence.

In the car, Cristina and Maria chatted quietly in the back. Margaret sat beside Luis in the front. Whenever he changed gear, which was often on these hilly roads, he would seize the opportunity to stroke her knee. He felt better. Margaret had seemed relaxed and happy with his family and with Antonio and Conchita too. Antonio had been polite and attentive and just before they left, he had glanced across at Luis and nodded, very decidedly. At least the marriage would have the blessing of his closest family and friends, if not hers, he thought.

They were spending a couple of nights on the island, but would have to sleep separately, Margaret sharing with Cristina. Anything else would have upset his mother, although he had caught Cristina grinning at him more than once, amused and understanding.

His almost constant physical desire for Margaret tormented him just now and in a strange way confused him, making him temporarily unable to distinguish the love from the lust. And yet he knew that the love was there, had been there almost the whole time, a small, tender melody, like one of his traditional tunes, running beneath the loud symphony of his physical passion for her.

CHAPTER SIXTEEN

We do not know what oranges are as a fruit in England.
Their flavour is poor, thin and watery compared with the golden
apples of the Garden of the Hesperides.
Olivia M Stone, 1878

The following morning, they set off soon after a breakfast of *ensaimadas* and coffee. 'I want you to see some more of my island,' said Luis. 'And I have something else to show you. Something very special.'

Margaret found that he had not exaggerated the island's beauty. Parts of it were covered in luxuriant sub-tropical woodlands of a kind she would not have dreamed existed here. Nobody visiting the hot south of Tenerife or even the port of San Sebastian on La Gomera could have guessed that such abundance grew just a few miles away. There was plenty of water at this time of year, with streams tumbling everywhere and the dampness that the forest itself created.

'When you chop down too many trees, you get a desert,' said Luis. 'That's what happened on Tenerife. Our Spanish *conquistadores* were very happy to cut down trees. Here, we managed to prevent it just in time. Now we have a National Park. Although there was a terrible fire a few years ago and still the risk of wildfires, mostly started by stupid people. But things are already growing again.'

The island was very green. Precipitous roads went spidering between the horizontal lines of cultivation terraces, punctuated by white blocks of houses, diving down through lush growth, with jagged pinnacles towering high above. On the way to wherever Luis was heading, they stopped in the town called Vallehermoso so that they could stretch their legs. They walked down the main street and together they gazed into shops that seemed to sell everything from plant pots and pushchairs to bread and bananas.

Luis said, 'My cousin Pilar lives here, Paco's daughter. But we won't go to her house just now or we'll never get away! It's possible to have too many relatives.'

Instead, he took her to the Valley of the King, the old name for the wide, fertile valley where the road swooped in long meanders towards the sea. At some point in the rich tapestry of that day, as they were heading back towards San Sebastian, they stopped for a late lunch, half way up a green hillside, in a whitewashed restaurant, a long, red-roofed building, with wooden shutters and a roof terrace. From there, the eye was drawn down the green slopes towards the sea and there was a sloping garden where vines grew and the air was heavy with the scent of flowers. She saw a profusion of trees and shrubs: orange, lemon and almond trees for sure, palm trees and more that she could not name.

They sat outside on a comfortable bench, padded with faded cushions, and drank soft red wine. An elderly woman came out and set a brown stoneware bowl of salad on the table in front of them: lettuce, sweet tomatoes, olives and artichokes, peppers and smooth avocados. She stooped down and embraced Luis, kissing him on both cheeks.

'At last!' she said. 'You've been a stranger for much too long, *Lucho!*'

'It's difficult for me to get over here very often.'

'I know. But we love to see you here. You know that. And this is your Margarita we've heard so much about?'

Margaret smiled and would have shaken hands, but the woman reached down and kissed her too.

'This is Carmen,' said Luis. 'She's the best cook in the world.'

Carmen pursed her lips. 'I can think of one or two others. Not many but one or two. Will sardines do?'

'With *papas arrugadas*?' asked Luis.

'What else? It'll be a little while but you're not in a hurry are you?'

'No, no. No hurry at all. We're staying on the island tonight. But we have to go away on the early ferry tomorrow, I'm sad to say.'

'Then you'll have to come back soon.' She winked at Luis, patted his head as though he were a small boy and went away.

'What did she call you?' asked Margaret when she had gone.

'*Lucho*. My – nick name?'

'Pet name.'

'Really?'

'Yes. It means you're close to somebody. Do you know everyone here?'

'I know quite a lot of people. It's hard not to. But there are thousands of people here.'

'I just wondered. You seem so familiar.'

'Of course. We should eat. There's more to come.'

She ate greedily and he watched her with obvious enjoyment. He had never liked women who picked at their food.

A little later, Carmen brought out platters with smoky grilled sardines, bowls of wrinkled salty potatoes and a piquant sauce.

'This is what I was telling you about. We cook the potatoes in sea salt,' said Luis. 'Lots of it. They used to be cooked in seawater. They'll make you very thirsty but it's worth it.'

He got up, was gone for a few moments, and came back with a big jug of water with lemon slices and a few sprigs of mint from the garden. 'The water is very good here,' he said. 'It comes from the hills and it's clean. No bugs.'

The sardines were large and luscious, the skin crispy, dusted with herbs and more sea salt, the flesh inside pale and cooked to perfection.

Margaret thought that she had never tasted anything so good and yet it was such a simple meal.

'I like simple food,' he remarked. 'As long as it's good. The seafood, the fish, the vegetables, the herbs, the olive oil – they all have to be first class and well cooked. Then who needs anything too complicated?'

She agreed with him, had never much liked 'fine dining' menus with their emulsions and juses and confits. Not that she had had much opportunity to sample these so far, given that her ex-husband had been reluctant to spend money on any kind of dining out, but it seemed that Luis knew what he was talking about.

For dessert, Luis – who had cleared their plates himself with a familiarity that surprised her – brought out a bowl of small, thin skinned oranges with a lovely astringent taste that matched their fragrance. When they had finished, he leaned over and kissed her on the lips and she could taste oranges on them, a golden taste, combined with the richness of the wine. It aroused in her a sense of happiness so acute, so overwhelming that it left her speechless and almost tearful.

'You like this place?' he asked at last, unable to contain himself.

'It's heavenly.'

'I'm glad.'

She realised then why he had brought her here.

'Oh,' she said. 'This is it, isn't it? *La Manzana Dorada*. The Golden Apple!'

'Yes. Carmen is my aunt. Paco's about somewhere too, but we wanted you to make up your own mind about it. I needed to know what you thought about the place without any pressure from anyone else. Do you like it?'

'Oh God, yes. Yes I do. I like it very much.'

'Do you really?' He looked at her doubtfully. 'I mean, could you live here, do you think?'

'Could I live here? It's like a little piece of heaven.'

'There's a lot of hard work going on behind the scenes. Like all restaurants. I always think that this place is so very beautiful that it would be worth it.'

She could see that he was delighted with her response. There had been no need for pretence. She *did* think it was like a little piece of heaven.

Paco joined them and shook hands. He was a handsome man, and Margaret saw again the family resemblance that she had noticed in Cristina, like variations on a musical theme. He was slender, with grey hair and a high cheek boned, weather-beaten face. She noticed the guitar calluses on his left hand. He brought another bottle of wine, sat down at their table and drank with them. Carmen came out, bringing a tray of coffee with thin almond biscuits, and a pot of honey for Margaret. Paco peeled an orange for his wife and she ate it delicately, passing a piece back to him every now and then. Like Luis's mother, she wore a print dress and a faded sun hat. She was small and plump and she looked younger than her years. Luis had said that she was seventy, but she looked at least ten years younger than that. Perhaps it was the honey, thought Margaret. Or perhaps it was just the island. Or a happy marriage. It was clear that this was the kind of marriage where they could finish each other's sentences. Where they could finish each other's thoughts. Would she ever achieve this with Luis? Had Paco been similarly impulsive and edgy in his youth, she wondered. Well, perhaps he had.

Afterwards Luis went off with Paco for a while, and Carmen went back to the kitchen. They were expecting a private party of ten tourists later that evening and although it was a set menu, it was always hard work. Somebody would be coming in from the village to lend a hand. Margaret offered to help as well, but Carmen shook her head. Her English was fluent, learned, she said, from tourists over the years and more recently from television. 'No, no. This is your holiday. Besides, I like my kitchen to myself. Even with Paco, he cooks or I cook but not both together. Otherwise we would quarrel. You understand?'

'I think so.'

'I will not be his *sous-chef*. No, not me. We divide the work, but we find our own way of working. Why don't you go and walk in the garden, Margarita? Have a proper look.'

She went into the garden that was alive with trees, flowers, shrubs: everything in its springtime flush of blossoms. It wasn't quite a garden, she thought. Something between a garden and a plantation. She sat down on a stone bench under a great flowering bush with a heavy, drowsy scent. She couldn't name it. Not yet. There were so many plants whose names she didn't know, but then she had never had a real garden. Her mother had a small plot only, a carefully manicured postage stamp lawn and a few perennials. She must look up some of these flowers and shrubs. For now, she just allowed them to dazzle her anonymously, until gradually the curiosity to name them, to pin them down in her mind, gave way to a kind of general appreciation. It didn't matter just now whether she could name them or not. She found herself seeing them anew, and as the anxiety to know, to define, was stilled in her mind, she looked more closely at each leaf, each stem, each blossom.

She leaned back and dozed briefly, replete with food and wine. Her dreams were full of dappled sunshine, the buzz of a passing insect, the goat bells in the distance. When she woke, the sun was sinking in the sky and Luis was bending over her.

'I think we have to go soon,' he said.

'Must we?'

He sat down beside her and slipped his arm around her. She leaned her head against him. 'We should spend some time with my mother. But we still have a little while. I'm glad you like this place so much.'

'Where are Paco and Carmen?'

'Bickering – that's the word, isn't it? Bickering in the kitchen.'

'She told me she doesn't like to cook with him.'

'No. They work best when they divide the work between them: his and hers. If she's in the kitchen, he's in the restaurant. And vice versa. Today they have a big party coming, so they are preparing vegetables together and arguing, very gently. It's the way they are.'

'I could stay here forever,' she said.

'You don't know how happy that makes me, *mi corazon*.'

'You make me happy.'

She turned into his arms and kissed him. The scent of flowers was overwhelming.

'*Dama de la Noche*,' he said.

'What?'

'This.' He gestured at a plant clambering over the shrubbery and rocks behind the bench, a big climber with small, greenish flowers. 'She's early here. She likes the warmth. We call her Lady of the Night. Because the scent is so powerful at night. Not much to look at, but it has the scent of heaven.'

'It has indeed.'

Carmen had switched on the lights in the restaurant. They could just see them, gleaming through the trees.

'It's not a bad house you know,' said Luis. 'It needs some work. There are things we could do to make it better. To make the house more comfortable, to make the restaurant kitchen more up-to-date. I don't want you to think you have to put up with anything just to please me. We'll come back, spend more time. See it properly. Decide what needs to be done.'

'I'd like that.'

'Are you quite sure that you want to live on this island? Are you sure that you wouldn't mind coming to live here?'

With absolute truth at that moment, she said, 'Luis, I can't think of anything at all that I'd rather do. Of anywhere I'd rather live. Or anyone I'd rather be with.'

When they got back to San Sebastian, Maria and Cristina were waiting for them.

'Did you like it?' asked Cristina, unable to contain herself.

'Yes. I loved it.'

Cristina sighed. 'I'm so relieved. It has been his ambition for so long. He loves the place too you know.'

'Well I'm not surprised.'

'But it's time for Paco and Carmen to retire or it soon will be. And they couldn't bear to sell it to just anyone. They want Luis to have it. Oh, I'm so glad he found you, Margarita! So glad! It all seems meant, somehow, doesn't it?'

Later, Maria fussed anxiously about them, wondering if they had had enough to eat. Margaret thought she would burst if she ate another morsel after their lunch, although Luis had been right and the salty potatoes had given her a fierce thirst. He brought out a pitcher of home-made lemonade and they sat outside the house, in the warm darkness, drinking and talking.

Just before bed, they went for a walk together, watching the lights of San Sebastian below.

'Well,' said Margaret. 'Have I passed, do you think?'

'Passed?' He didn't understand immediately.

'Passed the test.'

'What test?'

'Do they like me? Your family. Your friend Antonio. Your uncle and aunt. Do they like me?'

'It was no test.' He was embarrassed.

'Oh, of course it was. That was the whole point of this trip. I don't mind. You wanted to know what they all thought about me. Your relatives. Your oldest friends. Why wouldn't you want to know that?'

'I wanted to show you the restaurant. Make sure you liked it. But what do you think of them? My family and my friends. And my island.'

'Oh that's easy. I love them. They've all made me feel so welcome.

In fact they make me ashamed of my family. Of Ian and Fiona anyway. But then, my mum's different. You'll like her.'

'This wasn't a test.' He swung her round towards him.

'You're angry.'

'No. Why should I be angry with you? And why would that worry you?'

'Sometimes I find it hard to tell what you're thinking. Sometimes I find it hard to know if you're angry or if it's just you. The way you are sometimes. Maybe it's your language. The energy in it. You know? Sometimes you, all of you, seem to be angry when I know you're not.'

'Oh, my darling, I'm not angry. I'm never angry with you. Only sometimes with myself.' He tried to pull her closer but she resisted him.

'Lucho,' she said seriously, trying out the name. Liking the softness of it. 'There's something I have to say and now seems to be as good a time as any to say it.'

He felt his heart contract with fear. She was going to say that she didn't want to marry him. She was going to tell him that the differences between them were too great. She was going home to Scotland.

She felt his hands tighten on her arms, but continued in spite of him.

'It all happened very quickly, didn't it?'

'What did?'

'Us. You know? You were so impetuous. So impulsive. That proposal of marriage. I never expected it, you know.'

'What did you expect?'

'I don't know. When I knew that you wanted to make love to me, I couldn't say no. I couldn't betray myself because I wanted it too. I wanted it so fiercely.'

'And you don't want it now?'

'Don't put words into my mouth again. Of course I want it. All the time, if I'm honest. But when you said "marry me" it came as a shock. I can't tell you how much of a surprise. Of all the things I had expected, that never once entered my head. Not so soon and so suddenly anyway. And then when you said it, I knew that was what I wanted too.'

'Wanted?'

'You misunderstand me. I still want it. But what about *you*? It just struck me that you might be regretting it. Now that you've had time to think. Now that you've met some of my family. Oh, there must be all kinds of reasons why we should think twice. I've gone through most of them in my mind and I know that I love you and want to marry you.'

'Then where is the problem?'

'You.' She hesitated. 'You wouldn't go ahead out of some notion of pride? Because you couldn't go back on a promise? You wouldn't do that to me, would you, Luis? If you want to back out, tell me now and we'll wait, get to know each other better, still be friends. Just take more time.'

Her carefully assumed composure let her down and he saw her face crumple. He couldn't bear it and pulled her close, his fingers sinking into her skin. He bent and kissed her, biting fiercely at her lips, stinging the soft flesh there. When at last he released her, she leaned against him, panting with desire.

'There,' he said. 'That's what I think of your suggestion. You marry me now. *Te adoro.*'

'I'll marry you whenever you like,' she said.

CHAPTER SEVENTEEN

From top to toe
you are a bouquet.
Your mother was surely blessed
with the pain of your birth.

The wedding was in San Sebastian at the beginning of April. It was meant to be a very quiet affair, but all of Luis's immediate family and close friends were there. Maria was dressed in a smart linen suit that she had bought specially for the occasion and pretty shoes that were too small for her feet. At every opportunity, she would slip them off, flexing her toes and sighing with relief.

Fiona and Ian had decided that they couldn't spare the time to come. Margaret thought the truth was that they couldn't bear to come. The whole thing would have disturbed them too much. Her mother had a long online chat with her the day before the wedding.

'You know,' she said, 'If Ian and Fiona had been going, I'd have gone with them.'

'I wish you were going to be here,' said Margaret.

'I should have been braver. But Fiona was so insistent that I'd find it all a bit much. Too hot, too stressful. I don't know why I didn't insist, really.'

'They have you old before your time, mum. You're still a young woman.'

'Not really.'

'Well you're certainly not old! They'd quite like to do the same thing to me.'

'I know, I know.'

Annie had been diagnosed with angina the previous year. It was not serious but it had given her a fright. Margaret sometimes thought that ever since that bout of illness, Ian and Fiona had encouraged Annie to think of herself as delicate. It wasn't true.

'You have to stand up to them a bit more.'

'I know. It would be easier with you to back me up. I will come you know. I'll come and see you. Both of you.'

'Maybe I'll come over on a visit and bring you back with me. Just make sure your passport hasn't expired.'

'It's fine. I have to have it when I go to Dublin. I wish I was coming to your wedding now. I should be there.'

'It's all going to be pretty quiet. Luis's family will be there. His mother, Maria. She's lovely. You'll like her.'

'I hope so.' There was a pause. 'Is he good to you, Margaret?' Annie asked, tentatively.

'He's wonderful.'

'Are you sure? I mean you're not ... '

'I'm not going blindly into this, mum. I have thought about it. A lot. I do love him.'

'And he loves you?'

'I think he does, mum. I really think he does.'

Conor and Niamh and a few others from the property company had come over on the ferry to give Margaret moral support, they said. They had been given the day off – a rare gesture of generosity from Stella – and she was glad of their presence. At least if her family couldn't be bothered to come to her wedding, her friends had turned out for her.

If they had been surprised by her news, they had managed not to show it. She could only imagine what they might be saying about her in private. Conor had taken her to one side and, his face creased with worry, had said, 'You're sure you're doing the right thing?' He sounded a little like Ian.

'I wish everyone would stop asking me that. I'm certain of it. I love him. He loves me. Will that do?'

'Well then, all the very best of luck to you. I must say though, you've got hidden depths.'

'What do you mean?'

'It's just that we never expected it. We didn't expect you to do anything so ...

Crazy, she thought. They think I'm crazy.

'Unusual. Brave, I suppose, ' he said

'Boring old Margaret, you mean?'

'No. You were never boring. You just seemed a bit shy and quiet. Kind of old fashioned, Niamh says. Like your name. But it just goes to show.'

'What does it go to show?'

'Like my mum says, watch out for the quiet ones. She's right, isn't she?' He hugged her. 'We like you a lot, you know. We wouldn't want to see you get hurt in any way.'

'I don't think I'm going to get hurt.' She sighed. It was clear that before the day was out she would be lucky not to be swept away on a tide of other people's anxieties on her behalf. She hoped to God Luis's family and friends didn't feel the same. She didn't think they did, but who knew? Maybe they were just better at concealing their feelings. Sometimes she had caught Antonia, Luis's schoolteacher sister, watching her covertly when she thought she was unobserved.

'Listen,' she said to Conor. 'I've just decided to change direction, that's all.'

'Pretty radical though.'

'It's been a surprise to everyone, me included. Sometimes you just have to seize the day. You should hear what my family at home have to say about all this.'

'I can imagine.'

'Conor, he isn't any younger than me, you know. We're the same age. Besides, it wouldn't matter if he was.'

'But do you have anything in common?'

Oh yes we have, she thought, hardly able to hide the smile – or was it a smirk? – that threatened to break out. 'We have lots in common. We like a lot of the same things.'

She thought of all the things they both liked, especially when they were in bed together. It still made her heart pound. She was glad that the flush of sunshine on her face disguised her tendency to blush. 'And we both like his island. We both love La Gomera. And his music. I loved his music even before I loved him, you know. Don't you remember how we'd go to that restaurant and you lot never wanted to listen, but I did? And then there's food. He cooks up a storm and I like to eat.'

'Well yes, that sounds pretty good to me. Oh, I know your brother's put you through this already.'

'He has. Too much. Everyone warns women against getting involved with men while they're on holiday. Holiday romances. They'll love you and leave you. That's the conventional wisdom, isn't it?

'It's mostly true!'

'But I'm not on holiday. I live here. And he isn't loving and leaving me. He doesn't even want to go to Scotland. He wants to stay here and run his own restaurant. With me. There's a garden. I've always wanted a garden.'

'You still haven't known him for very long.'

'I knew my ex-husband for years. Didn't make any difference when he decided that he wanted to go off with a younger model. Besides, I've known Luis for long enough. I'm not a child.'

'You'll be fine.' He hugged her again. Perhaps she had convinced him. But still he seemed doubtful, as though encouraging her against his better judgement.

The ceremony took place in the old church, the one with the mural of the sea battle against the English. It smelled of incense and flowers and it reminded her of her childhood. She and Alastair had been married in a registry office, since Alastair was a self proclaimed atheist. And my, how he liked to proclaim it. Proselytising far more than any priest she had ever known. Despising any attempt to debate the subject. Patronisingly telling her how much he envied her the 'comfort' her rather vague belief brought her, with the implication that she was a credulous fool. She reflected that his intolerance was fortunate because it meant that her first marriage didn't 'count' in a religious sense, so there was no barrier to her marrying Luis in church. If there was a certain amount of hypocrisy about this, she decided that she could ignore it in order to please Maria, who would have been much more horrified to see her only son married in a civil ceremony than she had ever been about his decision to marry a foreigner.

Margaret wore a simple, not too expensive dress, in pale ivory silk chiffon, with a flared mid-length skirt, a fitted lace bodice and short lacy sleeves. She had bought it on a trip to Santa Cruz with Cristina and it suited her. They had found a rosebud and pearl tiara that Cristina threaded through her hair, worn long and loose. She carried a posy of tiny, creamy rosebuds. Looking in the mirror, before she left for the church, she hardly recognised herself. She looked young and voluptuous and very pretty.

The service was in Spanish and she was so nervous that she understood very little of it, though she made her own vows in English. Luis, who had spent the night before the wedding with Antonio at the mill, looked serious and handsome in his dark suit, his shirt very white and crisp. He spoke softly, looking at her all the time, and his hand shook as he placed the gold ring on her finger. Maria wiped her eyes with an inadequate lace handkerchief. The priest, a friend of the family, was jolly and brisk. He got through the ceremony very speedily, as though anxious to get on to the party, as perhaps he was. Afterwards they went to a restaurant in the town, where there was a sumptuous buffet of local dishes, some of which had been contributed by Paco and Carmen. Margaret had wanted to go to *La Manzana Dorada* after the ceremony, but they had decided that it was too far for the Los Cristianos friends to travel and still get back to Tenerife in time for work the following day. Besides, this was a much bigger restaurant.

The Canarians, on the whole, stayed together and talked in animated Spanish. Margaret's work friends sat together and conversed in English. Luis and Margaret moved happily between the two groups, trying to get them to mix. Luis's mother sat with one or other of her daughters for a large part of the time. With the help of Domingo, very grown-up in his Sunday suit, they orchestrated the children's games so that they didn't get too wildly out of hand. Sometimes Margaret would go and sit beside Maria and try to converse in a mixture of Spanish and English.

Her Spanish was improving, so Cristina told her. 'Soon you'll be speaking like a native!'

'I don't think so! But I'd like to know more.'

Maria watched Margaret anxiously and took every available opportunity of smiling at her. At last, when she and Margaret were alone together, she took the younger woman gently by the hand.

'Margarita,' she said. 'I hope that you and Luis will be very happy. I had almost given up hope of him marrying. He had one girlfriend from Barcelona for a long time. They lived together.'

'Yes. He told me.'

'She wasn't a good girl for him, although I didn't interfere. And then she went off with someone else, and he was desolate for a long time.' She struggled to say what she meant. 'Since then, there has been this or that lady, but no one special. Listen, he is my only son and I love him very much. I want you to be happy. I would like for you to be a daughter to me. It is easier to say this in Spanish. Do you understand me?'

'Yes. And I'm trying to learn more Spanish, you know. Luis will teach me now.'

'There is so much to tell you. To talk about. Luis, he is … ' She spread her hands. 'Well, he is still my boy in many ways. You will know what that means one day, please God. But sometimes it isn't easy when two such as you …' She moved her hands in a futile gesture, then smiled. 'Never mind,' she said. ' He is *un buen hombre*. I think you are a very nice lady. And I think you are happy today? *Si*?'

'Yes, I am.'

'Then welcome to our family.'

It was a blessing, freely given and wholeheartedly received. They embraced, and Margaret turned around to catch Luis watching them with a smile, but this time without a trace of mockery.

CHAPTER EIGHTEEN

How can you ask me to live
if I give you my soul?
A body cannot live without a soul.
A soul is for ever.

At first they made love anywhere and everywhere: awkwardly in the shower, daringly on the balcony at night. They couldn't help caressing each other wherever they went, touching knees or entwining feet under tables, holding hands, fingers laced together, seizing all opportunities for contact. It felt painful to be apart from one another.

It was a passion which, for a time, overrode all the cultural and linguistic differences between them. Sometimes she would go to the restaurant and watch him as he played and sang songs that were now directed wholly at her. To sit in the dim light and see his hands caressing the curves of the instrument, as later they would caress her, made her feel faint with desire for him.

On the way home, they would take off their shoes and walk along the beach, deserted in the moonlight save for the curled-up shapes of the stray dogs that slept comfortably there. Once, reluctant to go back to the stuffy flat because the night was so balmy and sweet-scented, they found a private place on flat rocks in the lee of a wall. Luis put his jacket down for them to sit on and they watched the pale light of the moon reflected in the water for a while. It was very late and nobody was about. Suffused with the pleasure of his touch, she saw the moon suspended over the sea, and thought that out there was his island, just waiting for them.

Their lovemaking was full of excitement but always tempered by tenderness and consideration. Inevitably, there were pitfalls. In spite of anything she had told her family and friends, she knew that marriage between two people of even broadly similar backgrounds involved compromising in a hundred ways, patiently accommodating each other's foibles. Now, she was feeling for footholds in the dark. It took loving and obliging hearts to cope.

After the first few weeks of blissful physical satisfaction, Margaret – while never once regretting it – found their marriage to be more of a trial than she might have imagined. There was a customary and cultural abyss between them. She had known that, but it was one thing to know it and quite another to live it.

Occasionally, she caught herself gazing at the gold band on her finger with astonishment. There was nothing she could or would have done to halt her headlong rush into marriage. Her passion for Luis had made her agreement as involuntary and inevitable as breathing. But in her darker moments she found herself wondering if he had wanted to entrap her quickly, given the obvious strength of his feelings for her. Their mutual desire was too powerful and overwhelming. Such moments came in the early hours of the morning when she would lie awake, looking at him as he slept. She couldn't help thinking of him as some bird of prey that had circled in, seized her and carried her away. She would remember her first fears on the mountainside and wondered if those early instincts to fly from him had been right after all. Maybe this was what she had sensed in him. But even those doubts were spiced with the tingle of sensuality. While she was troubled and sleepless, looking down at him with a mixture of anguish and tenderness, he would wake up and ask, 'What's wrong?' He would take her in his arms, and then she had no desire to escape from him. None at all.

On the whole, though, most of her reservations about him were much smaller, much more manageable. His occasional outbursts of voluble anger still alarmed her, though he had never so much as raised a finger to her, nor would he. She realised that their volume controls were set at different levels. Like the mountain storms, their few tiffs were soon over and – unlike her ex-husband who had been able to remain speechless for days on end – Luis was incapable of sulking for longer than half an hour or less at a time. They argued over his general untidiness. He loved to cook, even at home, and made splendid meals, but afterwards the kitchen looked like a battle zone. She remembered Carmen saying that she had no intention of being Paco's *sous-chef* and wondered if Luis took after his uncle. After the first couple of times, she refused to clear up his mess, telling him to sort it out as he went along, whereupon he did.

There was also a certain indifference about him where animals were concerned. She had seen him pet the dogs in his mother's house with casual affection, but once, after he kicked out at a small dog snapping around his heels in the street, she ran home, almost in tears.

He was genuinely astonished by her reaction.

'What's the matter?' he asked. 'It's only a dog, after all.'

He hadn't really hurt the dog, he knew, simply put it aside with his foot, quite gently at that. Surprise and hurt dignity had made it slink off and leave him alone. It was only a dog, not a child, he thought, helplessly.

'Why are you angry?' he repeated.

'If you don't know I can't tell you.'

'You English. You are all the same. Take care of the animals while you beat up your children.'

'I'm not English. I keep telling you. I'm Scottish and I've never beaten up a child in my life,' she said indignantly. Then she started to laugh. He joined in and the dog was soon forgotten.

She hadn't expected him to be like Alastair and he wasn't. He was different in every possible way. He was good humoured, sensuous, passionate and tender by turns, but he wasn't an easy companion. His energy could be exhausting. After their marriage, they had been given permission to stay on in Margaret's flat for the remainder of that year. She knew that owning *La Manzana Dorada* was his single biggest ambition, and she was willing to devote all her energy to the project. He told her that if he carried on cooking by day and playing at night, they should have enough money to move to La Gomera at the end of the current season.

'But I have money,' she said. 'I have some money in the bank at home. We could use it and put down a good deposit on the restaurant now if you like.'

He refused point blank to do any such thing.

'No,' he said. 'That's your money. Not mine. I can't take it. What would people think?'

'Who cares what people think? It's our money now. We can use it for whatever we want. And if we want the restaurant, why not?'

'But I remember what your brother said. And how he tried to buy me off.'

'Oh that was all nonsense. Fiona's meddling. We're married. What's mine is yours.'

He stood firm. It was a point of honour with him and mulishly, he would not budge. She was coming to know and hate his points of honour. They seemed to rule a good deal of his life, whereas she had always been pragmatic, doing what seemed best at the time.

'You're the one who's always telling me not to care about what people think!' she said.

'I know. But this is different. I can't use your money for this. Don't you see? They would think I had married you for your money. It would be exactly as I said when we came away from La Gomera that first time. They would think me *un picaro*. A thief.'

'Oh, rubbish.'

'It's true, Margarita. When we have the restaurant, then perhaps we can use some of your money for alterations. For developing the project. That would be OK.'

'Thank you for telling me what you'll *allow* me to do with my own money.'

'Exactly. It's yours,' he said, tight-lipped.

Enraged, she went off to work, slamming the door loudly behind her to relieve her feelings.

He had, she discovered, a streak of jealousy. He was intelligent enough to acknowledge it and try to control it, but just occasionally it broke the surface. He was jealous of her friendship with Conor and told her so. She laughed, then realised that he was serious. Soon after that, he suggested that she should stop working.

'Property sales. This kind of office is no place for you,' he said.

But that was one battle she won. 'If you think I'm going to sit in this apartment all day, waiting for you to come home, and then sit in here all night while you go out playing, then you're very much mistaken, Luis.'

'You won't do as I say?'

'No. I won't. I'm working and that's that.'

To her surprise, when she became firm, he complied almost instantly, though she didn't immediately learn – as perhaps she should – the valuable lesson that he was vulnerable to her anger, collapsing before it like a house of cards. Contrary to her expectations, he did all housework happily, except for ironing. Sweeping was apparently 'man's work' as was cleaning bathrooms, mopping floors and filling the washing machine and the dishwasher.

'So what's wrong with ironing?' she asked.

'It is not manly,' he said, simply.

'If you're a man,' she answered, 'And you're definitely that, anything you do ought to be considered manly.'

He thought about it, laughed at it, agreed with her, but still refused to iron. Not that either of them ever did much ironing. He was, however, very different from Alastair, who had hardly lifted a finger about the house. He had bought gadgets galore but had never really investigated their uses himself. He had done the occasional bit of washing up before they acquired a dishwasher, but cooking seemed to be beyond him at that time. Once, she had gone to stay with an old school friend for a week and had wondered whether she might come home to find a corpse sitting up at the dining table with a knife and fork in its hand, waiting for a meal that never came. Perhaps he had survived on takeaways. She had heard since then that things had changed with his new partner. She hoped so, for Jenny's sake.

Luis and Alastair were poles apart, and she certainly loved Luis more than she could ever remember having loved Alastair. The feeling was deeper. It seemed to strike at the very root of her being. She had some vague feeling that if Luis stopped loving her, her world would fall apart. It was nothing to do with fear of him. It was fear of losing what she had, what she cherished. She began to see that if she had hoped to escape from herself, then that hope had been vain. You took yourself and all your accumulated baggage of fears with you wherever you went. There was nothing she could do about it unless some outside force wrought a great change in her, and she didn't know what that might be.

Gradually, as the days grew hotter, and as April slid into May, she began to feel faintly discontented, not with her husband, but with the apartment and her job. It came as something of a relief when they went to spend a day on La Gomera. Maria paid her a great deal of loving attention and Isabel made a big effort with the small amount of English she had learned at school. Margaret made an even bigger effort with the Spanish she had managed to pick up from Luis. The children chatted away in Spanish, not caring whether she understood or not. The older boy, Domingo, was polite but shy. Miguel and Marie Carmen were a prince and princess, ruling in their own kingdom.

She thought they were a little spoilt but couldn't say as much to Luis, who plainly adored them. Besides, she didn't think there was such a concept here. It was a peculiarly British idea. Spoiling children by loving them too much. And maybe the Spanish were right.

Margaret listened curiously to the Gomero accent. It was becoming more obvious to her the more Spanish she learnt: the way certain vowels were changed, the way Maria called her eldest grandson *omingu*. Travel had subtly changed Luis's own speech, making it easier for her to understand, but she still found it difficult to understand him when he was in full, fast, conversational flow. It was embarrassing, she told him, to have to confess that the only words she knew well, the only phrases with which she was really familiar, were those connected with making love. It was nice, but limiting, she said. He laughed, said that he had better teach her some more useful words and phrases, hadn't he?

At lunchtime, Cristina came home and embraced her warmly.

'Lucho looks so well,' she remarked. 'Marriage to you must be good for him.'

'I hope so.'

'I know it is. But is it good for you? That's the important thing!'

'I think it is.'

They hadn't brought the car over this time, but Paco came into town in his elderly van to fetch fertilizer and netting for the garden. They squeezed into the cab and went back with him to *La Manzana Dorada*. This time, Carmen gave Margaret a tour of the house. It was a low, rambling building, very clean but a little shabby. Inside there were cool tiled floors, wooden beams, whitewashed walls. The restaurant area spilled out onto the terrace where they had sat on that first visit, with wooden tables and benches and vivid pelargoniums in terracotta pots. There were shutters on the windows against the heat, and bougainvillea clambering over the walls, the pink clashing wonderfully with the red roofs. Two sections of the building were linked by the small *azotea* or roof terrace. She followed Carmen up the steps to this sheltered platform, where there was a round table with a faded umbrella and a couple of chairs. An empty coffee mug and a pair of spectacles sat on the table. A newspaper lifted slightly in the breeze from the sea.

'He always leaves his glasses here,' remarked Carmen, putting them in her apron pocket. 'He'll be storming about the kitchen later looking for them.'

This was where Paco and Carmen came when they needed to escape from the restaurant. There was a view of orange trees, with tumbling terraces and the sea beyond.

Looking around, Margaret was once again amazed at the way in which life could change in an instant. How could such an opportunity have come to her so unexpectedly, so suddenly? Who would have thought it?

'It is very old, this house,' said Carmen. 'We think it once belonged to one of the important Spanish families. They loved their gardens, you know, those old families. I think some of the trees and plants are very old as well. There's a dragon tree and a – *morera*. I don't know what that is in English. It's a very tall tree, very old, but it has berries. You can only eat them when they are really ripe. But then they fall off the tree, so you have to be quick.'

'Mulberries, maybe?' said Margaret.

'Ah, *sí*! Luis and his friend Antonio could eat them till they gave themselves ...'

'A stomach ache.'

'Yes. Silly boys.'

'Are there records of the property?' asked Margaret.

'There will be, somewhere. Probably in the bank or with our lawyer. We have been here a very long time, since we were first married. It belonged to my father's cousin, but he wasn't living here, so my father bought it for us. It's the kind of place you hope always to keep in the family.'

'I'm not surprised.'

'And you know what else belongs here?'

'No, what?'

'Come down and have some lemonade and I'll tell you.'

They went out to join Luis and Paco on the terrace.

'I had no idea this place was so ancient!' she said, as she sat down beside Luis.

'Oh yes. Which, I suppose, brings its own responsibilities.'

'I was saying to her that there is something else that belongs here.' Carmen poured home-made lemonade into her glass.

Luis smiled. 'Oh yes. There is!'

'What?'

'My guitar.'

'Really?'

'You see, it was a gift to me from Paco. I was ten and I had already been playing for a few years.'

'But you were playing that wretched instrument your father used to have.' Paco pulled a face.

'And then one day, Paco arrived with a big guitar-shaped parcel, didn't you? My mother was horrified. Said it was much too good for me. And it probably was. It probably still is.'

'How come it belongs here. Isn't that what you meant?'

'We found it here. When we first moved here. When we were first married. I had played the *timplillo* and then moved on to the guitar. I had one or two instruments, even back then,' said Paco.

'Guitar mad,' said Carmen. 'He has more than he can ever play.'

'And where was it?'

'Very carefully stored away at the back of a cupboard in a room that wasn't used very often. No strings. Just the guitar, wrapped up in silk and put in an old wooden chest.'

'Really?'

'Really. We spoke to the cousin who had sold the place. Carmen's father had bought it from him when we got married. But he knew nothing about it and cared less. The place was very run down. As far as he was concerned it was just another old guitar. Keep it, he said. So I kept it and got the right strings for it, excellent strings, and then I played it.'

'He said it was the best instrument he had ever played,' said Carmen.

'It was. It still is.'

'But you gave it away to Luis?'

'Of course. There was something really special about Luis too.'

'No wonder you treasure it,' she said, looking from one to the other. 'And no wonder you love this place so much.'

'What do you think of it?' Luis asked. 'Our Golden Apple? Is this somewhere you could live and work?'

'I can't wait to move here. Can't wait to get started.'

'We could make some plans.'

'We could do that, yes. It would be a pleasure.'

'You get on well with Cristina?' asked Luis as they walked down the hill on their way back to the ferry.

'I do. She's very charming, isn't she?'

'Charming? I don't know. She has always been my favourite, if I have any favourites. She's very clever or I think so. But she needs to do more with her life.'

'How old is she, Luis?'

'Thirty. She'll be thirty next birthday.'

'And she's not married yet?'

'No. It's very unusual here for a woman to wait so long. And another great worry for my mother. Now that she's stopped worrying about me, of course.'

'She must have had plenty of offers.'

'I don't know. I think she doesn't want to be the wife of a small fisherman or farmer maybe. She sees the lives led by her sisters and she doesn't like them much.'

'There are worse things.'

'Ah, yes, you can say this from your own experience. As can I. But she went straight from school to working for Senor Gonzales at the bank. The furthest she has been is to Tenerife. The only city she has ever visited is Santa Cruz, with me. It's not much to show for thirty years of living.'

'Has she told you all this?'

'Not in so many words, but I know what she feels and thinks. I worry about her but there's nothing I can do. Perhaps you would speak to her. Perhaps you could be friends with her.'

'I hope we already are friends, but I'll see what I can do.'

The day had gone very well. They came away from La Gomera bearing fresh eggs, fruit and vegetables, companionably at peace with one another. At times like this, she felt blissfully happy, secure in the knowledge that all was well with her marriage. She trusted Luis, but the odd doubt would still creep in. She knew that by the very nature of his work, he would have plenty of opportunity for casual affairs. She had seen young tourists in the restaurants where he sang, strikingly pretty girls who stared at him with deliberate provocation, girls who bought him drinks and came up to speak to him afterwards or shy girls who glanced sidelong at him and smiled. Once, jokingly, she had expressed her fears but it seemed that was a point of honour too.

'You suspect me!' he said. 'Margarita, I can't bear this. There will never be another woman now. Do you hear me? Never!'

He walked out, sat in a nearby bar and drank brandy. She was in bed when he came home but not asleep. He stood in the doorway looking down at her, his handsome face clouded and sullen with resentment. He wasn't drunk. She had never once seen him drunk. But he was morose and resentful.

'Where have you been?' she asked.

'Why do you want to know? Perhaps I've been screwing around. Since it's what you think I do, perhaps I have!'

He was pulling off his clothes, dropping them in a heap on the floor, then climbing into bed.

'I didn't mean that,' she said.

She wanted to tell him that she didn't really suspect him but suspicion and insecurity had become such a habit with her that she couldn't easily shake them off. She knew it was unfair to Luis and she tried to keep her demons bottled up inside, but they were there all the same, hobgoblins that came out in the darkness.

Luis lay rigid and resentful beside her. She turned towards him, towards his unresponsive back, and slid her arms around him. 'Luis!' she whispered but he shook her off, slid away from her to the very edge of the bed.

'Be like that,' she said and turned away from him.

Five minutes later, she felt him turn over, slip his arms around her, pulling her close, kissing her gently on the neck.

'I'm sorry,' he said. 'I'm so sorry. I love you. I'll never be unfaithful to you. Never. You must believe that.'

In the morning he brought her breakfast in bed, put a red rose on the tray, anxious to reaffirm his love for her, anxiously seeking reassurance that she still loved him in spite of his bad behaviour.

CHAPTER NINETEEN

The wind blows in a marvellously angry way here every night from
about one or two o'clock until seven in the morning, but it does not
mean anything ; it is only bluster.
Olivia M Stone, 1887

Early May brought a late Sirocco from Africa, the hot wind that showered the islands with dust and sand. It was a wicked wind coming in March and November, fraying tempers, making people physically uncomfortable and spiritually unstable. It brought nightmares and arguments in its wake. It was a trial to the soul. Opening windows or doors in their apartment was like opening an oven door to admit a terrible blast of hot air. The property office was air conditioned and Margaret went to work with a sense of relief each morning. She had sold more apartments in the last few weeks than in the whole of her first two months in the Canaries.

'Marriage seems to suit you,' said Stella.

It was true that she was physically content most of the time, sleek and sated with Luis's lovemaking, but with the advent of the Sirocco, even that became intolerable. The apartment had electric fans but no air conditioning. The nights were almost as hot as the days, the air cooling marginally in the early hours of the morning only to heat up with renewed ferocity later on. The wind, forcing sand into every crevice of skin, was a constant irritation. A shower brought only temporary relief. Luis seemed much better able to cope with it than his wife, but perhaps it was just that he was used to it. She could understand now why those traditional houses with their cool stone walls and wooden shutters might be more comfortable in such weather.

All over Tenerife, rock formations altered the course of the fierce wind, forming mini-twisters that carried bits of wood and paper in small but alarming columns of blown dust, skedaddling uncannily along the beach or down the street. The office was much cooler, but after the short walk home from work Margaret wanted to lie down and pant like a dog. Sometimes she would meet Luis at a nearby hotel where they could swim in the cool pool for a while, when most of the guests were at early dinner. It was a blissful but short-lived respite from the heat. In the evenings, Luis went to work in his lightest shirts and cotton chinos or shorts. Occasionally she went with him to hear him play, and watched as he sat there under the lights, his hair damp with sweat, plastered in glistening curls over his forehead.

'It'll be much better on La Gomera. There's always a cool wind there. From the mountains,' he said.

She thought about *La Manzana Dorada*, perched on the side of a long, deep valley, with its gardens and terraces, the scent of oranges hanging over it and the sounds of goat bells in the distance.

'I wish we were there right now.'

She had been wondering what she would do, once they had the restaurant. Luis would want to do most of the cooking. She didn't have much idea of how to run a business, but she could learn, although she suspected Luis was financially astute. If he put his mind to something like this, he would probably make a go of it. Wine interested her; she would like to find out more about it, maybe even do a course of some kind. The idea of gardening, of growing produce, interested her even more. When they had last visited the restaurant, looking out from the *azotea* with Carmen, she had realised that quite a large area of land went with the property, a long slope of terraces and enclosures below the house. The natural fertility of the place was astounding. Paco and Carmen already grew oranges, lemons, papayas, avocados, tomatoes and even small, sweet Canary bananas, although there were bigger banana plantations elsewhere on the island. There were a few date palms too. Luis had told her they could be tapped for their sap which was made into a kind of syrup called palm honey. The idea of being able to carry on growing fruits and vegetables for the restaurant, cultivating things in this most fertile of places, entranced her. They could make a feature of it. Herbs too, she thought. Perhaps she could make things to sell to tourists and local people as well. Orange flower water. Essential oils. Palm honey. Carmen kept bees and had offered to teach Margaret. The more she thought about it all, the more it excited her. She had started keeping a notebook with ideas, reading gardening books, books about herbs. She thought of her money sitting in the bank at home. Not enough to buy much of a house in Glasgow, for sure. A small flat maybe. But here, if they put it together with Luis's considerable savings, it would be more than enough to put down a deposit, buy the place immediately and probably do the necessary alterations and modernizations as well.

When she raised the subject again, he said, 'Yes, we can use it when we take over. Employ some help. And some help in the garden. You have so many good ideas, but we would need help to achieve them.'

'Then why not now?'

'You must understand, Margarita. I can't use your money immediately. I've been working towards this for years. It'll be only a little while longer. It will be yours as much as mine. It'll be in both our names. Besides ...' He hesitated.

'What?'

'I worry about Paco and Carmen. The place has been their home for so long. They love it. They need to move. They've even seen the house they want. But it's a big thing for them, giving up the restaurant.'

'It must be.'

'They need a little more time to come to terms with it. For so long it's been something for the future. Something they planned to do. Now it's almost upon them ...'

'You mean they don't really want to go?'

'Oh they do. In fact they know that they *have* to go. Paco isn't as fit as he once was. Carmen has arthritis. They need to make the change soon. While they can still get their new place the way they want it. And have a pleasant retirement. Maybe still help out with the restaurant from time to time, although they've told me they don't want to interfere with whatever we decide to do. I thought, you know – new year, new beginnings. Do you understand? Not too long to wait.'

She did understand, and she was touched by his concern for the couple, by his sensitivity to their feelings but it didn't stop her from becoming prickly and cross with him as well as the Sirocco.

'How long does this go on for?' she asked.

'Who can say? It's very late this year. I have known it to blow for six weeks or more.'

'No!'

'*Si*, Margarita.'

'I can't bear it.'

'It will go only when it's ready. It could be gone by tomorrow. Say a prayer.'

'Is there a patron saint of the weather?'

'I have no idea! Probably. Look it up. And relax. Don't get so hot and bothered.'

'It's very hard not to get hot and bothered in this wind.'

She looked it up. It was Saint Medard, some obscure sixth century bishop who had been sheltered from the rain by an eagle. She didn't think he would be much help against the Sirocco but she said a prayer anyway. Medard's attention was clearly elsewhere. It had not gone by the next day or the one after that or even by the next week. She showered twice a day for the small relief it would bring and drank jug after jug of lemonade, orange juice, mineral water. It was too hot to eat, too hot to make love, and she became more and more furious with Luis for no very good reason other than the demonic wind.

She messaged her mother. Annie had been doing a basic computer course and now messaged her daughter on WhatsApp, as well as their weekly video call, begging her to come home for a holiday and bring Luis with her. She was desperate to meet him in person. Luis said that later in the summer they would certainly go to Scotland. Margaret wondered if she could wait that long. She went online and found that she could get a cheap flight for a short visit. A weekend perhaps. But Luis couldn't take the time off work. It was a busy time for him, the restaurants crowded, the guitar engagements coming thick and fast. She had an intense longing to see her mother and be babied, a sudden desire for Scottish rain on her face, for the taste of real bacon and proper toast, for the sound of Glasgow voices, as musical in their own way as the Gomeros.

She was forced to acknowledge that she was homesick.

'Go then,' said Luis. 'Go and see your mother.' She could tell that he was just a little disappointed, so she postponed the trip. It was enough for the moment to know that she could go whenever she wanted

By the end of May, Luis was working in a positive frenzy, taking all possible engagements, cooking by day, singing by night. All his thoughts were set on their restaurant. They met only in bed, where it was too hot to do anything but lie still, side by side. They ate breakfast together and if she went to the restaurant in the evening they would have a drink together after his performance. Irritation simmered inside her, though she knew that he was working only for their shared future.

Luis seemed blithely unaware of her frustration. She couldn't get through to him. Her tongue was tied by the heat.

'Are you well?' he would ask.

She would always reply, 'Of course. It's just that I'm so hot. I didn't know it could get so terribly hot in the summer.'

'This isn't summer yet.'

'Well, you know what I mean.'

She began deliberately to turn away from him at night.

'What's the matter? What's wrong?' he asked.

'Nothing. I'm just too hot. I don't feel like it.'

'How can we make a baby if we don't make love?'

'Who said anything about babies?'

'You did. You said you wanted a baby.'

'Just leave me alone will you!'

'OK. OK.' He turned away from her. 'Whenever you are ready. You tell me, mm?'

It was true. Aware that age was a factor, she had not gone on the pill, although they had been using condoms, electing to wait until they were settled in their new home. But sometimes they took risks, deciding that pregnancy wouldn't be a disaster.

He was determined to keep his temper. The following day, he brought her flowers, a big bunch of tightly curled Tenerife roses, red, white and pink. She found a vase for them and put them on the table. Almost immediately they began to open up in the heat. She softened towards him, kissed him. He cooked a chilled tortilla with fresh herbs for their evening meal and they opened a bottle of wine. But then he had to go out to work and by the time he came in, it was after midnight. She had finished the bottle of wine alone, and it hadn't really helped.

'You drink too much,' he said in the morning. 'It's always the same with you English.'

'Will you stop calling me English. Would you like it if I called you Italian, German, French?'

She felt sick and thirsty and she had a thudding headache, practically a migraine.

'Well, Scottish then. So much cheap alcohol. You can't handle it. It is a terrible thing in a woman.'

She rose to the bait. 'It's no more terrible in a woman than in a man.'

'Of course it is. It's much worse. If you can't see that then you're stupid. But then all women are more stupid than men. So it's only to be expected, isn't it?'

He had the peculiarly Latin failing of making outrageous and provocative assertions, saying things he didn't believe at all, simply to score a point in the heat of an argument. Usually, he wanted to withdraw these declarations moments after he had made them, but that never stopped him from doing it again, no matter how much he regretted it at the time. Later in the marriage, she would laugh at him whenever he did this and he would laugh with her. He knew when he was behaving disgracefully. Now, though, she was speechless with suppressed anger.

They had not made love for a fortnight. They had hardly touched each other. She had begun to avoid his eyes, to avoid touching him in passing. On her next day off work, she suggested a picnic at Adeje.

'You mean the *Barranco del Infierno*?'

'Yes. I've wanted to go there for ages.'

'Oh, Margarita. I'll be cooking in the restaurant until four today. That'll be too late to go. It's very beautiful though. We'll go but let's make it some other time.'

'That's all you ever say. That isn't what you said when we first met, is it? Oh, come out with me, Margarita. Let me take you up the mountain in my car, Margarita!'

'I have to work. Can't you understand that I'm working only for us?'

'Can't you understand that I'd rather you took my money and gave me your time!'

'But soon you can have all the time you want. We'll be together on La Gomera.'

'And working hard at something else. It's unreasonable. Take my money. Ease up on the work. We'll spend a little while together now and then take over the restaurant in the autumn or whenever Paco and Carmen are ready to move.'

'What would people say?'

'To hell with what people say.'

He tried to put his arms around her, but she pushed him away.

'Fuck you,' she said. She seldom swore and he never did, or not in her hearing, anyway. She knew it would shock him and it did, but he still smiled.

'I'd rather fuck *you*,' he said.

'Oh go to hell.'

If she embraced him, if she gave in to him, as she so often did, he would win the argument. But what was the argument? she wondered, her brain addled by heat.

'Margarita, *mi niñita*,' he said gently, with an understanding that irritated her even more. 'Listen, it isn't just me. I know. It's the Sirocco. That's what is doing this to you. And I know it isn't easy for you or for me to have to live with somebody else again.'

If there had been anywhere to go in the flat she would have flounced out of the room. It seemed foolish to flounce into the bedroom, however, and he might come after her. So she went into the bathroom instead, locking the door behind her, intending to take another shower. A half dead cockroach lay on the white tiled floor. It brought her out shrieking for his assistance. He disposed of it, trying to hide his smile. Then she went back to her shower. She had expected him to have gone to work by the time she came out, but he was waiting for her.

'Perhaps we can go out tonight,' he said. 'I'm not playing tonight.'

'Perhaps. If I'm back in time.'

'Back from where?'

'From Adeje.'

'Surely you're not going to the Barranco alone? If you wait till next week, I'll come with you, I promise. I'll make sure I have the same day off as you. But I said I'd be in the restaurant an lunch time. We're short staffed. And you mustn't go there alone.'

She shrugged. She had picked up the shrug from him. It was a useful gesture.

'Margarita, do you hear me?' he said seriously, catching hold of her arms.

'Yes, I hear you.'

He lost patience suddenly. He had only a small store of that commodity and her account was definitely overdrawn.

'Do what you like,' he said. 'Go to hell if you like!'

He went out of the flat, his face cloudy with suppressed anger. She watched him go with mixed feelings of satisfaction that she had finally provoked him into anger and despair at herself.

Oh, my dear, she thought. Why am I doing this to you when I love you so much? Why am I behaving like this?

CHAPTER TWENTY

One of these, the Barranco Infierno, from its great depth and narrowness is considered an object worth visiting. Its entrance, formed of two huge rocks, like gates, opens on the flat, cultivated plain surrounding Adeje.

Olivia M Stone, 1887

She stayed in the flat until lunchtime but the place seemed more and more unbearable. Every day she swept the tiled floors clear of the sand that blew in. Every afternoon, she would see the same fine layer of grey-black volcanic dust covering the shiny surfaces again. She got out the sweeping brush, a thin inadequate affair – typically Spanish, she thought crossly – and began to sweep the dust away. Even as she swept, it was blowing in again. She could feel it, gritty and horrible, on her skin. She gathered together fruit, bread, cheese and a bottle of water, stuffed them into a tote bag and, locking up the flat, ran down to the car park behind the apartment complex. As she thought, Luis hadn't taken the car, preferring to walk to the restaurant. She had a set of keys in her bag.

She slid into the driver's seat, so hot that she felt it burn her thighs through her shorts, and drove up towards the main road around the island. Less than half an hour later, she found herself in the expanding town of Adeje, from which the long *Barranco del Infierno*, the gorge called Hell's Valley, ate into the mountainside. Luis had told her that the *barranco* contained one of the few permanent streams on the island and the waterfall at the inner end of it was a novelty in this place. Most of the *barrancos* ran with water after the occasional rainstorms, especially in the wet season (which was never very wet by Scottish standards) only to dry up again a few days later.

She drove up the main street of Adeje, slumbering now in the *siesta* heat of the day. She parked the car in a quiet side street and, shouldering her bag of provisions, began to walk uphill out of the town. A couple of old men drank Dorada beer and played cards in a sheltered doorway, an elderly woman watched a small boy playing in the dust with a fat, panting puppy. Each one she passed nodded and smiled, giving her greeting. '*Hola senora!*'

Presently she came to a signpost with directions to the *Barranco del Infierno*, up Calle de los Molinos, Windmill Street. Just past the last house in the village, she went through a gate and was on the path that wound along the walls of the ravine towards the waterfall that lay at its farthest reaches. She hoped that it would be green and cool in there. She deliberately hadn't left a note for Luis and she saw that her phone had no signal.

Serve him right if he's worried, she thought, still fired by unreasonable anger.

She noticed that the wind had dropped; the air was more still than it had been for days. There was just a breeze now and then, hot to be sure, but not sandy. The *barranco* lay baking under the afternoon sunshine with an almost unnatural stillness about it. She had a guidebook, bought optimistically on her first visit to the island, though she and Alastair had certainly done no walking then. The hike was supposed to be an easy one and would take some two hours, perhaps a little more, there and back. She wore flat canvas shoes, shorts and a T-shirt and carried a light sweater, just in case by some miracle it got cooler later on. She looked at her watch and was surprised to see that it was already four o'clock. *Siesta* would be over. The shops and restaurants in Los Cristianos would be opening up again for their evening's trade.

Luis would be home by now, looking for her. Worrying. She felt a pang of remorse but put it firmly out of her mind.

At the start of the path she looked down into the ravine where it fell below the level of Adeje, dry here because the water had been diverted higher up the hill into a channel that eventually irrigated the plantations of the town. Her way lay up and to the left. She saw small black tails disappearing beneath stones and realised with a start of surprise not altogether pleasant that the hillside was full of lizards, creatures that had been startled out of their afternoon *siesta* by her approach. She was relieved to see that they were afraid of her, diving out of her way, each with a flick of its tail.

The path was well marked; this was obviously a popular tourist haunt. There were vast clumps of prickly pear such as she had seen on La Gomera, and the ubiquitous *tabaiba* and her namesake *margarita* growing beside the path.

After a while, she became aware of the sound of running water again and found that she was walking alongside the channel that carried the stream down to the village. In spite of the dry weather in Los Cristianos, it rained from time to time in the mountains and the townspeople of Adeje made use of this bounty. Her route crossed and recrossed the gravelly stream bed, although she couldn't remember afterwards where the running water ceased to be merely a man-made channel and became an actual stream, gurgling along beside her.

Most of the people she met at this time of day were walking back in the direction of Adeje. There was a voluble party of German tourists accompanied by several hairy dachshunds. They had stopped at a look-out place to drink beer and water and eat a picnic. She met a tall man and woman, obviously lovers, lagging behind the rest. The man was wearing a sleeveless T-shirt and his face was dripping with sweat. The tour guide had been keeping up a spanking pace. Now the couple stood still in a clearing among bushes. Just as Margaret passed them, his companion made him lift his arms above his head and then wriggled the shirt off him, like a mother with a large and cumbersome baby.

Very gradually, she began to realise that there were no other people heading inwards towards the waterfall and all those she met were returning. The air was preternaturally still after the turbulence of the past weeks. High up in the dazzling sky, pale with heat, she saw a bird of prey. She couldn't identify it at this distance, but only saw it circle and spiral above her, hovering for a moment and then circling lazily downwards again.

She was aroused by an outburst of furious squeals and saw two lizards engaged in a battle. Not wanting to witness the inevitably bloody outcome, she pressed on. Soon she reached the stream and then she was criss-crossing the water on flat stones, as it flowed over gravel. She realised how much she had missed the sound of running water on stone, so commonplace in Scotland, so unusual here. Sometimes there were deeper pools fringed with ferns and green bushes that she couldn't identify, although she knew which were willows. Flowers bloomed here and there and the bushes seemed to be full of penetrating birdsong. They sounded like blackbirds, but she couldn't be sure. She paused, sitting down on a tussock of real green grass. It was almost six months since she had been at home and she realised that this place bore a striking resemblance to any bushy valley in her country. Only when she looked up to the jagged volcanic cliffs, folding her ever closer and closer, did she know that it was not, and never could be, like Scotland. The stream with its green margin was an enticement, the noise of the water a siren song, leading her inwards towards the narrow defile that lay at the far end of the *barranco*.

She passed one more group of tourists making their way back to Adeje and then, save for the occasional cadence of birdsong, all was completely still, completely silent ahead of her. She looked at her watch. It was past five o'clock. She should just be able to see the waterfall, eat her sandwiches, turn around and quickly make her way back to the car before darkness fell. Except that she could not go quickly at all, because although the path itself was good, its edges often crumbled away to nothing and the drop below was precipitous, edged with dangerous prickly pear and scree, so it would have to be a careful walk back, imminent darkness or no. She had not thought to bring a torch. She considered turning around and making her way back right now, but she knew that she would have to confess to Luis that she had given up. Her pride wouldn't let her do it. She was learning from him about matters of pride and honour.

She heard again the calling of birds deep in the thicket, and sat down beside one of the pools to drink from her water bottle. Sometimes the path divided into two but because the gorge at this spot had become so narrow there was no possibility of getting lost. The cliffs were looming ever closer, green on their lower slopes, rocky and barren higher up, with darker patches that might be caves. Above her, at the negotiable head of the gorge, it was possible to see where a green, isolated valley continued at a higher level, but only a mountaineer would be able to get up there to explore its narrow interior. She knew from her guidebook that funeral caves of the original inhabitants of the islands had been found, high up on these precipitous walls. She imagined them, the Guanches, making the long procession inwards along this route, a procession of mourning or celebration, or both. How had they got up there, she wondered? Had there been ladders of a sort? Rope ladders perhaps? The bodies had been mummified, an indication that these earliest inhabitants had migrated from North Africa, long ago. Some said that the Spanish conquerors had killed all the original inhabitants, taking over these fertile islands. But that couldn't be the whole truth. She thought there must have been intermarriage. There always was. The mix was clearly visible even now, in these tall, handsome, Canarian people, like Luis and his family, as well as in the language, that was different from mainland Spanish. It was especially obvious in so many of the customs: the use of *gofio*, the *astia* and the whistled language. Men fought, she thought. But men and women? That was a different matter: a fertile land with handsome, fertile women. Cultures mixed. Blood mixed. When all was said and done, the urge to create life was stronger than the urge to kill. Sometimes only marginally so. But it won out in the end. Which was just as well.

As that thought entered her head, she looked up and back and then all around her, feeling the tingling in the spine and in the back of the neck that is a primitive intimation of being watched. She scanned the dizzying cliffs again but could see nothing and no one. Reluctantly now, she went on. I'll just snatch a quick look at the waterfall, she thought, and then turn around and come straight back out.

The abyss into which she was walking grew darker and cooler. The low sun could no longer find its way in here. The cliff walls had begun to lean together, to lean in on her. As she paused, on the threshold of shade, she thought that she heard, somewhere in the valley behind her, a vivid melodic whistling like the *silbido*, but it faded as quickly as it had come and she couldn't be sure that she had really heard it or perhaps just imagined it. With the sun gone, the rocks themselves seemed to exude a chill that made her shiver. She put her sweater on, glad that she had brought it.

At last, she was within the gloomy precincts of the 'Gate of Hell': the sheer rock walls glistening with damp, leaning inwards to form a triangle, blotting out the last of the light, blotting out the sky itself, the hot blue-white sky with its wheeling bird of prey. The cavern was full of the sound of water, tumbling in a graceful fall from a narrow outlet high above. It formed a pool, a cold, enigmatic eye from which the sunny stream below was born. This was a sacred place, the heart of the island perhaps. Those first inhabitants had realised its significance and had brought their dead here to a place close to the other world, the world of which we are only dimly aware when it spills over into this one. She sank down on the cold stones and rested her head in her hands, trying to clear it of the whirling miasma of lights that seemed to be filling her brain.

She didn't know how long she sat like that, listening to the pounding of her heart in her ears, trying to still the tremor in her limbs. What was it about the landscapes of this island that so alarmed her? First Teide, now this. It's nothing, she thought. Nothing at all but the heat. There's nobody here but you and the birds and the lizards. When she lifted her head, contrary to her expectations, it seemed even darker in the cavern, though she knew that the light outside couldn't yet be failing.

She didn't hear his footsteps above the incessant sound of water but, as she got to her feet and moved towards the entrance, she saw him looming over her as he had loomed that day on Teide, silhouetted against the light, and all those first fears came rushing back to her. In that instant she thought that she had married a stranger, through some irresistible impulse that was to do with the islands themselves, with the sensual compulsion locked into them. She put out her hand as though to ward him off, as she had that first day on Teide. He recognised the gesture and halted.

'Margarita. Thank God you're safe. I thought I was wrong after all. I thought you weren't here.'

'What are you doing here?'

'I came looking for you. I saw you had gone. Taken the car. So I followed. Well, I hoped I knew where you were.'

'How?'

'How?' He was momentarily at a loss. 'Oh – *how*?' He laughed. 'I hitched a lift on a banana lorry.'

He came inside, into the cold air of the ultimate point of the *barranco*, the air that was continually fretted and disturbed by the spray from the cascade of water.

He said quietly, 'The Sirocco is almost over. It will go tonight, I think.'

He came and stood before her. He seemed to her confused perceptions to be taller than usual and altogether bigger. Like a stranger, she thought again. His brown eyes shone, impenetrable in the gloom, brown eyes that cast everything back at her, like the pool. He made as if to take her in his arms but she stepped away from him. He was hot from climbing the *barranco* so quickly and fiercely in pursuit of her. He had shed his T-shirt and wore only soft blue jeans. His skin glistened with a fine film of sweat.

'Why did you come after me?' she asked.

'I was worried about you. I couldn't stay at home, worrying.' He spread his hands, then impulsively held them out to her. 'Oh, let me love you,' he murmured, so quietly that she could hardly hear his words above the pounding of water. She reached out to him and he pulled her close.

'Here?' she asked.

'Yes. Why not? There's no one here. And no one will come at this time, I promise. There was no-one behind me. Nobody at all.'

She shook her head and turned away as if to leave the cave, but he caught her hand again.

'Please.'

He pulled her gently back inside the cavern, deep inside to where the rock floor was smooth and shiny and damp.

'Here,' he said. 'Here. Let me love you here, please.'

There was a sudden silence between them. They stood, hands joined, arms extended. She caught his gaze, saw the desire in his eyes, felt her body responding to him.

'Here?' she echoed.

'Why not?' His voice was a whisper. Pleading with her. 'I beg you,' he said.

All at once, she capitulated, moved towards him. Moved into the circle of his arms again.

With a sudden, swift movement he swept her off her feet and laid her down, quite gently. She felt cold stone beneath her, watched his face, hovering above her.

'Please,' he said again. 'Please, please. I love you so much.'

He bent and kissed her, his tongue in her mouth.

Perhaps it was the sudden familiarity of him, the scent of his body, the taste of him. Perhaps it was the place too, numinous, implacable. Ancient and sacred.

Desire flashed through her. He was pulling her sweater and T-shirt over her head. She unfastened her shorts and he pulled them off. She felt her naked body chilled by the wet floor, the cool air and the cooling perspiration on its upper surface. He had thrown her clothes in a heap and now he was tearing at his own in the same frantic way as though it was essential to be completely naked. She lay on her back, seeing the dark precipice spinning and turning above her, half obliterated by his head. In a moment of utter stillness, she saw his face above hers and she looked into his eyes.

'Yes,' she said. 'Oh yes!'

He was on top of her and she felt the cool of the rock beneath her and the intense warmth of his body covering hers.

She was seized with a fierce overriding passion, a rekindled desire for him. Perhaps the place itself exerted a chemistry on them both which they were quite powerless to control, as though some ritual in which they were participants was taking place, because of their presence but in spite of themselves. She couldn't call it possession because afterwards she remembered each sensation so perfectly, but it was as though the place had trapped them for a time and demanded something from them for their release; as though a hand from the past had reached out and demanded payment in its own particular coin. During the whole encounter, they spoke no more words, but she remembered afterwards the sound of their breathing, their panting and groaning above the rushing noise of the water.

She was intensely aroused by him, as though it were some primitive game, as though there were some unspoken complicity between them, a ritual enacted by two willing protagonists. She felt herself rise with him, clambering and struggling to the very edge of sensation. Clearly in her mind she saw herself go hand in hand with Luis and they were leaping from the edge of some dizzy height, together they leapt and cried out, a terrible shout of exultation. She raked her fingers along his cheek, drawing blood. Briefly she saw Luis and herself writhing on the floor of the cave, and then she was falling to rejoin her body again, stretching herself to inhabit it, to feel the whole of it. From her toes to her fingertips she was all sensation and he was with her, his head buried in her shoulder, sobbing uncontrollably.

A little later, it was she who took charge, as though she understood more of the experience than he did, its savagery and wonder.

She took water from the pool and wiped his face where she had cut him. It was a scratch merely, a small wound, the blood already drying.

'Oh lord,' she said. 'What have I done to you?'

'Nothing. It's nothing.'

She took a little hand towel she had brought in her bag and washed his body and her own with it, repeatedly dipping it into the cool, clean water like a benediction. In near silence, they dressed and then crept away down the empty *barranco*, hand in hand. Even where the path was at its most treacherous and narrow, their hands seemed welded together. Each was reluctant to sever that contact between them. It was beginning to grow dark now and they knew that neither of them would have wanted to spent the night in that place, even together. Who knew what spirits of the island might reclaim the place by night?

Half way down, and when they were well clear of the green ravine, and could see open country below, they stopped and sat close, side by side on a rock.

'I'm sorry,' he said.

'What for? You did nothing wrong.'

'I felt out of control. I felt as though I could have hurt you.'

'But you didn't.'

'I've never felt like that before. Never.'

'Me neither. But I wanted it as much as you, Luis.'

'Are you sure?'

She saw that there were tears on his cheeks. She pulled him close and kissed him on his eyelids, on his lips. She felt his hair soft beneath her fingers.

'Of course I'm sure. But I think it was the place as much as us. Don't you?'

'Maybe. Yes. Maybe so.'

She had brought with her a small melon that smelled of strawberries. They gouged pieces out of it with a butter knife and ate greedily of the sweet, clean fruit, feeling better for it, tired and sated.

They reached Adeje just as darkness was falling. Behind them, thunder was beginning to rumble among the mountains, to be quickly succeeded by lurid flashes of blue lightning leaping from hill to hill. Even before they reached the car, the rain was already falling in huge droplets and the clean scent of slaked earth was beginning to rise all around them. They sat in the car for a while, feeling protected and close, and listened to the longed-for sound hammering on the roof. Then Luis drove home, carefully, down slippery roads.

She was very tired, but Luis couldn't sleep. He undressed her tenderly, and searched her back for bruises, still worried that he might have hurt her. But he found none, save perhaps for the very faint marks of his fingers on her arms, and even that might have been his imagination.

'My darling, you didn't hurt me,' she said. 'You didn't hurt me at all. If anything, I hurt you. Don't worry about it. I wanted it. I wanted you.'

He had frightened himself. He sat up for hours with his arm

around her, alternately watching her as she slept and staring at the faint luminous glow of his own reflection in the mirror opposite. He felt clean and empty, as though something had turned him inside out like an old sack and shaken him very vigorously.

CHAPTER TWENTY ONE

I have in my bosom
a little chair made of glass.
Who will sit down there?
My lover must surely come.

Things improved between them after Adeje, though sometimes she wondered if it might be a remission rather than a complete cure. She told her mother a little of her feelings when Luis was out of the flat.

'You have to give it time,' said Annie, speaking to her online. 'It takes time for a marriage to settle down, you know.'

'I do know. But I sometimes think it's because I love him *too* much. It overwhelms me. I have to back away. I'm afraid of losing myself. Does that make any sense?'

There was a long pause. 'Aye, it does,' said Annie. 'It makes sense to me.'

'Did you feel like this with dad?'

'Not with your dad, no. Oh, I loved your dad dearly, but not like that. Not madly like that. But I know what you mean.'

So who, Margaret thought. Who did you love madly like that? And when? But she didn't say it, couldn't ask. It seemed too intimate, too intrusive.

'And you'd better hold fast to that, hen, because it only ever comes along once in a blue moon,' said Annie, but didn't choose to enlighten her daughter further.

Margaret still sold property. Luis still went out most evenings, playing in restaurants, and worked for his friends through the day, mostly prepping, sometimes going to the market for vegetables or seafood.

A few weeks after Adeje, she began to feel very strange. It was a sensation she had never felt before, which made it all the more alarming. She could only describe it as a feeling of dissolution, disintegration at once physical and spiritual, as of some vast upheaval taking place within her. This was accompanied by a daytime fatigue so profound that she felt as though she had been drugged. Paradoxically, she found it hard to sleep at nights and lay awake for hours.

'It isn't too hot for you now, is it?' Luis asked.

'No. But I feel quite ill.'

'How ill?'

'I don't know. Very odd.'

'You'd better see a doctor.'

'Soon. I'll go soon.'

She wondered if she were sickening for something. She couldn't have described the way she was feeling in her own language, let alone made it clear to Luis in his. Certain foods and wines made her feel much worse, as though she were at one remove from the world, no longer fully at home within her own body. She dropped things: glasses, cups, boxes of eggs. Her dreams became even more vivid and profoundly disturbing. Once she tripped up in the street and fell down and had to be picked up, much to her shame, by two holidaymakers.

'I'm not drunk,' she kept saying, confusedly. 'Honestly, I'm not drunk.'

They were a kindly English couple. 'No,' they said. 'We can see that, dear.'

At home, Luis bathed her grazed knees tenderly and put ointment and sticking plaster on them.

'What have you been doing to yourself?' he asked. 'You must watch where you're walking. Our pavements are terrible.'

A little while after this, she realised that her period was late. It had been due two weeks after the trip to the barranco and she was usually regular. She said nothing to Luis, excitement vying with fear of disappointment. They had used no protection at the Barranco. Every trip to the lavatory became a nervous investigation, but still no sign came and the oddness of her feelings, surely explicable now, was always with her. Eventually, unable to stand the suspense and unsure of how to ask for a test in the Pharmacy, with thoughts of Bridget Jones in her mind, she visited the English-speaking doctor who had bound up her sprained ankle.

He was very late for his surgery that day and she had to wait for him in the street, along with two Spanish ladies: one elderly with swollen, ulcerated legs, the other much younger and rather pretty. The girl passed the time by singing songs to herself in a tuneful, husky voice, the older lady making occasional and obviously admiring comments on her performance. Margaret was so entertained by them that she didn't mind the wait on the dusty steps. She smiled at the two women and they smiled back.

When the doctor arrived, he remembered her and asked about her ankle.

'It's fine thank-you.'

'Then what's your problem?'

'I was wondering ... could I be pregnant?'

'Ah, I see!' He looked at her hopeful face and smiled. 'But you could have bought a test. You didn't need to see me for that!'

'I didn't know what to ask for and I didn't want my husband to know until I was sure.'

'Your husband?' he said, a little surprised, clearly remembering the last time he had seen her.

'Yes. I'm married now.'

'Are you indeed?'

'To the man I was with that day. Luis.'

'Luis Herrera Garcia. The musician. I've heard him play, here in Los Cristianos. He's very good.'

'He's a fine musician. And a good man.'

'Ah yes. And a good man is hard to find. That is what my English teacher used to say. And now you think you could be pregnant?'

'Maybe.'

'Will this be a good thing for you? Is it what you want?'

He was Spanish and to him, a child in such circumstances could be nothing but a blessing, but he was perceptive enough to know that it wasn't always so for the woman involved.

'Oh yes, yes,' she said. 'I do hope so. We both want a child. But you never know, do you?'

'How old are you, señora,' he asked?'

'Thirty five. It's a bit old, I know.'

'Not really. Not these days. But is this the first child?'

'Yes. I was married before. We had no children.'

'Did you try?' He shook his head. 'I apologise if these questions seem intrusive but I must ask, so that I can advise you.'

'No, no, it's fine. We didn't try. I was on the pill for a while. Then we used other protection. But this time ...'

'You want a child.'

'We both do. We thought we might wait a little while, but we'll be very happy if it's positive.

'Women like to think about their careers. My wife certainly does. You have nothing to worry about. You're just at the very edge of the age when risks increase but it's negligible. You need to take good care of yourself, that's all. I expect you will.'

'Oh I certainly will.'

'Well, before we think about anything else, let's do a test, shall we? Then you can come back and see me.'

She found his words very comforting and took her sample up to the next-door clinic with a note from the doctor. That same afternoon, after *siesta*, and while Luis was still at work, she went back to the clinic where the white-coated technician handed her a piece of paper in a brown envelope. She gazed at it blankly, barely able to read it. Then she looked at the girl's impassive face.

'*Si* or *no*?' she asked.

The girl looked momentarily confused, but then her face broke out into a dazzling smile.

'*Si*,' she said. '*Si, señora.*'

It was one of those crazily busy days. Luis was going straight to the venue where he sang, from the restaurant where he was cooking. He would come in exhausted, but the playing seemed to help him to wind down from the frantic cooking. She prepared and ate a salad. Wine would be off her menu for a long time now but she didn't mind. It had been making her feel queasy for a couple of weeks. Even the thought of it was revolting. Wine and coffee both. She walked down La Paloma and sat watching him play. He seemed surprised and delighted to see her there.

'You don't often come these days.'

'I should come more often. I do love to listen to you.'

They walked home, linking arms. She thought he must be able to feel her happiness through her arm.

'What's wrong?' he said at last, stopping, turning her towards him.

'Nothing's wrong. But I went to the doctor today.'

'What's the matter?'

'Nothing. Everything's just as it should be. I'm pregnant.'

He stood still, absolutely speechless for a moment, then he let out a whoop of joy and hugged her.

All the next day he kept looking at her over and over again as though he couldn't quite believe it.

'You could stop work if you wanted,' he said.

'No way. I'd go mad, alone at home all day. Besides, I'd only worry.'

'What is there to worry about?'

'Oh, about the birth. About the baby. Everything. I'm not ill, you know. There's no reason at all why I shouldn't work. Everybody does.'

'But you're tired.'

'It'll pass. I'll be fine.'

She wasn't troubled by regular morning sickness, although occasionally, if she was sitting in a warm place with too many people, she would feel nauseous and dizzy. Once or twice, waiting for Luis in a crowded restaurant, she felt the need to fight her way towards the door and breathe in fresh air.

'Are you staying here for the birth or are you going home to England?' asked the doctor when she saw him again so that he could take her blood pressure, arrange for a scan.

'Scotland,' she corrected him automatically but without committing herself either way. She hadn't made up her mind yet. Luis wanted her to stay. Fiona and Ian, who seemed shocked by the news, thought she should go home. Her mother said she ought to make up her own mind.

'After all, you don't know what maternity services are like there, do you?' Fiona said, speaking close to the telephone as though somebody might be listening.

'I think they're very good,' said Margaret cheerfully. 'I see lots of healthy babies round here, so they must be doing something right.'

'Your mum wants you to come home. She worries about you.'

'She says I should make up my own mind.'

'Oh well, she would say that, wouldn't she?'

'I'll think about it.'

Fiona had received the news of Margaret's pregnancy with something approaching horror.

'I wonder if she knows what she's letting herself in for,' she asked Ian sourly, over the breakfast table.

'I expect so. I think she wanted kids much more than Alastair ever did.'

'Did she? She never said anything to me about it.'

'Well, she wouldn't, would she?' The words were out of Ian's mouth before he could stop himself.

'Why not?' Fiona asked, indignantly. 'I would have thought she'd feel able to confide in me. Besides, Alastair changed his tune quickly enough, didn't he?'

Ian focused on his wife. He had been on his laptop, reading a long email from Margaret. It had arrived the morning, after she had phoned them with the news.

'I suppose Alastair wanted kids but just not with Maggie. It happens.'

'Hm.' Fiona was noncommittal.

'Anyway, children, that kind of decision, it's very private.'

'It's such a permanent decision. That's what worries me.'

'What do you mean?'

'Much harder to back out. Once you have children. If it all goes wrong.'

'Fiona, why are you so convinced it's all going to go wrong?'

'Well, aren't you?'

'I don't know. No. If I'm honest. I don't think so. She seems very happy. Ecstatic, really.'

'Oh you would say that. You're a man. You can't read between the lines.'

Ian scanned the email as though searching for a literal subtext but it yielded nothing more than his sister's intense happiness, which her new husband seemed to share.

'She seems fine to me.'

'She just doesn't know what she's letting herself in for.'

'Did we? Does anybody?'

Rory burst into the room demanding to know where his football boots were.

'Where you left them,' said Fiona, automatically. Rory went out, muttering. She turned her attention back to her husband. 'I wonder if she'll come home for the birth?' She poured more tea.

'I thought she said no, she wouldn't. That's what she says in this email. Planning to stay. There's a good doctor.'

'She might change her mind.'

'Why should she?'

'She'd be better having the baby over here,' said Fiona stubbornly. 'You don't know anything about it.'

'What does mum think?'

'She says Margaret will just have to do what she and Luis decide. Make up their own minds. You know what she's like.'

'Then that's just what they'll have to do, isn't it?'

CHAPTER TWENTY TWO

We gladly turn to the luxuriance around. The scents are delicious; it is impossible to tell whence they come, for every plant seems to be giving out perfume, save perhaps the immense magnolias, which reserve theirs for night.
Olivia M Stone, 1887

Margaret was well for almost the whole of her pregnancy, but by no means serene. She wouldn't have believed that something so natural could play such havoc with her emotions. Her mother understood though.

'It doesn't take much to knock you off your perch at a time like this,' she told her daughter. 'And let's face it, you were only just getting used to living with another person. It's bound to be a bit of an upheaval.'

The doctor assured her that everything was going smoothly, but she was prey to many doubts and fears. She had seen so many of her friends producing their offspring, some of them, so it seemed to her envious eyes at the time, as easily as shelling peas. But she knew now that she had been wrong. No matter how unmoved and serene a face you presented to the world at large it was never so easy. Luis was deeply sympathetic, but he could hardly make the imaginative leap into the turmoil of her mind. She didn't blame him for it. She had not even been able to put herself in another woman's place, so how could he? She knew it was mostly down to her hormones, but that didn't make it any easier. Luis would recognise the occasional panic in her eyes and he would fold her in his arms until it was over.

'I know,' he would say. 'I know, *querida*. I have seen my sisters the same, especially Isabel. I know.'

She loved him for his sympathy, but she also knew that Luis couldn't think himself into her head, couldn't understand what lay behind her unpredictable behaviour. It was a solid wall of fear, impassable as the cliff wall of the *Barranco del Infierno*. Fear of pain. Fear for herself. Worse, much worse than that, fear for the baby. As the weeks went by, she understood more intimately than she ever had before that the phrase to 'give birth' implies a risk of death, unusual these days, but present, a link with all those other mothers down the years. Mostly she was happy, enjoyed her pregnancy tremendously, the deep, undeniable womanliness of it, enjoyed the little attentions she received as soon as her condition became apparent and the novelty of each new development within her body. There were other times when uncertainty threatened to drag her down. On those occasions she clung to Luis.

He would stroke her hair and sing her lullabies in a voice like honey.

'*Arrorro niña chiquita, arrorro!*'

Ever since that evening in Adeje she had felt free to take the physical initiative with him. She would turn to him in the night, slipping her arms around him, delighting in the sensation of his body against hers. It was she who kissed him, inveigled her warm tongue into his mouth, she who made love to him. He took pleasure in it too, but as the months progressed and her body grew bigger, she saw him begin to withdraw from her and she found herself wondering if he didn't like this new self that the *Barranco del Infierno* had shown her.

Had she known it, rather the reverse was true. He liked it too much. Had they spoken about it she would have known, but they didn't speak. They hadn't yet learnt to whistle across the valleys to each other, to understand each other's language enough to avoid misunderstandings. That would take time.

The problem for him was that, as her pregnancy advanced and become more obvious, his desire for her warred with his innate respect for her condition. He hadn't expected to feel like this, but it had all happened so quickly and he felt overwhelmed by events. There was a primitive part of his mind that cautioned him about touching her, made him fear damaging the child above all things. The doctor's reassurances made no difference, for it was not rational. She seemed vulnerable to him. He was afraid of hurting her or hurting the baby in some way. Nothing was more calculated to dampen his feelings.

Then he would feel angry, not with her, but with himself, and impatient with other people at work. There was nothing to it, this anger. It was quickly over and done. He knew that it bothered her. She had told him that her first husband had been quite capable of not speaking to her for days at a time.

'Days?' he kept repeating, incredulously. 'You're joking.'

'No I'm not. He could sulk for Scotland if he didn't get his own way.'

'*No lo creo*. But how can he do it?'

'Very easily.' His disbelief and astonishment made her laugh but it hadn't been very funny at the time.

'How can he possibly live with you in the same house – *you* of all people – and not speak to you for whole days at a time? I could never do it! I can hardly do it for five minutes!'

She gazed at him. 'I know you couldn't, but *he* could. Quite easily. He had it down to a fine art.'

Alastair would maintain his sullen and speechless demeanour until she felt guilty. Then he could forgive her for something that had been his fault in the first place. He was a great one for the inexplicable strop, the unexplained sulk.

'If you don't know what's wrong, then I'm certainly not going to tell you,' he would say, craftily. She wouldn't know what she had done and he wouldn't tell her. It was enough to drive a person crazy. It almost *had* driven her crazy. She would be reduced to apologising for things she might have done. It was a form of abuse, as real as anything physical, although she couldn't see it at the time, only in retrospect and then with difficulty.

Luis was so much the opposite that he was constitutionally incapable of understanding such behaviour, but he was sensitive enough to see how his occasional volatility disturbed her. The events at the Barranco, which they were both pretty sure had been when the child was conceived, had unnerved him. She always reassured him that things had been different and uncanny that evening; that the place itself had exerted some influence on them that was neither malign nor benign, but simply a force that had manipulated their mutual passion for its own ends, or perhaps for no ends at all.

Her breasts and belly had begun to expand, not softly but with a definite firmness about them. One afternoon in September, after she had been swimming, she lay back at the poolside and felt, quite distinctly, the first butterfly movements of the child inside her. She told Luis and he sat with his hand on her belly, talking to his baby, but it wouldn't respond to him until a few days later when they were in bed together, lying side by side. She took his hand and placed it on the small bump. And there it was, the movement, a subtle flicker through her skin, against his hand. Life. Moving inside her. Later, the child would turn and somersault through the days. They would visualise it like a miniature dolphin or porpoise, already taking pleasure in its own existence.

At the end of October, the weather, which had been pleasantly cool for a week or two, turned hot again. For Margaret, in the sixth month of her pregnancy and growing heavier by the day, it was uncomfortable.

'This is going to be a big baby,' the doctor had remarked on her last visit.

The baby was due in February, and it was November before she could bring herself to give up her job. Even then, it was only because her ankles were swelling whenever she stood for too long and her fingers had become puffy. She had taken to wearing her wedding ring around her neck on a chain. Besides, there were going to be some changes in the office. Stella was leaving. She had been promoted and was going on to better things in the Dublin headquarters of the company. Conor was moving up to a senior sales position. He looked very different now from the lad who had arrived from Glasgow such a short time ago. He wore smart linen suits, his hair was neatly cut, his hands well manicured. He looked, thought Margaret rather regretfully, squeaky clean these days. Niamh too had been promoted. And for two months now, she had been wearing Conor's engagement ring. A new manager was arriving from Germany. Nothing would be the same, and she thought it was finally time to say goodbye to that part of her life.

To Margaret's surprise, her colleagues presented her and Luis with an intricately hand-carved wooden cot. It was beautiful and she could only imagine what it must have cost them, but Conor said he and Niamh had been collecting not just from their colleagues, but from some of Margaret's clients as well. Stella had made a big contribution. It was kind of them and she was moved by the gift.

The doctor had said that she should rest, try to keep her blood pressure down. Luis suggested she go to La Gomera for a while and she found the idea very appealing.

'I'd miss you though,' she said.

'I know, but I'll come over whenever I can.'

Where would I sleep?'

'In Cristina's room like before. She won't mind . I'll phone and ask her. When you get tired of it or when the weather changes again you can come home. Give it a week or two, anyway. My mother will look after you.'

'I'd really like that, Luis. If you don't mind me being away.'

'I always mind you being away, *querida*, but I think this is the best thing for both of you at the moment.' He patted the bump, kissed her.

In the event, she stayed with her in-laws on La Gomera until late

November. In that time she saw Luis for only a handful of days. He spoke to her, when she could get a signal, every day, sometimes twice a day, often from a restaurant where he was working. Maria mothered her, and both Cristina and Isabel gave her their friendship, shy and tentative on the part of Isabel, but with a whirlwind of affection from Cristina. Like her brother, she was an intensely physical person, enthusiastic and impulsive in her likes and dislikes. The weather was mostly very mild, and Margaret sat outside the house among the potted pelargoniums, listening to the musical twittering of the canaries. Sometimes she went for a quiet walk in the early morning or late afternoon, strolling over to feed the goats or down into town to do a little shopping for the household.

She and Maria talked in a mixture of Spanish and English, confiding in each other more, perhaps, than they might have done had each been more familiar with the other's language. Maria told Margaret all about her girlhood on the island and about her own courtship.

'When I was a girl,' Maria said, 'I was helping with my stepfather's small-holding but even though the work was hard and I had very little free time, I went into town sometimes. There was a social club. Dances. The older ladies would act as chaperones, keeping an eye on us all. And that was where I met my Eduardo.'

'Your husband.'

'That's right. He sang to me. Serenaded me.'

'What did he sing?'

She sang softly:

'I know that Maria is your name
but I do not know your surname.
Give me a jug of water
because I am dying of thirst.'

Margaret recognised the song: Luis had sung it to her too, though he had sung 'Margarita' and not 'Maria'.

'What a voice he had then,' Maria said, her face alight with the memory of the young man she had loved, still did love. 'Better than Paco's, I think. Paco was the better musician but Eduardo was such a fine singer. The two of them always went around together. Paco was a bit of a ladies' man until he met Carmen. She sorted him out. But Eduardo was different. Very kind. Very nice. A good man. Luis is like him in so many ways, you know.'

'Maria, this is so romantic!' said Margaret.

'Well it *was* romantic! He always called me *Mariquilla*,' she added, wistfully. 'His butterfly. Even when we were no longer young, he always called me his *Mariquilla*. Isn't it strange – even when somebody has been gone for quite a long time, you still miss them, still find yourself wishing with all your heart that you could see them again. I miss him all the time. It's the small things. I sometimes feel that when I'm here in the house in the late afternoon, I'd give anything for him to come walking through the door like he used to. That sadness never goes away.'

From time to time, Margaret cooked for them all. The family introduced her to more of the local cuisine. There was *gofio* with hot milk for breakfast. She wasn't sure that she liked it at first, but Maria swore that it would be good for her, good for the baby. Their evening meals were often fresh fish, grilled gently in olive oil, with sauces made with tomatoes and olives. She helped to peel and wash vegetables and made salads with olive oil and herbs. She tasted the piquant sauces that went with the fish and meat, although they gave her violent indigestion just now, but she had begun to enjoy the *gofio* porridge. There were pancakes with sweet palm syrup, mild goat's cheese, very fresh, like solidified curds, but smoked gently around the edges to seal the flavour in, and big flat bread cakes called *bollos*.

Down in the town was a shop that sold delicious home-baked biscuits. She would bring bags of them up for the children every few days, including strangely powdery concoctions called *bizcocho fino* that disintegrated on your tongue. She didn't like these much, although the children seemed to be quite fond of them. Another acquired taste, she thought, and probably very like the old style *gofio* that was often eaten in powdered form. For her part, she baked scones or made soups and stews, introduced them to the delights of stovies – potatoes, onions and a little meat, simmered gently for a long time on top of the cooker – and even shortbread. After school she played with the children, beginning to enjoy their company enormously. She no longer found them spoilt. They were just more open and physical than her niece and nephew at home.

They swarmed about her, the girl brushing her hair, pinning and combing it into all kinds of styles, fascinated by its colour and texture, the boy running his toy cars very gently up and down her arms. She taught Marie Carmen to knit and to make pompoms around a piece of card. She found an old fashioned wooden bobbin in a drawer and got her brother-in-law to put some nails around the top so that she could teach the child to make long fine tubes in many coloured wools that could be fashioned into bracelets and necklaces and hair ornaments. She taught them to sing Away in a Manger and she drew London taxis and country tractors as best she could for Miguel. The older boy, Domingo, was more silent and shy, but one day he brought her a bunch of wild flowers, thrusting it into her hands, his face scarlet with embarrassment, and she had a sudden vision of how Luis must have looked at the same age.

She brushed the little good natured dogs until their coats shone, and fed them titbits. Each evening she took her mug of 'English Tea', as they called it, and sat outside with Cristina and they talked, mostly in English, because Cristina wanted to practise. The more Margaret knew of her, the more she found to like in her new sister-in-law. She was gentler than Luis, and yet the same spark of vivid intelligence lit up her lovely face. There was an enthusiasm for life about her that was very attractive. Margaret wondered why she hadn't married, but thought that perhaps she had met nobody compatible on the island. Not yet, anyway. And perhaps she wanted something other than marriage. She couldn't help comparing Cristina's cheerful, loving presence with Fiona's rather fretful company.

One night, as they undressed for bed in the dimly lit room, Margaret turned to find Cristina poised, like a swallow ready for flight, staring at her uncertainly. She thought how beautiful the woman was and how very like her brother. Cristina was tall and straight and slender as a sapling, with the white cotton of her nightdress falling to her brown knees, and her hair lying loose about her shoulders. As Margaret sat down on the bed, her loose pyjama top draped itself around her swelling breasts and the firm bulge where the baby nestled.

'May I?' said Cristina. Margaret nodded, Cristina knelt down and rubbed her hand slowly and gently across the other woman's belly.

'Oh! I felt him. Or her. You don't know yet, do you? Whether it's a girl or a boy?'

'No. We didn't want to know. But he or she moved for you.'

Cristina went to her own bed, while Margaret did the same on the opposite side of the room. After a while she said, 'Goodnight, Cristina. Sleep well.'

She heard the soft rustle of sheets as her sister-in-law stirred.

'What does it feel like?'

'What?'

'To have a baby inside you?'

She didn't know how to answer. At last she said, 'Safe. And real. You know it's never going to be so safe or so real again.'

'Real?' Cristina sounded puzzled. 'I would have thought it would be the opposite.'

'No. It's real. It pleases itself so much, the baby. And yet you know that you're necessary for its survival. Perhaps you'll never be so necessary for anyone again. All those feelings tied up together. As well as love and fear.'

Presently she switched off the lamp and they lay companionably in the darkness. The starlight cast a pale silvery gleam through the small window where they had left the shutters open. Margaret lay there for a long time, enjoying the sensation of the baby moving inside her.

The morning after, Margaret persuaded Maria to let her help clean the house, swabbing the stone flagged floors with bleach and water, polishing the wooden furniture with beeswax, wiping the old, comfortable armchairs, washing curtains and cushion covers and hanging them out to dry in the sunshine: a kind of autumn cleaning. Maria had been unwilling to let her join in at first, but Margaret felt full of energy and they paced themselves, she, Isabel and Maria. The slow, steady rhythm of the house and the family, their work and pleasures, absorbed her. She began to see what Tenerife must have been like before the changes that tourism brought in its wake, before strangers with their all day breakfasts and their English pubs began to outnumber natives in a second relentless invasion, coming so long after that first Spanish conquering of the earlier inhabitants.

She could see in all the women of this family the goodness of heart that she loved in Luis, that she now found herself loving in Maria. They were capable of a thousand unthinking kindnesses. There were inconveniences and discomforts, for sure. The house was a little cramped and dark and always seemed to be too full of children and dogs, as well as adults. Now her rather cumbersome self was added to the melee. Sometimes the babble of sound when they all debated together was deafening, but Margaret was growing used to it, used to the edgy, spirited quality of their conversations, understanding how that too had made Luis the man he was. She was used to them now, even Juan.

Isabel's husband was a thick-set man with a rather surly manner disguising a quiet sense of humour. He had ignored her for a few days, but after the first week, he would place her chair carefully in position for her outside the door each morning.

'He likes you,' said Isabel. 'But he's very shy.'

Margaret had apologised several times for intruding on Cristina's room. Cristina always dismissed her words with a smile, but still Margaret felt guilty. After all, privacy and light were at such a premium and Cristina's room, at the front of the house, was the only place where she was free to be completely herself. It was as pretty as the girl could make it, with clear colours and everything carefully positioned: clothes hung neatly in the wardrobe, the few pieces of jewellery, mostly delicate necklaces and brooches of semi-precious stones, festooning a silver stand. Cristina kept her books here too: old schoolbooks and a collection of paperback novels with a few in English. Margaret guessed that Cristina bought and eagerly read whatever arrived on the island. Or perhaps Luis brought over what he could from Tenerife. She made a mental note to buy her new sister-in-law a Kindle for Christmas. In one corner was a pile of Vogue and other fashion magazines. They dated from a couple of years ago, although some months were missing.

'I have a friend who works at the Parador, at the big hotel. Guests leave them sometimes or give them to her and she passes them on to me. I'm so interested in fashion.'

'No wonder you always look so nice, Cristina. So elegant.'

'Do I? Thank you!'

Margaret wasn't sleeping too well now, and sometimes had to take a nap in the day. At first she had found it very hard to get used to the absolute silence of the nights on this hillside. She missed Luis, wondering what he might be doing.

Luis slept alone at nights and in almost equal discomfort without her. When he had finished playing, he would sit up at the bar and have a drink or two with the staff. Then, to the disappointment of pretty young tourists, he would bow out gracefully. Even before his marriage he had done it for some years, skilfully avoiding casual encounters without giving offence.

'I must go home. I am a married man, *señorita,*' he would say with mock regret, showing his ring. It was what he had always said when he wanted to avoid entanglements, but now it was true. He would wink at the barman and go. He didn't regret it at all. He regretted Margaret's absence much more.

After his wife had been away some ten days, Luis took the ferry over to la Gomera. She was sitting outside the house among the crimson flower heads of the geraniums, inhaling the bitter scent that she found enormously satisfying just now, perhaps because of some quirk of her pregnancy. She felt that she could never get enough of the fragrance and even had to restrain herself from wanting to sample the blossoms. Maria had managed to coax a garden out of the poor soil here. Juan and Isabel were on the terraces that passed for fields, working there with the children. Maria was inside the house, cooking. She had switched off the radio that usually blared out all day, taking the opportunity of the children's absence to please herself, and to please Margaret too, by singing for her.

She was singing songs of La Gomera that recollected events of ages before. Maria was remembering them as she sang, cataloguing them in her mind, refreshing her memory of the words, adapting and embellishing the melodies anew. Margaret recognised them because she had heard Luis singing them. But there were others that he had not sung for her. Most of them were love songs and many of them were sad.

Diecisiete primaveras Isabelita cumplio
cuando los ojos abrio
a su juventud primera.
Era una rubia hechicera

elegante y bien formada

risueña y bien dibujada ...

It was a song all about Isabel, who was seventeen years old, blonde and beautiful in her first youth, bewitching, elegant and well shaped. But she was sold by her father to a much older man.

Margaret was knitting. She had bought wool and needles in a little shop in San Sebastian and had found a pattern for a baby's cardigan in a very out of date woman's magazine, tucked away on Cristina's bookshelf. She wasn't a great knitter and she kept making mistakes and having to take it back, but it didn't seem to matter very much. Nothing mattered very much here. Even *mañana* was a concept that was imbued with too much immediacy. What was it Luis had said? Not today. That was what it meant. She would just finish it another day. She relaxed and drowsed in the sunshine and listened to the magic of her mother-in-law's voice.

She was aroused by a kiss on her forehead so gentle that she raised her hand to brush it away, thinking that it was some insect alighting there. She opened her eyes to see Luis bending over her. Delighted, she reached up and embraced him. He kissed her again and then stood back to look at her, aware of the change in her that just a couple of weeks had wrought. She seemed plumper and rosier and yet paradoxically more fragile, more obviously removed from him, slipping into the remote self absorption of late pregnancy. The child had taken greater possession of her body. She too had felt this over the last few weeks. The baby moved often now, especially when she sat down after walking. Perhaps it was soothed by the motion of her body, and resented the change. It moved even more in bed at night, sometimes with the gentle fluttering she had first recognized but more often with a series of vigorous kicks. Now that Luis was here, she showed him, and he saw with amazement the uncanny rippling across her belly, the skin there beginning to be stretched tight as a drum.

She no longer felt that her body was her own, though she didn't resent the intrusion. With relentless and insistent compulsion, the baby took what it needed and pushed everything else out of the way, but her body accommodated itself willingly, though not always with great regard to the comfort of the original inmate. It was clear to her that the baby was already an independent life, a non-paying guest, making use of all her facilities, a small sea creature inhabiting a world within her world. The mystery and wonder of it, the deep femininity, often brought a lump to her throat. She found it natural now to sit with her hands protectively across her stomach and when she was alone she would talk aloud to the child, telling it to listen, listen to her.

Now that Luis was here, she said, 'Talk to him in Spanish. Talk in Spanish, why don't you?' He spoke softly in his own tongue, his hand on her stomach and his voice warm and sweet. Later that night he sang songs, the melodies his mother had sung, lullabies and love songs, in a voice that was as full of sun as an orange, redolent of growing things and all the scents and sounds of the island.

'Tell me,' said Luis that night, when they lay in bed together. Maria, at her own insistence, had vacated her double bed and gone to sleep with Cristina, giving the couple her bedroom. Little Marie Carmen was sleeping with her parents. 'Tell me, now that you've spent some time here, are you still sure you want to live on this island? Are you absolutely sure that you don't mind coming to live here?'

'Luis,' she said, with absolute truth, 'I can't think of anything I'd rather do. I can't think of anywhere I'd rather live. I can't think of anyone I'd rather be with.'

She fell asleep with his arms around her swollen belly. In the night, they turned the other way round and he was woken by the sudden magical movement of the child, keeping late hours against his back.

CHAPTER TWENTY THREE

I put my hand into a
cup of gold and
took out my lover's heart
which I will never forget.

Luis left a few days later. He had to go back to work. She didn't argue with him. There seemed little point in pressing him yet again to make use of her money, buy the restaurant right away and move to La Manzana Dorada. Besides, things were progressing. Paco and Carmen had put a deposit on their new house in Vallehermoso and were decorating it before moving some of their furniture. A few old wooden items, too big for the new house, would be left behind. Margaret was glad of it. They looked as though they had been in the house for ever: a couple of carved chests, a beautiful big cupboard that smelled of beeswax polish, a Baroque wooden bedstead, a bit florid but clearly an antique.

'Do you want new furniture?' Luis had asked, anxious to please her.

'Not at all. These pieces belong here. Besides, I like the bed. I'll feel like Mrs Zorro in it! We can get new mattresses, maybe redo the kitchen. And I can make new curtains and cushions if we can get a sewing machine.'

'I'll get one. I didn't know you could sew.'

'Oh, you don't know everything about me yet, Luis!'

The restaurant was still open for business, but only for limited hours. Paco and Carmen were winding down and were almost ready to move.

Margaret broached the subject with Maria one day when they were alone in the house, to find that Maria seemed horrified, not so much at the thought of the couple moving to the island immediately, as at the idea of Margaret giving birth to the baby on Tenerife.

'I thought you would surely be going home for a little while. Home to Scotland,' she said. 'When exactly is the baby due?'

'The end of February.'

'Less than three months. Not long. I just thought you would be going to Scotland soon.'

'I was planning to have the baby here. Well, on Tenerife, anyway.'

'But they may not speak your language at the hospital.'

'I speak some Spanish.'

'Yes. But not when you are giving birth. It will all desert you then, believe me.'

'Do you think so?'

'I know so. You'll feel very much alone. I don't think this is a good thing. You should have your own mother, your own family about you at this time.'

'I'll have Luis. And you're my family now.'

Maria still looked anxious. 'We love you very much, and you are one of this family now, it's true. All the same, you would be better to have this first baby at home in Scotland and then come back here afterwards.'

'Why?'

'Well,' said Maria judiciously, 'everything in the hospital here is very good.'

'I'm sure it is.'

'But it is different.'

'I know. But I live here now.'

'Nevertheless, you are not Spanish.' Maria spread her hands expressively. 'I tell you, giving birth is not easy.'

'I know that.'

'No, my dear. You don't know it.' She spoke so firmly that Margaret was forced to take her seriously. 'I know the modern way is to play it down, make it all seem very easy and natural.'

'Well, I was hoping for a natural birth.'

'Yes, but the first time might be difficult.'

'I know that.'

'No. Excuse me, Margarita, but you don't know it. I mean that it will be like nothing you have ever experienced before. No matter how much you have read or heard beforehand, you don't know what it will be like. When I was a girl I saw my mother giving birth, so I was better prepared. I knew more.'

'I've seen films.'

'Oh yes, films. I too have seen films. There are some screams and gasps and a few big pushes or perhaps a great deal of pushing and heaving and then the baby is out and all is sweetness and light. These are films made by men.' She paced the room, more roused than Margaret had yet seen her. 'Listen to me. Listen,' she kept saying. 'I know. I have four children. The second time it was easier and quicker and the third time it was worse all over again, but each time the pain was the same. So I know. And that first time it can go on for so long.'

She paused, remembering.

'Margarita, you cannot imagine.'

'There'll be painkillers if I need them. And besides, I've been doing the exercises and breathing and everything.'

'How can I make you see?' She was speaking in Spanish, but slowly so that Margaret could understand. 'It is so difficult and strange that when it happens the first time it is almost impossible to remember what you have been told. I can't explain it to you. I don't have the words. There is *una conspiración* among women because they have no words to describe the feelings, the pains, the fears. The way it takes you over. So that you don't have the pain. Rather you *are* the pain. Women don't tell because if all goes well, there is the baby at the end and then you forget until the next time. And the men can't say because they don't know. Even if they are there.'

'Luis would be there.'

'But even if they are there, they don't really know because they don't *feel* it. They watch and listen and that is bad, maybe even worse for them, in a way, watching someone you love. But they don't feel and so they can't tell. And then for the woman, of course, it all fades away very quickly. If it didn't I think there would be no more babies. Not after that first one. For many people, anyway. Do you understand me? This is important.'

'You're frightening me.'

'No, no. You mustn't be afraid. It isn't frightening. This is just how it is. You have a baby and you have a lot of pain and then you forget and you get another baby. And you are fine and happy until six months like you are now. Then you begin to remember the pain. It is as if your body has been asleep and then it wakes up and reminds you. Sometimes it is like no pain you have ever had before. Nor would you wish to have it again. Do you understand?'

'But surely,' said Margaret, who had ordered or downloaded all the right books on natural childbirth and had been reading through them, 'Surely it isn't like that for all women every time?'

'No. For some it is very, very easy. A short labour and almost painless. They have a special blessing perhaps. Sometimes if the child is small it's easier. But you can't know what it will be like for you. You should be with people who can speak to you in your own tongue. You should be in familiar surroundings. Once you have a baby – if you decide to do it again – it will be a different matter.'

'Let me have this one first.'

'Exactly.'

'Do you really think I should go to Scotland?'

'I know you should.'

'But what would Luis say? I'm going back to Los Cristianos next week.'

'Would you have to go home to Scotland soon?'

'I think I would. I'd have to be booked into a hospital there. Besides, if I don't go soon, the airline won't take me.'

'Yes. I'd forgotten that.'

'Luis won't like it.'

'If it's for your comfort and peace of mind, he will have to like it.' She took Margaret's hand in hers. 'I'll come with you and tell him. He'll do as he is told. And he won't upset you by being angry. I'll see to that.'

Margaret saw that she had underestimated Maria, thinking her quiet and gentle. She was all that, for sure, but she was also a match for her son. She would be more than a match for any man.

Maria was as good as her word. The following week, much to Luis's surprise, she came over with Margaret on the ferry, staying with the couple for a few nights. It was Maria who broached the subject of Margaret's return to Scotland with her son. She braved his disbelief, then his irritation but finally, hard on its heels, resignation.

'If you think she should go back and she agrees, then that's what must happen.'

He had never been a particularly obedient or biddable son, some-times doing the exact opposite of whatever his mother proposed out of sheer bloody-mindedness, but he had always loved and respected her and he was forced to accept her judgement in this matter, since it was something about which he was so ignorant. Maria lectured him in rapid Gomero that Margaret found well nigh impossible to follow, and when she woke up the next morning to see him eyeing her with a mixture of affection and regret, she knew that Maria had won. She was rather sorry. She had half wanted the baby to be born in Spain as well as being made in Spain and if he had been adamant that he wanted her to stay here, she would have given in. She felt too tired to make any momentous decisions but she thought that her family in Scotland would be relieved.

'At least if the baby's born in the UK it will have dual citizenship – I think,' Ian had said, when he had tried to persuade her to come home. 'Mind you,' he added thoughtfully, 'if a kitten's born in a pigsty, it still doesn't make it a pig. So I'm not at all sure.'

She hadn't known whether to laugh at him or fall out with him.

'This kitten's half Spanish, anyway,' she had replied, very crossly, but she had wondered if he was perhaps only repeating his wife's words. She could well imagine Fiona talking about kittens and pigsties.

Now, by the sheer sincerity of her persuasion, Luis's mother had succeeded where her own family had failed. Implicit in her brother's warnings had been the idea that when the marriage failed, as Fiona was sure it would, she and the baby would be able to come straight home to Scotland with no difficulty. She had scorned this idea, but was there, at the back of her mind, a twinge of misgiving? Scotland no longer felt like home, but how could she think of this small flat with all its associations of holidays and impermanence as 'home', either?

When they had *La Manzana Dorada*, it would be different.

'I'll fix things up,' said Luis. 'I'll go and get you a ticket. When do you want to travel? This week? Next week?'

'You'll never manage to get me a ticket for this week.'

'It's OK,' he said. 'We'll pay the standard fare. You can go to London and from there to Glasgow.'

She heaved herself clumsily up in the bed. 'You can't do that, Luis. I'll wait for a cheaper seat. Honestly. I can wait a bit.'

'If you wait too long, they won't let you on the plane, in case you have the baby in mid-air.' His irritation gave way briefly to amusement.

'I wonder what happens about citizenship then? That might give your Home Office pause for thought.'

'Luis, if you don't want me to go, I won't go at all. This was your mother's idea, you know. If you want me to stay then I'll stay and have the baby here. I don't like the idea of going back without you anyway. And we haven't really talked about it properly, have we? We haven't talked about what's to happen afterwards.'

She took him by the arm, making him sit on the bed next to her. They left too many things unsaid all the time, mostly because of the language barrier.

'What do *you* want me to do?' she asked, again.

He paused, sighed. 'I think my mother might be right. I think you should go to Scotland and have the baby there. I think it would be easier for you. But I must stay here and work.'

'Will you come over for the birth?'

'Yes, of course. I'll come over in good time. I'll come as soon as I can.' He had picked up a tissue from beside the bed and was twisting it round and round, nervously. He began to shred it into tiny pieces. Then he stood up abruptly and dropped them into the waste paper basket. 'Listen, I must go and get your ticket. If you think you can wait just a little, I'll see if I can get you on a direct flight. It would be much better if you could go straight to Glasgow. I have a friend at the airport. I'm sure he can do me a deal.'

Margaret still marvelled at Luis's ability to fix things through the good offices of this or that friend. Whatever the problem, it seemed it could always be solved by 'doing a deal.'

When he had gone out, she got dressed and went through to the living room where Maria had breakfast ready and waiting: fresh bread, preserves, tea and a boiled egg.

'I can't possibly eat all this.'

'Of course you can. You must keep up your strength.'

'Tell me,' said Maria, when they had finished and were sitting together, Maria with a coffee, Margaret nursing a cup of weak tea.

'Tell me, has that son of mine taken you to Candelaria yet?'

'Candelaria? No.'

'To the Basilica. To the church of the Holy Virgin there.'

'No. Why? Should he have taken me there?'

'Oh, yes. If you are going to have a child, you must certainly go there. You have to go and take some flowers and leave them for the Virgin.'

'Will that ensure a safe delivery, then?' she asked, trying to keep the scepticism out of her voice.

'Not always,' said Maria, looking at her severely, daring her to mock. 'But often. And it is worthwhile, is it not? Anything is worthwhile.'

Margarita remembered church services of her childhood, remembered making her First Communion, in a pretty white dress, in an incense and flower scented church. Perhaps a visit to the Virgin might be no bad thing.

'Why is it so special?' she asked.

'There was a miraculous statue of the Virgin Mary. It was washed ashore hundreds of years ago. Many miracles happened, especially for mothers and babies. Then a century ago the statue was washed away again in a storm. Now there is only a replica. A very beautiful replica nevertheless.'

'And do miracles still happen, now that the statue isn't there any more?' asked Margaret.

'Of course they do,' said Maria, very sternly. 'And why would they not? It is our Blessed Mother in heaven who is responsible for the miracles, and not the statue. Through her intercession with her Son. For what son will not listen to his mother?'

Margaret thought of Luis and smiled. 'That's true,' she said. 'I went to a convent school you know, Maria.'

'Then you'll know.'

'Know what?'

'That there are certain places on earth where some spiritual power seems to be concentrated. And Candelaria is one of them.'

'Yes,' said Margaret with a shiver, remembering Adeje. 'Oh yes, I understand that very well.'

Sometimes she wondered if the whole island group were not a focus for some concentration of spiritual power. She knew that the place had a violent and bloody past, but long before the advent of the Spanish conquerors, the ancients had called this archipelago the Isles of the Blest, where the daughters of Hesperus kept watch over the garden of the Golden Apples. Hera's Orchard. Assisted by a dragon, of course. There had to be a dragon. The tourists who came and stayed in their hotels, hardly budging from beside the swimming pools, fancied that they had found paradise in these Fortunate Isles. She too had felt as though she had regained her own lost paradise in the garden of the restaurant on La Gomera. The sunshine had entered into her and she would never be the same again. The scent of oranges was in her head. She would never be rid of it either. Along with her love for Luis. Heart and soul, she thought.

This evening,' said Maria, 'We will go to Candelaria. All of us together.'

'Luis too?'

'Of course. Don't worry. He'll come.'

They went to the Basilica just as the sun was setting. In the town square was a flower market and Margarita bought a large bunch of roses like those Luis was in the habit of bringing for her, and one of carnations. Maria looked on with approval. The Basilica was big and cool, decorated with striking frescoes of the Last Supper and other Biblical scenes. The Madonna herself, remote beside the altar, had the face of a darkly serene doll. She was dressed in sky blue and gold vestments, beautifully bejewelled in the custom of many Spanish Madonnas. She had a crown on her head, a crowned baby in her right hand and a golden candlestick in her left. At her feet was a silver crescent and below the statue were massed banks of flowers, mostly carnations and roses.

At the foot of the altar were buckets of water left there for more offerings of flowers. Many of them were already full and Margaret, slipping easily into old habits, genuflected in front of the altar and put her flowers into one of the empty buckets.

'When you are safely delivered, then you can come back and offer more flowers,' Maria whispered in her ear.

Luis stood back, embarrassed by all this. He didn't take his religion very seriously. Maria had confessed to her daughter-in-law that it was a constant source of worry to her.

'You mustn't worry,' Margaret said. 'He's such a good man, you know.'

Maria's face lit up. 'Yes, he is, isn't he?' She beamed at her daughter-in-law. 'That's true. He's a very good man.'

They knelt before the statue for a few minutes and Maria bent her head in prayer. Margaret did the same thing, wondering what to say. She hadn't prayed formally like this for years. Soon the old familiar words came into her mind. *'Remember, oh most loving Virgin Mary, that it is a thing unheard of, that anyone ever had recourse to thy protection, implored thy help or sought thy intercession and was left forsaken ...'*

She repeated the whole prayer but her thoughts behind the words were less coherent. Help me in my time of need. Make everything turn out right. Let the baby be well and strong. Let my marriage be a good one. All that I hope for. All that he hopes for. Help us. A sudden sentence flashed into her head, profoundly disturbing, from some untapped depths of her subconscious.

'Mother Mary, let me come back to him.'

The words shook her. She hadn't thought that there was any doubt in her mind. The church was very calm, each small movement, as somebody stirred in her seat or knelt down, echoing up to the high ceiling.

Luis knelt beside her, staring at the statue, his mind a million miles away. He was thinking of Scotland with sudden apprehension. He had never been there. She had said that it was a cold place, even colder than London. As she moved, he looked at her and raised an eyebrow.

'Ready?'

She nodded.

'Let's go then.' He helped her to her feet.

In the grotto, to one side of the church, were banks of candles, lit by visitors as offerings. The grotto had been built on to the church, or perhaps incorporated into it. There was a raw stone face with candles arrayed against it. The roof was open to the darkening evening sky, the rock thrown into relief between it and the soft glow of the massed candles. Following Maria's example, Margaret lit candles for herself, for Luis, for the baby, then came out with the candlelight still blossoming behind her eyes, imprinting itself upon everything else for a moment or two.'

'What a wonderful place,' she said to Luis.

'Once a Catholic, always a Catholic,' he observed drily. 'They never let you go, do they?'

'Luis should take his religion more seriously,' said Maria, digging him in the ribs. 'I can't remember the last time I saw him in church. Well, I can. It was at your wedding.'

'I don't have to go to church. We won't argue about it now. Besides, I've already told you that I like this church. If all churches were like this one, I might go more often.'

The church had quietened the child that had been moving and toiling all day. It was already leading its own life with its own rhythms and patterns, self-contained, safe. Did it know where it was? She had read somewhere that unborn children dreamed and she wondered what they dreamed of. Did her own dreams perhaps cross the placenta to penetrate the baby's consciousness, predisposing its character in one way or another? Did it know what was coming? Already she pitied it the loss of its sanctuary, its emergence from the warm, wet cave, subconscious memories of which would subtly pervade its entire life. She knew the light penetrated there only dimly, a red glow when she lay in the sun. Now the baby was sleeping and she felt calm and quiet and very happy.

They drove back to Los Cristianos and then Luis and Margaret went out and walked along the seashore. For once he wasn't working. They sat on the sea wall as they had done the previous spring, before they were married, and watched the yachts again.

'Less than a year,' she said. 'How could so much happen in such a short space of time? My whole life has changed in less than a year.'

'Are you unhappy about that?'

'Of course not!'

'I wish you weren't going away.'

'I wish I wasn't.'

'Then why did you agree?'

'It seemed the right thing. It still does. I just wish you were coming with me.'

'My mother can be very persuasive when she wants.'

'I know. She was so firm about this.'

'Sometimes when I think of you going back to Scotland, I'm afraid.'

'Afraid of what?'

'That you'll go away and decide that all this has been a big mistake and that you don't want to come back to me.'

'Don't be daft. Of course I'll come back to you. You're my husband and I love you.'

'Are you sure you won't wake up and think that all this has been a dream and decide that you must go back to your nice normal life again?'

'My normal life wasn't very nice. I didn't like it much. I love this one.' She patted her stomach. 'Besides, there's somebody else to think of now. I didn't dream this, did I?' She slipped her arm around him, pulled him close, kissed him. But even as she did, she was thinking of her prayer in the Basilica, wondering what had prompted it.

He had bought her a ticket for the following week. She had phoned her mother, who was overjoyed to hear of the change of plan.

'What a sensible woman his mother must be,' Annie had said. 'She sounds so kind.'

Margaret thought of Annie's bungalow with its patch of garden, wretched in winter. She thought of her familiar bedroom with its pink floral wallpaper. She thought of Ian and Fiona. Without Luis to bolster her confidence, would she be strong enough to stand up for herself against the weight of their well-meant disapproval, their certainty of what was right for her? All the way from the shore to the apartment she walked with her arm threaded through his. Why should wintry Scotland seem any more real than Tenerife or La Gomera? Which was enchantment and which reality? Was it an innate Calvinism that dictated the unreality of pleasure as opposed to the authenticity of discomfort?

The night before she left, they made love gently and circumspectly: a warm and kindly coupling. She felt her heart somersault with love for him. How can I even think of leaving him, she asked herself. Then they lay together, miserably sleepless, until finally he got up and made tea and toast for them both.

'I've got such heartburn,' she said. 'But I've got an aching heart. I don't know which is worse.'

He managed to laugh at the feeble joke. He reached across and took her hand.

Her flight was an early one. She had to be at the airport by six o'clock. They set off in the dark, her teeth chattering with misery more than cold. He drove carefully but whenever he could, he reached over and briefly took her hand or patted her knee. Contact. He must make contact while he still could.

In the airport, she kept compulsively checking her handbag. Passport, paperwork, phone.

'It's fine,' he said. 'I love you. Everything will be fine.'

Nothing felt fine at all. He held her close, with the bump between them. Kissed her and kissed her and kissed her. She thought she would die for love of him. She thought she might die without him. Except that there was the baby. His baby. Their baby.

The officials checking passports took one look at her condition and waved her through. She looked back once at Luis's solitary figure as he stood watching her go, but could not look again.

Her flight was full of holidaymakers. The stewardess eyed her bump, suspiciously.

'How long do you have to go?' she asked, as though considering whether to refuse to have her aboard at all.

'Another two months or so.' Margaret spoke in Spanish in a placatory tone. It had the desired effect. The attendant smiled.

'You are expecting a big baby. A big boy, maybe?'

'Maybe. A big Spanish boy. My husband is Spanish, you see. I'm only going back to Scotland to have the baby.'

It was the right thing to say. The attendant was very kind to her after that, bringing her mineral water and a cushion for her back.

Without her, Luis felt as bereft as an abandoned child. He was ashamed of his own misery, ashamed of his reliance on her. It was not manly to feel like this. He got into the car and dashed humiliating tears from his eyes, switched on the radio, turned it up very loud and drove too fast and too aggressively back to Los Cristianos, leaning on the horn at every available opportunity. It gave him a kind of perverse satisfaction to think how angry she would have been if she could have seen him behaving like this.

When he got back to the apartment, he took out his guitar and played for a little while, finding some comfort in the sensation of the old instrument in his arms, in the smooth sounds, in the familiar vibration beneath his fingers. It calmed him. The child would come soon and safely. Their child. He felt a thrill of excitement. A child conceived in love, made in love, born in love.

But what if it wasn't enough?

Later, she messaged to say that they had landed safely in Glasgow, a brief message with many kisses. He went to the restaurant to work, glad of the opportunity to keep himself busy, and ate there when they had finished. That night he sat in the apartment that seemed desolate without her, and got a little drunk – just drunk enough to think that he might be able to sleep. He got into bed with her pillow clutched close against his body. It smelled faintly of her perfume. On the verge of sleep, he was roused by the buzzing of his phone. He fumbled for it on the bedside table.

'It's cold and wet but what's new? I can hear the rain against the window. Everything looks grey. I wish you were here beside me, my darling. I love you. *Te quiero. Te extraño.*'

'*Te quiero. Te extraño.* I want you, I miss you.' He whispered the words into the empty air. 'Please, Margarita, don't forget to come back to me.'

THE END

Acknowledgements

Many thanks to Dolores Torres Medina and her family for so much invaluable information about La Gomera, for recollecting traditional poems and songs of the islands and for much appreciated assistance with translation. Many of these songs can be found in the original Spanish in *Cantares Tradicionales Canarios Uso y Significado* by Francisco J Castro Perez. Some of the later translations are my own.

Posthumous thanks to an enterprising Victorian lady traveller called Olivia M Stone, whose two volumes written about the Canaries in 1883 and 1884 and published in 1887, Tenerife and its Six Satellites, have proved to be an invaluable resource, full of precise and enchanting details, not just about the landscape, but about the people of the Canaries at that time: their way of life, food, dress, customs and music, all lovingly depicted. They contain everything a fiction writer's heart could desire in the way of information.

Chapter headings involve a mixture of traditional Canary Island songs, and quotes from the above books.

Thank-you to Edgar Salsas Boada (our dear T-shirt Boy) for some help with Spanish phrases and expressions and to Martin Hannah who knows about guitars, and gave me the information I needed at exactly the right time. Thanks too must go to the people of *Las Islas Canarias* for proving to be such an enduring inspiration, and to my husband, Alan Lees, whose sailing career took us and later our baby son to these most beautiful islands. A special mention must be made of my late, sorely missed friend Anna Goudie, who first told me how much she loved the story, and last but by no means least, Eileen McKoy, who enjoyed this book and has been waiting for the second book for far too long.

Catherine Czerkawska is an extensively published writer of fiction (novels and short stories) non-fiction, poetry and award-winning plays for BBC radio, theatre and television. Born in Yorkshire, of Polish and Irish parentage, she has spent most of her life in Scotland, with time also spent working in Finland, Poland and the Canaries.

Her many novels include The Physic Garden, set in early nineteenth-century Glasgow, The Curiosity Cabinet, The Posy Ring, Ice Dancing and The Jewel, a meticulously researched novel about the life and times of Robert Burns's wife, Jean Armour. Bird of Passage and The Amber Heart are family sagas of cruelty, loss and enduring love. A Proper Person to be Detained and The Last Lancer are poignant true histories that take us from 19th century Ireland and WW2 Poland to the industrial heartlands of England and Scotland.

Her stage plays include two full length plays commissioned by Edinburgh's Traverse Theatre: Wormwood, a play about the Chernobyl disaster, staged in 1997, and Quartz. She has written plays for Glasgow's Oran Mor, as well as various community theatre projects, television drama and more than 100 hours of drama for BBC R4.

Her other interests include antique textiles, collecting vintage perfumes, local and social history. She has served on the committee of the Society of Authors in Scotland and spent four years as Royal Literary Fund Writing Fellow at the University of the West of Scotland.

https://www.catherineczerkawska.co.uk/

Bitter Oranges, the sequel to *Hera's Orchard*, is out now in eBook and Paperback. Look out for the next Canary Island novel: *The Golden Apple*, in early 2026.

www.ingramcontent.com/pod-product-compliance
Lightning Source LLC
Chambersburg PA
CBHW070638260626
47161CB00007B/2754